MURDER
ON
RATTLESNAKE
ISLAND

A Maisy Malone Mystery

Starring

Mabel Normand and Mack Sennett

LARRY NAMES
USA

.

ISBN: 978-0-910937-82-5

To my late dear friend

Marilyn Slater

who was Mabel Normand's greatest fan

and who developed and managed a website,

<u>Looking for Mabel Normand</u>,

which has been an invaluable source

for everything there is to know

about Mabel and the early days

of the movie industry in California;

may she rest in peace,

our beloved Marilyn

Special thanks to

JAMES SHERMAN

Of the Los Angeles Public Library for providing the exact location of and many other details about the library during the time of this story.

A gentle breeze blew up from the south, promising a sunny, warm Christmas Day in southern California. Mack Sennett hated Christmas when it fell in the middle of *his* work week at the Keystone Moving Picture Company studio in Edendale. He loved the holiday when the calendar showed it on a Sunday, and he was okay with Christmas being on a Saturday because when it did, he only lost a half day of shooting the most farcical comedies ever made. But Christmas on a weekday meant no filming and—much worse—*no profit* for a whole day.

Since he couldn't make his cameramen, directors, actors, and extras work on a holiday, Sennett saw no reason for him to waste the day lollygagging around somebody's house waiting for a gluttonous dinner of ham, mashed potatoes and gravy, green beans, candied yams, and creamed corn, followed by a dessert of mincemeat pie or carrot cake. Instead, he had arranged a picnic for four on a beach that would surely be absent of bathers on this auspicious day. Normally, the director-general of the Keystone Moving Picture Company would call Willie James, the studio's chauffeur, and have him drive the company's fallow brown Cadillac Model 1913 for him. That would be on any other day. This was Christmas Day. Willie had a family of his own with whom he wished to celebrate this special occasion. For Sennett, the people at Keystone were his family. Today, he would drive the Caddy himself.

Sennett's favorite member of the Keystone ensemble of actors was, of course, the charming and vivacious, brown-eyed Mabel

Normand. He invited her under the original plan, thinking they could spend some time together—just the two of them—without all those furtive glances from everybody at the studio or in a restaurant or night club. Didn't happen.

Mabel batted her beautiful brown eyes at Sennett. "Oh, Mack, a picnic at the beach on Christmas Day is a wonderful idea. I'll tell Maisy, and maybe she can get Milo to join us as well."

Sennett knew better than to argue with his leading actress. He sighed and gave in without any of the usual debate between them, which often made strangers think they were married. They weren't.

The Keystone crew had only been making moving pictures in southern California since the end of August when Sennett, Mabel, Ford Sterling, Fred Mace, Henry "Pathé" Lehrman, and cameraman Irving Willard stepped off the California Limited at the Santa Fe Railroad's La Grande Depot in Los Angeles. Maisy Malone joined them a month later, arriving by train at the same station on the day Leslie Clover was murdered. Milo Cole had been in the state since late April, trying to catch on as an actor with other companies but having little success until Sennett and company showed up and gave him a real opportunity to break into the business. Maisy became a close friend to Mabel, and Milo found a niche as Sennett's personal gofer.

Sennett navigated the Cadillac from the studio to Mabel's apartment building on Seventh Street. Maisy lived in the same building, and Cole took a Red Car to meet them there.

Mabel looked into the back seat. "Where's the picnic basket?"

"We'll pick it up at the Hollywood Hotel. I called the chef there and asked him to throw one together for us. Told him to pick out a couple bottles of their best wine to go with the meal. I brought the studio still camera, too."

"Good idea, Mack. So what beach are we going to?"

"I don't know yet. We'll drive to Santa Monica and then decide whether to go up or down the coast from there."

Maisy queried. "Up the coast?"

"Yes, Tom Ince's studio is up the coast, and Venice and Redondo are down the coast. Let's see how we feel about it once we get there."

"Fair enough."

Sennett peered sideways at Maisy. "You know, Miss Malone, you say that a little too often, and it's beginning to get on my nerves."

Maisy turned her head and squinted a few daggers in Mack's direction. "Say what, Mr. Sennett?"

"You know, those two words you always say when most people would say something like ... 'Okay' ... or 'That would be fine.' You know, something different that means the same thing."

Mabel entered the fray. "Never mind him, Maise. He's in one of his snits. Just ignore him."

Maisy considered the advice of both Normand and Sennett before replying. "No, Mabel, I think he might be right. I do say 'fair enough' a lot. I can see how it might get on someone's nerves."

Mabel giggled a bit precociously. "Yes, especially his."

"Fair enough, Mack?"

Mabel's snicker grew into a sarcastic laugh.

"Sorry, Mack. It's a habit. I'll try to say it less. How about me saying okie dokie, instead? Or maybe sure thing?"

Mabel stepped up her laughter to a roar.

Sennett grimaced, squeezed the steering wheel so hard that he was certain he would break it. Through tight lips, he muttered a profane word, "Women!"

* * *

When the picnickers came to the junction of Santa Monica Boulevard and Ocean Highway, Sennett pulled the Cadillac to the side of the road, stopped, and put the gear box in neutral. He took a half-dollar from his right trousers pocket. "Heads we go north. Tails we go south. Okay?"

Maisy sat behind Sennett. "Okay by me."

From the passenger seat, Mabel concurred. "Me, too."

Seated behind Mabel, Cole nodded and waited for the outcome of the coin flip.

Sennett flicked his right thumb, and the silver disk sailed a foot into the air. He caught it with the same hand and slapped it on the back of the other. "We go north." He held it out for the others to see.

Mabel, Maisy, and Milo expressed their agreement.

"Sounds fine to me."

"Me, too."

Cole just nodded.

Sennett replaced the half-dollar in his pocket, shifted the transmission into low, drove back onto the street, turned the corner onto Ocean Highway, and headed the Caddy north, driving three and a half miles along the coast road until they came to an outcropping of stone with a roadside sign stating it to be Castle Rock.

Maisy leaned over her door. "Looks like the beach comes to an end here, Mack."

Mabel pointed. "There's a place on the other side of the road where you can park the car."

"That's all well and good, girls. But is there a trail down the bluff to the beach?"

"Only one way to find out, Nappy."

Maisy scrunched up her face. "Nappy? I've never heard you call him that before."

Sennett pulled the car to a halt. "That's her nickname for me. It's short for Napoleon. She calls me that whenever she thinks I'm getting or acting too high and mighty."

"Oh, Mabel, that's clever."

"If you want to keep your job, Maisy, you'll forget you ever heard her say it."

Mabel rolled her eyes. "He's fired me a dozen times at least in the past year. Go ahead and call him Nappy. If he fires you, then I'll quit and we'll both go work for Griffith."

Sennett countered. "Griffith doesn't make comedies."

"Maybe not, but the old man always had his eye on me. I'm sure he wouldn't mind having me around again. And where I go, Maisy goes. Right, dear?"

"I'm with you, Mabel."

Sennett swung the Cadillac around to the other side of the road and parked it in the wide spot between the highway and the cliff.

Without waiting to be ordered, Cole opened his door, jumped out, and went in search of a way down the side of the bluff to the beach below. In seconds he completed his mission. "There's a trail right here. Looks like it gets used a lot."

Without hesitation, Sennett shut down the engine, followed Cole to the edge of the cliff, and caught a glimpse of his own. "You know, I think this might be a good place to do some shooting of a beach scene or two. Those rocks along the water's edge would give the background some perspective as well as some scenery. The path down there isn't too steep for a man of good size to carry the camera and other equipment down there and bring it back up here when the day is over." He turned and looked at the parking place. "Room enough there for three, maybe four cars. We could get a whole crew and cast over here some morning and get set up before the sun comes over the mountains. What do you think, Milo?"

"I think you've found a terrific location, Boss."

"So do I. Lots of room down there to shoot the other direction as well, and we can get Santa Monica in the background, too."

"I think you've got something here, Boss."

Sennett patted Cole on the shoulder. "That's what I like about you, Milo. You know which side of the bread to spread the butter. Come on. Let's get the picnic stuff and get down there on that beach. I'm hungry."

Several minutes later the four of them had their blankets spread on the sand, their beach umbrellas erected, and their portable canvas bath house standing. One by one they changed from their driving clothes into their bathing suits.

"Does this remind you of anything, Mabel?" asked Sennett.

"Yes, The Water Nymph."

Perplexity warped Maisy's face. "The Water Nymph? And that is … the title of a movie?"

"Good guess, dear," said Mabel. "Yes, it is. When we came out here back in August, the studio was far from being ready, so Mack hauled us over to Venice Beach to shoot a half-reeler he titled The Water Nymph. I played the lead. He directed, and my supporting cast was Ford Sterling and Gus Pixley. Mack played himself, a crotchety old man."

"I was not crotchety, and I am not old. Besides, I played the boyfriend, and Ford played the boyfriend's father."

Mabel giggled. "Can you imagine Mack playing my boyfriend? See what makeup can do for the elderly?"

"All right, that's enough out of you, young lady. One more smart remark like that and you'll be going for a swim."

"Okay by me. Didn't we come here to swim and get some sun?" She took Maisy by the hand. "Come on, dear. Let's go for a swim and leave these two to talk shop."

"Fair enough."

Sennett held up a hand. "Wait a minute, you two. Before you run off, I want to get a picture of you together with me. Milo, did you bring the studio camera down with you?"

"Sure did, Boss."

"Good. Go get it and take our picture. A couple of them."

Cole retrieved the Kodak Folding Brownie, opened it, set the focus, and then took three pictures of Sennett flanked by Mabel and Maisy.

"That's good enough, Milo." Sennett waved a hand as if he were brushing away an annoying bug. "No need to waste any film. All right, girls, you can go for your swim now."

The two young women ran to the water's edge and danced in the shallows of the outgoing wave.

"Should we join them, Mack?"

"You go ahead, Milo. I'm not much of a water lily. I think I'll just have a look around for good shooting angles."

"Are you sure, Mack?"

"Yes but give me the camera first. Then you go ahead and prance with the princess and her lady-in-waiting."

Cole handed over the Brownie and took a few steps toward the water, stopped, and turned to face Sennett. "You know, Mack, I don't think you're old."

A frown drooped Sennett's face. "Get in the water, Milo."

"Yes, sir." Cole raced after Mabel and Maisy.

Sennett returned the camera to the shade of the beach umbrella and then surveyed the area for possible places to set up a moving picture camera in order to get the best angles for filming. He held up his hands, thumb-to-thumb, and peered through the gap between the two forefingers, imagining they framed a scene for the motion picture screen. Gradually, he worked his way to the base of Castle Rock. He repeated the same framing motion with his hands, starting with the bottom of the cliff to his left and slowly turning from there to the right, keeping the foot of the bluff in focus the whole time until the pier at Santa Monica came into view. Stopping there, he lowered his hands for a moment, smiled, and nodded to himself, assured he had found an excellent location for filming.

Satisfied with that spot, the director-general moved closer to the water and the rocks that broke the waves and prevented them from eroding Castle Rock faster than they already were doing. Once again, he held up his hands, thumb-to-thumb, and framed the scene before him, this time capturing Mabel, Maisy, and Milo splashing each other in the light surf. He congratulated himself again, totally oblivious to the shadowy object floating in the flotsam lathering among the rocks. Lowering his hands again and nodding to himself appreciatively, he scooted closer to the water's edge, thinking he might be able to get a shot or two from the boulders protruding from the ocean should the ebbing tide allow his cameraman to set up there. He climbed onto the most easily accessible rock, steadied himself, and again framed a possible scene with his hands. This time the dark shape bobbing in the water between the rocks caught his eye. His brow furrowed and pinched together over his nose.

"What the …?"

Sennett lowered his hands slowly to his sides as his brain brought perspective to what his eyes were seeing. When the connection completed, astonishment widened his steely blues. Disbelief followed. Then fear.

"Good God Almighty!" He stumbled backward, forgetting he had been standing on a solid surface, and stepped into the water. The shock of wet and cold forced another fright into his senses. He turned to run, stubbed his foot on the rock behind him, and fell atop the boulder, landing with his hands extended to break the fall. His first thought was to call out to the person closest to his heart, but since his mother was back in Canada, he shouted the name of the second most important woman in his life.

"Mabel!"

She didn't respond.

Sennett pushed himself erect again. "Mabel!" When she still didn't answer, he yelled the next name that came to mind. "Milo! Milo, come here. Now!"

Having synchronized his ears to the sound of Sennett's voice, Cole responded instantly. "Mack? Did you say something?"

"Come over here. All of you."

"Are you hurt, Boss?"

Sennett had Mabel's attention now. "Mack darling, are you all right?"

Maisy said nothing because she wasn't closely attuned to Sennett's voice. She simply scampered from the surf and ran toward the director.

Cole bolted behind Maisy a good two steps.

Mabel followed Cole.

Now righted physically and mentally but not yet emotionally, Sennett backed farther away from the object floating in the surf.

Maisy came up alongside Sennett. Her amber-flecked whiskey brown eyes followed his gaze to the floating entity. She immediately recognized it as a corpse, floating face down and bloated from having been in the water for a deadly length of time.

Milo and Mabel joined Maisy and Sennett.

"What is it, Boss?"

Mabel didn't bother with a verbal question. Like Maisy, she let her eyes follow theirs. She saw the body and reacted instantly by drawing her left hand up to her mouth to cover a gasp with the back of it and to shield her face against the horror before them.

Cole finally saw the corpse. "Omigod! Is he dead?" His roguish blues dulled with fear.

Annoyance twisted Maisy's lips. "No, Milo, he's just out for a Christmas plunge the same as we are."

"Hey, you don't have to get sarcastic about it."

Sennett grouched at them "Never mind that prattle, you two. What do we do about this?"

Maisy knew. "We need to get him out of the water before the tide goes out and takes him with it."

Mabel shook her head. "Not me. I'm not touching him." She waved off the chore with both hands in front of her. "I'm an actress, not an undertaker. You can do it, if you like, but not me." She backed away to punctuate her stand.

Sennett looked at Maisy and leaned away from her. "I'm not touching him either. If you want him out of the water, Maisy, then you and Milo do it."

Maisy turned to Cole. "Are you going to be squeamish about this, too? Or are you going to help me?"

"Well ..."

Maisy shook her head slowly. "City people! You never chased a headless chicken around the yard when you were kids, did you?"

Although he had been raised on a farm in Quebec, Sennett had to admit that was one thing he never did as a boy.

Maisy waded into the water to the body.

"Aw, hell!" groused Cole. He followed her against his will.

Maisy held out her right hand to halt Milo. "Let me take a close look at him before we try moving him."

Cole held up his hands. "Be my guest."

Maisy bent over and touched the arm. "Cold as ice." She pulled on it slowly. "No bend. He's still in rigor mortis."

"What does that mean?"

"It means he's been dead at least two hours, but having been in this cold water, he could have died anywhere from two hours ago to two days ago. Rigor usually only lasts for six to twelve hours, but that's under normal conditions, meaning dry and about seventy-five degrees."

"Oh."

"How do you know this stuff?" asked Sennett.

"I read books, and I asked a lot of questions from people who know the answers," said Maisy. "Come on. Let's turn him over."

Cole hesitated. "Would it be easier to do that on the beach?"

"No!" she snapped. "Are you going to help me or not?"

Cole came closer. "What do you want me to do?"

"Get his feet. When I give you the word, we flip him onto his back."

Milo took the corpse by the feet and waited for her command.

Maisy took the deceased by his shoulders. "Now."

Together they flipped him onto his back.

Maisy straightened up. "I kind of thought so. He's Asian. From the smell of him, I'd say he was a fisherman." She looked south along the beach. "There's a fishing village back down the road about half mile or so. He's probably from there."

"So you think he fell off his boat and drowned?"

Shaking her head, Maisy focused on the corpse again. "No, I don't think he drowned. Didn't you notice that gash on the back of his head? Somebody clubbed this guy before he went into the water somewhere."

"Then you think he was murdered?"

"Looks that way to me. Come on. Let's get him on the beach."

They guided him through the shallows until he rubbed against the sand. A wave lifted him off the bottom, allowing them to get a few feet closer to the dry beach.

"Maisy, why do you think he floats like that?"

"Good question." She felt the man's clothing. "Oily. That and the gases beginning to build up inside his gut from decomposition probably brought him up from the ocean floor early this morning or late last night. Could be that he never sank to the bottom. The combination of his oily clothes on ocean salt water could have kept him afloat. After all, look how small he is. I'll bet he's no more than five-feet-two, five-feet-three and probably didn't weigh more than one hundred ten, one hundred fifteen pounds soaking wet."

Each of them took him under an arm and dragged him onto the dry sand of the upper beach.

"Mack, we have to notify the authorities about this."

Sennett threw up his hands. "Oh, no, we don't. We're not getting involved in another murder. One murder in a lifetime is too much for me as it is. We lost two days of work because of Leslie Clover's murder. I'm not losing any more shooting time getting involved with another killing."

Mabel jerked his arm. "Mack, you're being ridiculous. Leslie's death had a direct bearing on the studio. This one has nothing to do with the studio. We don't even know who this poor man was. We're only doing the right thing here. Isn't that so, Maisy?"

Sennett freed himself from Mabel's hold. "I don't care. He's just some poor Asian who got himself murdered, and he has nothing to do with us. So let's just pack up our stuff and go somewhere else for the day. Let somebody else find him and report his body to the police."

Maisy shook her head. "Will you listen to yourself, Mr. Sennett? If this corpse was someone related to you, would you want him left here like this for someone else to find? It could be days before someone else comes along here and finds his body. Do you really want that?"

"Why don't we just go back to that fishing village and tell the people there about this dead man on the beach and let them deal with it?"

Maisy verged on the edge of anger. "This was a murder, Mack. The authorities have to be informed."

This time Mabel punched Sennett softly in the upper arm. "Maisy's right, and you know it. Quit being such an old fuddy-duddy, and let's inform the authorities about this poor man's death."

Sennett looked at Cole for help.

Milo shook his head slowly and shrugged. "I'm sorry, Boss, but I have to agree with Mabel and Maisy on this one."

The man with the power sighed, resigning himself to accepting the fact that he was fighting a lost cause. "Yes, of course, you're right, Maisy. Milo, you take the car and drive into Santa Monica to the local police station and tell them about this body we found. They'll know what to do from there."

Mabel shook her head. "No, Mack. Why don't we go into Santa Monica instead? The police will be more cooperative with you." She gave Cole an apologetic tilt of her head. "No offense, Milo."

"None taken, Mabel. You're right, all the same. Boss, you're the head of the studio, and I'm just a bit actor and gofer. The police will jump all over themselves if you report this body to them."

Sennett knew he was having his feelings soothed by Mabel and his boots licked by Milo, but he accepted the patronization as a show of their love and respect for him. At least, deep down he hoped those were their motives. "Yes, I see your point. All right, Mabel and I will go. Will you two be all right here?"

Maisy nodded. "We'll be fine, Mack. We'll cover him with a blanket and then wait under the umbrellas for you and Mabel to return with the police." She motioned to Milo with a tilt of her head. "Just don't take too long. Milo's liable to eat all the food and drink both bottles of wine, if you do."

Sennett frowned at Cole. "You don't get to open that wine until we get back. There are four Coca-Colas in the basket. Drink those if you get thirsty."

"Sure thing, Boss."

"Come on, Mabel. Let's go find the cops and tell them about the body."

Mack and Mabel found a lone police officer patrolling Santa Monica Boulevard on foot a block off Ocean Avenue. Sennett pulled the Cadillac to the side of the nearly vacant street and leaned through the window.

Sennett spoke for the two of them. "Excuse me, sir, but where do we go to report a murder?"

The question staggered the policeman. "A murder? Where? When did it happen? Where's the body? Who did it?"

Sennett threw up his hands. "Hey, take it easy, pal. We just want to tell someone about finding a body on the beach by Castle Rock. Actually, it was right at Castle Rock, floating in the surf among the rocks."

"Castle Rock? Are you sure?"

"That's what the sign said. Castle Rock. Very appropriately named, I might add."

"And you just left the body there?"

Mabel answered the officer's question. "Yes, but our two friends are still there keeping an eye on it so nobody else disturbs it."

The patrolman lifted his high-crowned policeman's hat and scratched his head. "Castle Rock, eh? You know, Castle Rock is outside our city limits, sir."

Sennett replied. "We didn't know that Officer. We've only been here in California for six months or so."

The lawman nodded. "That explains a lot."

Mabel knew Mack was offended by the policeman's attitude, so she intervened. "So what do we do about this body we found?"

"Well, miss, finding a body on a beach near Castle Rock would come under the jurisdiction of the county sheriff."

Sennett didn't like where this conversation was headed. "The county sheriff?"

"Yes, sir." The officer replaced his hat. "Or because you found it on the beach, it could come under the jurisdiction of the Coast Guard. Depends, I think, on whether the victim was smuggling anything or not."

"I don't think he was smuggling anything. He was Asian."

"Asian, you say. Well, then he was most likely a fisherman. Lots of them Asian fellows up and down the beaches around here. There's a little village of them yellow fellows living in shacks south of town. They used to be abalone fishermen, but the state passed a law back in O-five forbidding the Japanese to fish for abalone. Most of them moved to Terminal Island, but a few stayed around here. Could be he's one of them. Little fellow was drowned, you say?"

Sennett frowned at the policeman. "I didn't say he was drowned. I said he was murdered. Somebody caved in the back of his head with something."

"Well, murdered or drowned, he was an Asian. Probably Japanese if he was a fisherman. Even so, his death comes under the jurisdiction of the county sheriff."

"And where would I find the county sheriff's office?"

"Downtown Los Angeles."

"Really?"

"Yes, sir."

"Did you hear that, Mabel? We have to drive downtown Los Angeles to report this murder. I knew this was going to be trouble right from the moment I laid eyes on that corpse."

The officer interrupted Sennett. "No, sir, you won't have to do that unless you really want to."

"Keep talking, officer."

"Just drive over to the station and report the body to the desk sergeant on duty, and he'll place a telephone call to the sheriff's deputy who lives in town here to tell him about the body on the beach. His name is Mike Van Vliet. The deputy, I mean, not the sergeant. Mike will take it from there."

A smile curled one corner of Sennett's face. "Now you're talking, pal. Where's the station from here?"

* * *

"Help me roll this man onto his front side, Milo. I want to take a closer look at that gash on the back of his head."

Cole shook his head. "No, thank you, Miss Malone. I've touched that corpse enough already. If you want to turn him over, then you do it by yourself. Besides, didn't Mack say he didn't want us getting involved in another murder?"

Maisy took a turn shaking her head. "No, he said *he* didn't want to get involved in another murder. He didn't say a word about you and me staying out of it."

"Oh, yes, he did. I remember precisely him saying *we* aren't getting involved in another murder."

Turning away from Cole for the moment, Maisy offered a rebuttal. "You're right. He did say that." She faced him again. "But then he went on to say that *he* wasn't going to lose any more shooting time getting involved in another murder. And by saying that, he retracted his previous statement where he more or less forbade us from getting involved."

"That's not the way I see it."

Maisy cozied up to Cole. "Milo dear, if you have any aspirations of … ever … seeing more of … *me* … then I suggest you start seeing a few more matters my way."

Cole grimaced as he looked down at her pert nose. "That's blackmail, and you know it."

"Yes, I do know it, but …"

"Okay, how do you want to do this?"

Maisy raised up on her tiptoes, gave him a quick kiss on the lips, and dropped back onto her heels just as fast. "I knew you'd come around."

Cole raised his eyes skyward. "I'm spineless. A jellyfish. Gelatin on a plate. The things I do for one tiny little kiss."

Maisy slumped onto the beach beside the corpse. "Hush up and get down here with me."

Without another word, Cole obeyed, resting on his knees next to her.

She brushed a cheek on his bare biceps. "Come on, dear. It's not all that bad. We do just like we did that day back in September when we rolled Leslie Clover onto his side. Ready?"

Cole slipped his hands under the dead man's lower back and thigh, while Maisy took his shoulder and ribs. "Let's do this."

"Go."

They flipped the dead man onto his front side, and immediately, Maisy leaned over the back of his head to make a closer examination of the wound she had seen there previously. "That's a really nasty gouge in his scalp, don't you think?"

"I don't want to think about it, Maisy. You leave me out of this."

She twisted her head slowly to focus on Cole. "Milo, if we're to continue being something of an item, then you'd better start taking an interest in the things I like to do as much as I take an interest in the things you like to do."

"Oh, really? And what things that I like to do *do you* take an interest in, Miss Malone?"

"I take a very active interest in your acting career."

"My acting career? We work at the same studio. The only difference between you and me there is you get more roles than I do, while I run errands for the boss. You're all chummy with Mabel Normand, the leading lady of comedy, while I'm the boss's golden retriever."

"You could quit, you know, and go elsewhere to work."

"And spend more time away from you? Not on your life."

Maisy smiled sweetly at him. "Milo, you say the nicest things at times." The smile vanished. "And then there are other times when you're as stubborn as a Missouri mule. Now would you please humor me while I try to figure out what made this injury to this poor man's head?"

"I forgot. You're Sherlock Holmes."

"No, I'm Shirley Holmes, Sherlock's smarter sister."

"Oh, yes, of course. How foolish of me to forget, Miss Holmes!"

"Good. Now pay attention." She brushed away the sand that had adhered to the dead man's hair while he was on his back. "Take a look at the edge of the wound. See how it's got a kind of crescent shape to it?"

"So what?"

"So, it's curved like the moon in an early phase, and it's off to the left side of his head."

"Yes, I see that, but why isn't there any blood?"

Maisy frowned at him. "Think for a second, Milo. He's been in the water for several hours. Don't you think the ocean would have washed off any blood by now?"

"Oh, yes, of course. I should have thought of that."

"If Mr. Selig ever decides to make another *Wizard of Oz* movie, I'm going to suggest he cast you as the Scarecrow."

"Very funny, Miss Malone. Let's get back to the wound. So what about the crescent shape of it?"

"So what do you think made a wound shaped like that?"

Milo's brow pinched together. "I don't know. A hammer, maybe?"

"Too big for a hammer head and the curvature of it would be rounder if it had been made by a hammer. I was thinking it might have been made by a lead pipe."

"A lead pipe? Pipes are smaller than a hammer head."

"Pipes can be anywhere from a half inch in diameter to three or even four inches in diameter."

"Yes, but a pipe that large would be too bulky for a man to hold in one hand."

Maisy nodded in agreement. "And too heavy, even if it was only a foot long. I wish I had something to measure the wound. That would give me a better idea what might have caused it." She thought for a moment. "Get me one of those Coca-Cola bottles, would you please?"

"Do you think he was killed with a Coca-Cola bottle?"

"A bottle with thick glass like that could have been the weapon, but I'm thinking it had to be something harder than a glass bottle. I would think a bottle might leave a few tiny glass splinters behind, but I don't see any here, do you?"

"No, I don't. I'll be right back." Cole popped erect and dashed off to retrieve the bottle from the picnic basket. He returned in less than a minute. "Here you go."

Maisy took the bottle and held the bottom of it close to the gash. "Whatever made this wound was a bigger than this bottle. How wide do you think the bottom of this bottle is?"

"I don't know. Two, two and a quarter inches at the most."

"That's what I figure as well. So we're looking for something bigger. Something about three or four inches in diameter. Maybe bigger. Something a man can hold in one hand and swing without much trouble and with lots of force. Something like a blacksmith's hammer."

"Okay, somebody killed this man with a blacksmith's hammer. So how did he wind up in the ocean?"

"He was a fisherman. Where else would a fisherman be except in a boat on the ocean?"

Cole nodded. "Yes, of course. That makes perfect sense. So you're thinking he was out fishing, and somebody clubbed him with a blacksmith's hammer and dumped him in the ocean? Is that it?"

"Something like that." Maisy thought for a moment. "Then maybe he was fishing from a pier and somebody clubbed him and then dumped him in the water, and he washed up here. Maybe somebody killed him on land and then took him out to sea on a boat and threw him overboard. There's no telling at this point where he was murdered. The only real fact we have is, he was murdered with a blacksmith's hammer or something like that."

"Well, at least the police will have a start on finding out who killed him. They can take it from there once they get here."

"Sure, but in the meantime, let's take a closer look at his clothes and hands. Regular leather workman's shoes, oily like his trousers and shirt. Do you see any pockets in his pants?"

Cole examined the man's blue jeans and found a four-inch pocket knife in the right front pocket. He opened it and studied the blade closely. "There's blood on it."

"Probably fish blood, but you never know. Could be human. I'll keep it in mind for later. For now, put it back. Find anything else?"

He dug into the other front pocket. "Found some money." He extracted the coins. "Looks like three pennies, three nickels, and a dime. Twenty-eight cents."

"Well, we can probably rule out robbery as a reason to kill him. Anything else? A wallet perhaps?"

"No, no wallet. Nothing else."

"From the tan line just below his hairline, he usually wore a hat. Did you see one in the water near him?"

"No, did you?'

Maisy shook her head. "Probably lost in the ocean." She lifted each hand and examined the fingers and palms. "He used these to make his living. Lots of callouses but no crud beneath the nails. Tells me he probably wasn't working when he was murdered."

"How do you know that?"

"I don't know that much about Japanese people, but I do know they are an exceptionally clean people. They bathe a lot." She had another thought. "It could also mean he might have been wearing gloves when he was working. That's why the fingernails are so clean."

"He sure does smell like dead fish, doesn't he?"

"The stink is getting worse as his clothes dry." She backed away. "I guess that's enough for now. Let's leave the rest to the police."

* * *

Almost an hour after leaving to inform the authorities about the body on the beach, Sennett and Mabel returned to the pullover area beside Castle Rock. Deputy Michael Van Vliet from the Los Angeles County Sheriff's Department followed them there in a Ford, his own car. Two officers from the Santa Monica Police Department drove up behind the deputy in the local department's paddy wagon. All of them emerged from their vehicles and gathered at the edge of the bluff overlooking the strip of sand below.

"So where is this body?" asked Van Vliet, a short man wearing a big Stetson that appeared to be too big for his body. He had a swagger about him that said he would have been more comfortable sitting on a horse than driving an automobile.

Sennett pointed toward the base of Castle Rock. "I'm pretty sure it's down there under that blanket." He cupped his hands around his mouth. "Milo, Maisy, we're back!"

The pair were sitting on the other blanket under a beach umbrella, watching the waves ebb and flow with the outgoing tide. They jumped to their feet, turned around, and looked up at Sennett, Mabel, and the three lawmen staring down at them. Maisy waved an acknowledgement to them.

"Everything all right?" queried Sennett.

"We're fine. Come on down."

Sennett and Mabel started down the trail.

Van Vliet turned to the policemen. "You'd better bring a stretcher to carry the body back up here."

The two cops nodded simultaneously and then hustled off to their van to get the stretcher.

In a couple of minutes, the four picnickers and three lawmen were assembled by the blanket covering the dead fisherman. Sennett introduced Maisy and Cole to Deputy Van Vliet. "And these two men are officers from the Santa Monica police. They came along to pick up the body and take it into Los Angeles for the county medical examiner." He pointed to the water. "We found him floating among the rocks over there. He was face down. Maisy and Milo pulled him up here to keep him from going out with the tide."

The deputy nodded. "Good idea." He knelt down and flipped a corner of the blanket off the corpse's head. "Yep. Definitely an Asian like you said, Mr. Sennett." He peeled away more blanket. "And from the looks of his clothes, I'd go along with him being a fisherman. Probably, he was Japanese. He could be from the village down at Playa del Rey. That's on the other side of Santa Monica. That village was started by some Mexicans a good twenty years ago. Japanese started moving in there about six, maybe seven years back. Now it's all Japanese. They fish for tuna and other fish there and sell most of their catch in Santa Monica." He looked up at Sennett. "You said he was murdered. How do you know that for certain, sir?"

"I don't, but she does." Sennett nodded toward Maisy.

Maisy took her cue. "He's got a big gash on the back of his head, Deputy. Somebody clubbed him with something like a lead pipe."

"And how do you know this, Miss Malone?"

"I inspected his wound. See for yourself, Deputy."

Van Vliet shook his head. "That's not my job, Miss Malone. I'll leave that to the medical examiner to determine. I'm just here to make sure this fellow is dead and to see that the body is recovered and taken into Los Angeles for the coroner's office. Those boys will deal with it from there." He stood up. "Okay, officers. He's all yours."

Astonishment and disappointment colored Maisy's face sunburn red. "That's it? You're not going to investigate the area for any clues or go through his pockets or anything? You're just going to haul him into the morgue and dump him there?"

The deputy nodded. "That's pretty much the size of it, Miss Malone. What else would you have me do?"

"Aren't you going to investigate his murder?"

"That's not my job."

"Then whose job is it? Doesn't your department have detectives like the Los Angeles Police Department?"

"No, we don't. Usually, the sheriff leads any investigation with a team of deputies to do the leg work."

"Oh, I see. So your sheriff will investigate this man's murder, is that it?"

"Probably not, Miss Malone."

"Why not?"

"Well, look at him. He's just another Jap fisherman. Nobody will care about his death except some family member if he even has a family here. Most of them don't, you know."

"He's just another Jap fisherman? I can't believe you just said that."

"Why not? It's not like he's a white man or even a Mexican. He's a Jap or a Chinaman or a Korean. He's Asian, Miss Malone, and most people around here could care less about them. In fact, most would probably like to see them all go back to wherever it was they came from."

Maisy was beside herself with indignation. "That's just not right. He was still a human being. He deserves justice just as much as you and I would deserve it, if somebody murdered either of us."

"It's not the same thing, Miss Malone. We're white, and he's just a Jap. A dead Jap. And now if you don't mind, we'll take care of this from here. Okay?"

"No, it's not okay. If the sheriff isn't going to investigate this man's murder, then I'll find someone who will."

Van Vliet mocked her. "Oh, really? Like who?"

"Never you mind, who. For now, suffice it to say, I'm going to see that this man gets justice and that's that." She turned to Cole. "Milo, where's that camera? I want to take pictures of this man's face, his hands, and the wound on the back of his head."

Cole hesitated. "Why do you want to do that?"

Sennett jumped into the conversation. "That's the studio's camera, Maisy. You might ask me for permission to use it before you start ordering Milo to fetch it for you."

Mabel took Sennett by one arm with both her hands. "Oh, come on, Nappy. You're going to let her use it, aren't you?"

"Well, of course, I am, but it would be nice if she would ask first."

"Okay, Mack. May I use the studio camera to take pictures of this poor man here?"

Sennett smugged up. "Certainly, you may, Miss Malone."

The deputy stepped forward. "Who says I'm going to let you take pictures of this corpse? I'm the one in charge here, you know."

Mabel released Sennett's arm and moved closer to Van Vliet. "He's right, Maisy. You should ask the deputy for permission to take pictures of the dead man."

Van Vliet tipped his Stetson to Mabel. "Thank you, Miss Normand."

"You're welcome, Deputy."

Maisy played along. "Sorry, Deputy. Would you mind if I took some photographs of the dead man here?"

"Be my guest, Miss Malone. Of course, I think you're wasting your time and your film. But do as you must if it suits you."

"Milo, get the camera."

* * *

After Van Vliet and the two policemen from Santa Monica carried the corpse up the bluff to the paddy wagon, Sennett focused on Maisy. "I know you're upset over this, so I'll tell you what I'm going to do for you. I'll have those pictures developed for you first thing tomorrow morning, and then after work you can take them to the sheriff yourself and be done with this murder business. I assume that's who you're planning to give them to."

"Yes, that's exactly who I'm going to take them to. This deputy who was just here doesn't have the authority to let this go by the wayside. So, I'll go to the sheriff and see what he has to say about it."

Mabel stepped forward. "And I'll go with you."

"Thank you, dear. Having you along should carry more weight with an important official like the sheriff."

Sennett grimaced. "And if he won't investigate this murder, then what?"

"Then I'll do it myself."

The movie-maker appeared confounded with a touch of anger. "Do it yourself? Are you kidding? You snooped into one murder and got lucky enough to catch the killer and now you're a detective?"

"No, I'm not a detective. I'm a concerned citizen who believes everybody deserves justice, including that poor dead man they just carried up the bluff on a stretcher."

Sennett threw up his hands. "Justice? How do you know he didn't deserve to be killed? Maybe he wasn't a fisherman. Maybe he was criminal, a killer, a smuggler, a rapist or just a thief. Maybe he was killed while he was committing a crime. Have you even considered that possibility?"

"Yes, I have, which is all the more reason for his death to be investigated by the sheriff."

Sennett removed his hat and scratched at his head. "Now we're back to that. Mabel, you talk some sense into her."

"Sorry, Nappy, but I'm with Maisy on this one. That poor man's death needs to be investigated, if for no other reason than to find out why his body washed up on this beach."

"Do you hear that, Milo? They're both crazy." Sennett stomped around in the sand for several paces. "She's your girlfriend, Milo. You talk some sense into her."

"I'm not his girlfriend. We're only friends. Good friends, but still only friends. Whatever gave you the idea Milo and I are an item?"

The studio head flinched, backed away a step, and then charged ahead again. "Never mind that now. I forbid you to get involved in this murder. You work for me, and I say you can't get involved with it. Do you understand me, Miss Maisy Malone?"

Very calmly, Maisy responded. "You can't tell me what I can or what I can't do on my own time, Mr. Mikall Sinnott. I am not your property."

"No, you're not my property. You're my employee, and if you want to keep on as my employee, you'll do what you're told."

"Is that so?"

"It is."

"Fair enough. Fire me, if you must, but I'm going to get justice for that man whether you like it or not."

"No, you're not."

"Yes, I am."

"I'll fire you, if you get involved."

"You said that already."

Mabel jumped into the growing affray. "Nappy, if you fire Maisy, then you'll have to fire me, too, because I'm going to help her."

"No, you're not."

"Yes, I am, Nappy, and you can't stop me."

Sennett was had, and he knew it. Keystone was just another cut-rate moving picture studio without Mabel. As much as he hated the position, she had placed him in, he knew he had no choice but to give in—part way, at least. "All right, you help Maisy. Do what you have to do. We can shoot around you until the first Monday of the New Year. You two have until then to get this murder business wrapped up and out of your systems, and I want the both of you back on the set at eight o'clock sharp Monday morning, January ..." He peered skyward for a second before shifting his focus to Cole. "What day of the month will that be, Milo?"

Cole thought for a second before answering. "January sixth."

A smug smile curved Sennett's mouth. "You've got the twelve days of Christmas to solve this murder or you're both fired."

Mabel nudged Maisy. "What about Milo?"

"Me?"

Sennett nodded. "Mabel's right. Milo same goes for you. You've got twelve days to help them solve this thing or you're fired right along with them."

"But Boss—"

"You heard me."

Mabel appeared pensive. "Does this mean I don't have to ride with you in the *Tournament of Roses* parade?"

Sennett considered her question for a few seconds. "Hm-m! I forgot about the parade." He shook his head. "You're our main attraction, Mabel, so I think you should be there."

Mabel glanced at Maisy. "He's right, Maise. I should be there. We can take one day off from sleuthing, can't we?"

Before Maisy could reply, Milo offered a thought. "Who knows, Maisy? You just might have this murder solved by then."

Maisy nodded. "The *Tournament of Roses* parade is a big deal in these parts, isn't it?"

Sennett answered her. "That's what D.W. tells me."

"Well then, you'd better ride in that parade, Mabel."

Good to his word, Mack Sennett ordered the \the film Milo Cole used to photograph the dead fisherman the day before on the beach north of Santa Monica. He promised Maisy Malone and Mabel Normand they could have the pictures as soon as their directors called it quits for the morning and broke for lunch. "The photos will be in my office. Come there to get them."

Quite promptly at noon, the two actresses and Cole approached Sennett's private domain on the top floor of the building everybody in the company called *The Tower*. The tallest structure on the lot, it resembled an enclosed lookout tower in a national forest. Thus, the nickname. From its height, Sennett could observe nearly everything in his five-acre realm below. Many of the people who worked at Keystone dreaded climbing the six flights of stairs to the top, often comparing it to *The Tower of London* and all that immortal edifice implied; while the more lewd crowd at the studio deemed it "Sennett's erection," an analogy for a phallic symbol and all that term inferred derogatorily toward the director-general of the Keystone Moving Picture Company.

If he had been alone at Sennett's office door, Cole would have knocked and waited to be called into the boss's presence. However, Mabel had long since passed that point in her relationship with Sennett. She barged in on him any time she pleased. Recently, with her rise in status at the studio, Maisy had begun doing likewise as Mabel. Today was no exception.

Sennett looked up from his desk and focused on Maisy. "All

right, here's the deal. You get the rest of the day off, but without pay. If you need to take tomorrow off, same thing, no pay. Same goes for Saturday. Since I've decided to close down the studio for all of next week because hardly anybody who works here will be able to concentrate on their work, what with looking forward to New Year's Eve and recovering from their hangovers afterward, why bother trying to work? I'm going to give everybody who's on salary half-pay for next week, and I'm being generous at that. Day workers will also get a third of their average pay for a week, and I'm really being generous there."

Mabel sat on a corner of Sennett's desk. "Now that just won't do, Nappy. Nobody is asking you to close down the studio for the week. You know these people. They're used to coming in here at the crack of dawn and working until it's too dark to shoot without setting up lights. You're paying Hank Mann twelve dollars a week when he's worth thirty for all he does around here acting and painting and pounding nails for you. And you're only going to give him six for staying home? What do you expect him to do for food that week? He barely gets by as it is. And he's only one guy around here. What about all the others? A third of what they make in a week on average? And you call that generous? Simon Legree lives and breathes in you, doesn't he, Napoleon Sennett? With what this studio is making, you should be paying them a big fat Christmas bonus plus their usual pay for next week and still give them the week off. I know I certainly deserve it, and so does just about every other person on the lot. Don't you agree, Maisy?"

"Sounds about right to me, Mabel."

Sennett frowned at them. "Ganging up on me, is that it?"

"I wouldn't put it that way, Nappy, but if that's how you see it, then, okay, we're ganging up on you."

Maisy sidled up to Mabel. "And what about a little Christmas bonus for everybody?"

"Do I look like Santa Claus?"

Mabel ran her fingers through his graying hair. "You're getting there, Nappy." She gave him a childlike grin.

"Oh, all right. I'll see that everybody gets paid for Christmas Day."

"And New Year's Day?"

"All right. New Year's Day, too. But not until next payday."

Mabel smiled at Maisy. "What do you think?"

"Fair enough ... so far."

Sennett fell back in his chair. "That's more than fair. What more do you want?"

Maisy drew much closer to the boss. "You're a sporting man, aren't you, Mack?"

"What makes you think that?"

"Well, for one thing, your partners are a couple of New York City bookies, aren't they?"

"So what?"

"Oh, come on, Mack. Everybody knows how you fell in with Kessel and Bauman. You lost too many bets with them, and you had to talk your way out of getting your legs broken by getting them to back you in the moving picture business. Isn't that right?"

Sennett glared at Mabel. "You couldn't keep your trap shut, could you, sweetheart?"

Mabel took the offensive. "Everybody in New York knew about your deal with Kessel and Bauman before we came out here, so don't go blaming me for spreading tales."

Sennett knew she was right, so he changed tactics and focused on Maisy again. "Okay, so what about this bet you want to make?"

"I'll bet you my salary for the next two weeks that we can get the murder of this poor Japanese fisherman solved by the law or by us by midnight on the twelfth day of Christmas. If I do it, you pay me double. If I don't, you keep my slave wages. Fair enough?"

Mabel giggled. "I'll make you the same bet, Nappy."

Sennett grimaced and looked up at Cole. "What about you, Milo? You throwing in with them on this?"

Maisy tilted her head at Cole and smiled coyly. "Of course, he is. Aren't you, sweetie?"

The man was helpless whenever Maisy spoke to him with an

endearment of any kind attached. "I guess I am."

Sennett shook his head and then pushed a folder with the photos across his desk toward Mabel. "Okay, you got a bet. Now take your pictures and get out of here. Just keep me informed about what you're doing, will you? I have to know when my star attraction will be available for filming again. Now beat it. All three of you."

"Can Willie drive us there?"

Sennett threw up his hands. "Sure, why not?" Then another thought crossed his mind. "The car has to be back here by Sunday morning. I just remembered that we've got an entry in the *Tournament of Roses* parade over in Pasadena on New Year's Day. We're going to have a meeting at the studio on Sunday to decide how we're going to decorate the Cadillac for the parade."

Mabel appeared a little sheepish. "That's right, Maisy. I have to be here for that, but you don't."

Sennett piped in one more question. "Anything else you two want from me before you go?"

Maisy and Mabel exchanged questioning looks. Each shook her head. They giggled and then they kissed him, simultaneously, each on a cheek, before Mabel answered. "I guess that will do for now, Nappy."

* * *

Shortly after one o'clock Mabel, Maisy, and Milo entered the Los Angeles Sheriff's Department at the County Courthouse and approached the desk sergeant.

"Can I help you folks?"

Maisy stepped forward. "Yes, we'd like to see Sheriff Hammel please to speak to him about the body that was found on the beach north of Santa Monica yesterday."

"What about the body, miss?"

"He was murdered."

"Yes, we are aware of that, miss."

"Are you investigating the murder, sir?"

"I'm sure something is being done about it."

"Could you please tell us *what* is being done about it?"

The sergeant's voice took on an edge. "That's department business, miss. We check out all murders within our jurisdiction, and when we have proof of who did it, we pass it along to the district attorney's office. Then it's up to the district attorney whether he wants to prosecute or not."

Mabel stepped forward beside Maisy. "We'd still like to see Sheriff Hammel, if you don't mind, Sergeant."

"The sheriff is a busy man, miss. I'm sure he doesn't have time for you today." Before Mabel could say anything else, the lawman held up his hand to stop her. "I assure you, miss, we're doing everything that needs to be done with this case. Now would you please run along? I have work to do."

His attitude put a huff in Mabel's demeanor. "We're not budging until we see the sheriff."

"Is that so? And just who do you think you are, miss?"

Cole took his turn. "These ladies are Miss Mabel Normand and Miss Maisy Malone from the Keystone Moving Pictures Company in Edendale."

The officer of the law glared at Cole. "I don't care who they are, pal. They still aren't getting in to see the sheriff. Now beat it before I have the three of you thrown out of here."

Mabel knew exactly what this situation called for. She swooned, collapsing against Cole who caught her before she prostrated on the floor.

A bit jealous that Mabel had beaten her to this maneuver Maisy glared at the desk sergeant. "Now look what you've done!" She dropped to her knees beside Mabel.

Suddenly having gone pale, the lawman sputtered to speak. "What I did? What do you mean by that? I didn't do anything."

Maisy ignored his plea and kept up with their charade. "Ease her down slowly, Milo. We don't want her to have a serious seizure right here in the sheriff's department." She glanced up at the sergeant again. "This is all your fault."

Hearing her cue, Mabel began shaking violently, stuck her tongue out of one side of her mouth, and allowed her saliva to escape through her lips in spurts and rivulets.

Maisy gasped. "Omigosh! You did it. You scared her into having a raving fit. Quick! Give me a pencil or a pen or something hard that I can put between her teeth and keep her from biting off her tongue."

Other deputies gathered around three visitors as the sergeant found a pencil and handed it to Maisy. A deputy raced to the door of the sheriff's private office, opened it, and made a short report to the department's head man. "Better come out here, sir. A young woman is having a seizure."

Maisy put the pencil between Mabel's teeth and let her bite on it as they continued the ruse. "It's okay, Mabel. The rude man didn't really mean to frighten you." She glanced over her shoulder at the sergeant leaning over his desk and watching the scene before him. "You didn't, did you?"

"No, of course not."

Sheriff Hammel entered the scene, his face pale and rippled with anxiety. "What's going on here, Cochran?"

The desk sergeant jumped to his feet and faced his boss. "This young woman is having a seizure, Sheriff."

Hammel came closer to the trio in front of Cochran's desk. "Who is she?"

Cochran spoke in self-defense. "She says her name is Mabel Normand ... the actress."

Sheriff Hammel leaned over to look at Mabel's face. "You idiot! This is Mabel Normand the actress."

Maisy looked up at Hammel. "She certainly is, Sheriff. And I'm Maisy Malone, and this is Milo Cole. Your sergeant here frightened Mabel into having a seizure, sir."

"He did what?"

Mabel took the pencil out of her mouth. "Your sergeant is a rude man, Sheriff. All we wanted is to see you about the murdered Japanese fisherman we found on the beach yesterday just north of Santa Monica, and your sergeant here wouldn't let us see you. And then he threatened to have us thrown out of the building. That's when my seizure started."

Hammel appeared flustered and unsure of what to do or say next. He did manage to blurt out the few words that popped into his head. "Are you all right now, Miss Normand?"

A coy smile and a twinkle in her eyes sparkled Mabel's face. "I am now that I see you, Sheriff." She focused on Cole. "Help me up, Milo." Once she was upright again Mabel batted her eyes at the head lawman. "Could we please speak to you in private, Sheriff Hammel?"

Already appearing more like a Methodist minister than an officer of the law, Hammel called up all the dignity he could muster. "Yes, of course, Miss Normand. Please come into my office. This way." He waved an arm toward the doorway to his work space. "All three of you. Please come in."

In a minute, Mabel, Maisy, and Milo were seated in Hammel's office. "Now what may I do for you good people this afternoon?"

Maisy took the lead. "Sheriff Hammel, my friends and I were with Mack Sennett, our employer, yesterday on the beach north of Santa Monica when he discovered the body of a dead Japanese fisherman. We reported this to the Santa Monica police, and they then reported it to your department. A Deputy William Van Vliet came out with two Santa Monica policemen to retrieve the body."

"I am aware of all this, Miss Malone. So what is your point?"

"Deputy Van Vliet stated there would be *no* investigation into this fisherman's murder because he was Japanese. When I asked him why, he replied ... and these were his exact words ... he said, 'He's just another Jap fisherman. Nobody will care about his death except some family member if he even has a family here. Most of them don't, you know.' And when I confronted him with the fact this man deserved justice, your deputy added, 'It's not the same thing, Miss Malone. We're white, and he's just a Jap. A dead Jap.' Deputy Van Vliet insinuated you would take the same stance in this matter. Is this how you feel about this man's murder? That he doesn't deserve justice because he's Japanese?"

Hammel cleared his throat before speaking. "In the first place, Miss Malone, we haven't established that this man was murdered."

"His head was caved in from behind, and he was found dead,

washed up on a beach. That pretty much says he was murdered to me."

"All right murdered or not, it's not the man's race that matters here, Miss Malone. It's his status in the community. Many of the less fortunate in this county die under mysterious circumstances all the time. We have neither the time nor the manpower to investigate every single one of them. Therefore, his death is not a priority that is germane to this department."

"In other words, since he was a poor Japanese fisherman, he doesn't deserve justice. That's it, isn't it, Sheriff?"

"It's not that he doesn't deserve justice, Miss Malone. It's—"

"Never mind, Sheriff. I understand. He was a nobody, so nobody cares who he was or why he was murdered. There's only one problem with that, Sheriff. *We ... do ... care ...* who he was and why he was murdered. We can't let his death go without knowing *why* he was murdered, and once we know why, then we'll want to know *who* murdered him."

"If it was that simple, Miss Malone, I assure you this department would be investigating his death."

Mabel stepped forward. "It's obvious you're not going to do anything about this murder, Sheriff Hammel. So who do we have to speak to about it above you? The mayor?"

Hammel shook his head. "No, the district attorney. Mr. John D. Fredericks. You can find him two floors up."

* * *

Fifteen minutes later Maisy, Mabel, and Milo were shown into the office of District Attorney Fredericks, the man who had gained nationwide fame in 1910 and 1911 for prosecuting the bombers of the Los Angeles *Times* newspaper building. "I understand you people are here about the possible murder of a Japanese fisherman. Is that correct?"

Again, Maisy took the lead. "Yes, sir, it is. We are three of the four people who discovered the body on the beach north of Santa Monica yesterday when we went there for a picnic."

"I see. And how do you know this man was murdered?"

Maisy quickly explained the evidence.

"How do you know he wasn't killed in some kind of accident or he fell into the ocean and drowned?"

"I don't know that for certain, but that's not the point, sir."

"Then what is the point, Miss Malone?"

"The point is your sheriff's department isn't going to investigate this man's death. They aren't even going to try to find out who he was so his family can identify him and give him a funeral and say good-bye to him and all that."

"I'm sure Sheriff Hammel and his deputies are doing all they can in that area, Miss Malone."

"No, they aren't doing anything about it. The sheriff said so. He said he doesn't have the manpower to scour the county looking for anybody who might have known this man. He said his men have more important things to do than to find anybody who might have known this man."

"Los Angeles County is larger than the states of Delaware and Rhode Island combined, Miss Malone. Over four thousand square miles of land, not including the islands off our coast. That's nearly a hundred square miles per deputy. When you remove the incorporated cities of our county from the equation, each man would still be responsible for more than fifty square miles of territory each day, twenty-four hours per day, seven days per week, three hundred sixty-five days a year. Furthermore, several of our smaller municipalities have only token police departments for the time being, so they rely on our sheriff's department for much of their law enforcement needs. In my opinion, Miss Malone, our sheriff's department has more than they can handle already. Investigating the death of one Japanese fisherman, if he was Japanese in the first place, would be a poor use of the sheriff department's manpower."

"But he was murdered, Mr. Fredericks. Doesn't that mean anything to you at all?"

"Certainly, it does, Miss Malone. But until someone brings me solid evidence of the murder, the identity of the victim, the motive for the murder, and the culprit who committed this crime, I can do nothing."

Mabel came forward. "Mr. Fredericks, can't you order Sheriff Hammel to begin an investigation?"

"Miss Normand, Sheriff Hammel and I have an excellent working relationship. Although I am technically his superior as the chief law enforcement officer of the County of Los Angeles, I do not tell him how to run his department any more than I give out orders to Chief of Police Sebastian on how to run the City of Los Angeles Police Department. So to answer your question, Miss Normand, no, I cannot order Sheriff Hammel to begin an investigation into this man's death."

The anger in Maisy rose to the surface. "You mean you won't order him to do it, don't you?"

Fredericks leaned back in his chair, allowing his charcoal gray suit coat to open and expose his maroon vest. He gripped the arms of his chair. "I can understand your disappointment and frustration, Miss Malone, but I will not tolerate your attitude toward this office."

"My attitude isn't aimed at your office, Mr. Fredericks. It's aimed at you. You're the one with the bull's-eye painted on your chest. You won't do anything about this because it won't help you get re-elected or it won't help you get elected governor or senator or something."

The district attorney snapped forward and came erect. "That will be enough, Miss Malone."

"No, I'm not through."

Mabel and Milo each took Maisy by an arm to hold her back.

"I warn you, Miss Malone. I am the district attorney for the—"

Maisy shook herself free of her friends, jumped to her feet, and cut Fredericks short with a snarl. "You're just another racially motivated politician. You only do what's politically expedient to get yourself elected to a higher office. If that poor dead man we found on the beach had been a white man, you'd have absolutely no compunction about ordering Sheriff Hammel to do a full investigation into his death. But he was Japanese, so it's not a big deal, is it, Mr. Fredericks? And to think, I read an editorial in the *Times* that compared you to Abraham Lincoln. Man of the people, the writer called you. What a crock that is!"

Fredericks appeared suddenly shaken by her outburst. He sat down again and glared at Maisy for several seconds before speaking calmly to her once more. "Miss Malone, if you will allow me, I will tell you what I will do in this matter."

"You're just like Hammel. You won't do a thing."

Mabel stood up and gently took Maisy by an elbow and a hand. "Let him speak, dear." She eased Maisy back into her seat and sat down herself.

"Thank you, Miss Normand." Fredericks leaned forward in his chair. "As I was saying, Miss Malone, I will tell you what I will do in this matter. I will tell Mr. Hartwell, the county coroner, to have one of his medical examiners make a close inspection of the dead man's body to determine whether or not he was murdered. At the same time, I will speak to the newspapers about this man's death and request that they print something asking anybody who might have some information about this man to come forward and identify the body. If any of that leads us to the conclusion that this man was indeed murdered and we can make a positive identification of the deceased, then I will ask Sheriff Hammel to assign a deputy to begin inquiring into this man's death. How does that sound to you, Miss Malone?"

"How long will all that take?"

Fredericks shrugged. "It could bring immediate results, or it could take days, even weeks."

"Or it could result in a big fat nothing."

"There is that as well."

"That's not doing much, Mr. Fredericks."

"It's the best I can do at this juncture, Miss Malone."

Calm again and in complete control of her temper, Maisy stared at Fredericks and actually saw that he was being straightforward and honest with her. "I can't say that I'm happy about it, Mr. Fredericks, but it's more than I had when I came in here. Thank you for that."

"You're welcome."

"But what if *we* bring you information and evidence that this man was murdered, and *we* can learn his identity? What then, sir?"

"Then I will pass that information to Sheriff Hammel and have him do as I described previously."

"And if *we* can find the killer and prove that killer did it, then what?"

"Then we will prosecute the villain to the limit of the law."

"Is that a promise?"

"You have my word on it."

Maisy studied him for a few seconds. "I believe you."

* * *

Back on the street, Milo spoke first. "What now?"

Maisy looked up at Cole. "Now we go to the one man we should have gone to in the first place."

Mabel shook her head slowly. "Maisy, are you sure you want to do that? I mean, he wasn't the friendliest person on earth the last time you saw him."

"If you mean that day at the cemetery, then you'd be right. But I've seen him and his wife since then. Eddie's gotten over losing our bet, and Nealy says his sense of humor has improved a lot since then."

"Nealy? His wife?"

"Yes. She and I have become good friends over the last few months. She invited me to spend Christmas with them and some other policemen and their wives, but I said no. I would have been out of place with those people, nice as they are and all."

"So are we going to Central Station to see Detective Browning?"

"Well, I'd like to go to their home and talk to him about it there because then I can visit with Nealy as well. But I'm not sure that would be appropriate because it's a police matter."

Cole nodded. "I think you're right about that, Maisy. It's a police matter, and we should talk to him about it at the police station."

With all three being in agreement, Willie drove them to Central Station where they spoke with Sergeant George Willett at the front desk. "How can I help you, Miss Malone?"

"We'd like to see Detective Browning please?"

"Is this police business or personal, Miss Malone?"

"It's about the death of that Japanese fisherman who washed up on the beach north of Santa Monica yesterday."

"Oh, yes, I read about that in the newspaper this morning. What has Detective Browning got to do with it?"

"Nothing yet."

"Then why do you want to see him about it?"

Mabel came forth. "Our boss found the body, and we were there with him."

"I see, but the newspaper said the body was found outside of Santa Monica, which would mean it comes under the county sheriff's jurisdiction."

"Yes, we already know that."

Maisy put her arm on the sergeant's desk. "We've already been to the sheriff's office and to the district attorney's office. They told us they wouldn't be investigating this man's death, but they said if we brought them any kind of evidence that might lead to a conviction, that they would look into it. We'd like to ask Detective Browning for some advice on how we should go about doing that."

Willett shook his head. "Miss Malone, don't you think you should leave this alone? After all, he was only a Japanese fisherman who drowned in the ocean."

"He was murdered, Sergeant Willett."

"But the newspaper said he drowned."

"Well, the newspaper got it wrong. The poor man was murdered. Somebody caved in the back of his head with something like a blacksmith's hammer. We've got photographs to prove it."

Willett shook his head again. "Photographs or not, the body was found in the sheriff department's jurisdiction. It's their case, not ours."

Mabel leaned on the desk and batted her eyes at the policeman. "Aw, come on, Sergeant. Why don't you let Detective Browning decide that?"

Willett heaved a sigh. "Oh, all right, Miss Normand. You win. I'll call him down here." He lifted the receiver from the cradle of the desk telephone and put it to his right ear while he grabbed the base with the other hand. "Connect me to Sergeant Browning." Pause. "Ed, Miss Mabel Normand and two friends are down here asking for you." Pause. "Sure thing." He replaced the receiver on the cradle and set the base back in its proper spot on the desk. "He'll be right down to speak with you, Miss Normand. You can have a seat over there." He pointed to a bench against the wall.

Impeccably dressed as always in a dark blue suit, white shirt, and a slightly lighter blue tie, Detective Sergeant Ed Browning appeared in less than a minute, his olive green eyes sparkling with delight. "George, why didn't you tell me Miss Malone and Mr. Cole were the two friends with Miss Normand?"

The desk sergeant shrugged but made no verbal reply.

"So what brings the three of you here today?" Browning chuckled. "Another murder?"

Maisy spoke first. "Yes, Eddie, another murder."

Browning's thick umber mustache twitched noticeably. "You're kidding, aren't you?"

Mabel shook her head. "No, we're not."

The policeman tilted his head to the right. "Well, I was."

"We aren't," said Mabel.

Maisy spoke up. "Eddie, do you know about the Japanese fisherman who was washed up on the beach north of Santa Monica yesterday?"

Browning pinpointed his gaze on Maisy. "I read about it in the newspaper. The story said he drowned."

Maisy held out the folder with the photographs to him. "Take a look at these pictures we took of him, and I'm pretty sure you'll agree he was murdered."

The detective's brow furrowed. "You have pictures of the body? How did you …?"

"We were there having a picnic when Mack found the body floating among some rocks. We had a camera, so we took some pictures."

"So why are you coming to me about it?"

Maisy related everything from talking to Deputy Van Vliet on the beach to their meeting with District Attorney Fredericks. "And now we're hoping ... or I'm hoping ... you can point us in the right direction on where to start investigating this man's murder."

"*You* want to investigate this murder?"

"Yes, that's right."

Browning shook his head. "Maisy, you're wasting your time."

"How do you figure that?"

"In the first place, the victim is an Asian. Whether he's Japanese, Chinese, or Korean, it doesn't matter. Those people don't talk to white people unless they absolutely have to. And they definitely don't talk to the police about things like this, like a murder. They keep to themselves, and they usually take care of things like this man's death themselves. They don't get involved with white folks except when they work for them. We could send an army of officers and deputies to the fishing villages asking all sorts of questions about this man and do you know what we'd get for it?" He shifted his gaze from Maisy to Mabel to Milo and back to Maisy. "Bunkum. That's what we'd get from them."

"Fishing villages?"

Browning was astounded, and a hint of frustration slipped into his voice. "Didn't you hear what I just said, Maisy?"

"Yes, you said you could send an army of officers and deputies to the fishing villages and you'd get bunkum for your efforts. I heard you, Eddie. So what about these fishing villages you mentioned?"

"A lot of the Japanese men are fishermen, and they live in little ramshackle villages on the beaches. There's one north of Santa Monica at the mouth of Santa Monica Canyon. There's another at Playa del Rey south of Santa Monica. There was one at White's Point west of San Pedro, but that one is gone now. There was one at Timm's Point, but many of those people all moved over to Terminal Island in 1906. Terminal Island used to be called Rattlesnake Island. The name was changed in 1891 when the Los Angeles Terminal Railway bought the island and put their terminal on it. A lot of the old-timers around here still call it Rattlesnake Island."

Maisy raised her eyebrows and focused on Mabel. "Rattlesnake Island sounds a lot more colorful to me. What do you think, Mabes?"

"Well, being in the motion picture business, I have to go along with you on that one, Maisy. Rattlesnake Island is a lot more colorful. Can't you see it on theatre marquee? *Murder on Rattlesnake Island*. Sounds a lot better than *Murder on Terminal Island*. How boring is that?"

The detective cleared his throat. "As I was saying before, ladies, these are places where white people aren't exactly welcome. You'd be lucky if even one of those people spoke to you."

"Really? They can't be any more tight-knit than some of the ethnic neighborhoods of New York or Chicago or London that I've been in. In those places, the bad people look just like the good people. At least in these fishing villages, we'd stand out and know who to keep an eye on when we're there."

Milo shook his head. "You're not planning to go to these villages, are you, Maisy?"

"How else are we going to find out who this man was and who killed him?"

Cole shook his head. "I keep telling people she's nuts, but nobody believes me until she's done something rash. I tell you, she's Crazy Maisy Malone."

"I can't allow you to go into any of those villages, Maisy. It's simply too dangerous for a young woman like you."

Maisy shook her head. "You have no legal right to stop me, Eddie. Besides, I'm not going alone. Mabel and Milo are coming with me."

Browning focused on Mabel. "Miss Normand, can't you talk some sense into her? It's simply not safe for you to go into any of those villages."

"If Maisy goes, then I'm going with her."

The detective shifted to Cole. "Can't you talk them out of this idiocy, Milo?"

Cole smirked. "You're a married man, Ed. You should know that you can't change a woman's mind once she's dead set on doing something inane. And the more inane it is, the more she's going to set her sights on doing it. Even I know that much about women."

Browning heaved a sigh. "All right, I give up. If you're really going to do this, then I'm going with you, too. But I can't do it today."

Disappointment put a frown on Maisy's face. "Why not?"

"It'll be dark before we can get out to the closest one to Santa Monica."

"What about tomorrow?"

"Tomorrow is Friday, and I still have my duty to the City of Los Angeles. I can't go with you until Saturday."

"Well, we'll just have to go without you then." She turned to Mabel. "I think we'll start with the village south of Santa Monica. Since the body washed up on the beach north of Santa Monica, it's more than likely he came from that village. Don't you agree?"

"Good idea. We can start there, first thing tomorrow morning. I'll get Nappy to let us have Willie and the car to take us over there. How soon do you want to get there?"

Browning threw up his hands. "Now hold on for a minute and let's talk this through. You can't go there without some kind of protection. Can't you wait and go Saturday?"

Maisy shook her head. "No. I don't want to waste a single day."

Suspicion furrowed the detective's brow. "What's so urgent about all this, Maisy?" His mustache twitched. "Don't tell me you've made another wager on solving a murder."

Caught with her hand in the cookie jar, the little girl in Maisy went on the defensive. "So what if I have?"

Browning chortled. "I should have known." He shook his head in mild disbelief. "Who did you sucker into betting with you this time? Milo here?"

"Hey! I resent that!"

"No offense meant, Milo."

Maisy put her hands on her hips and glared at Browning. "If you must know, I made the wager with Mack."

"Sennett?" When she affirmed his query with a nod, he burst out laughing. "He's a bigger fool than I was when I made a wager with you over the Leslie Clover murder. You were an unknown when I bet with you, but now you've proven you're a pretty sharp cookie. Sennett should have known better than to let you dupe him into betting with you. What a fool!"

Browning's insensitivity toward her off-and-on fiancé offended Mabel. "You have no call to refer to Mack as a fool, Eddie."

Feigned remorse overtook Browning. "I'm sorry, Miss Normand. You're right. I had no right to say he was a fool. I think sucker was the correct term after all."

Mabel stomped her foot. "If I were a man, I'd—"

Maisy cut her short. "Take it easy, Mabel. I told you his sense of humor had gotten better. He's only trying to get our goats, and it looks like he got yours."

"Maisy's right, Miss Normand. I meant no harm. Mr. Sennett is a first class gentleman, and I'm honored to know him."

"That's better."

Browning turned serious again. "Look, Maisy. I can't go with you tomorrow, but I'll tell you what I can do instead. I'll talk to Sheriff Hammel about sending a deputy with you to see that no harm comes to any of you. How would that be?"

"Sheriff Hammel and District Attorney Fredericks already said they don't have the manpower to investigate the fisherman's death. So what makes you think you can convince him to send a deputy with us?"

"Bill Hammel used to be my boss."

"You were a deputy before you were a cop?"

"No, he was chief of police for a couple years between his terms as sheriff. We have a good professional relationship. I'll ask him for this favor, and when he needs one in return, I won't hesitate to give it to him. That's how law enforcement agencies get along, Maisy."

She beamed at him. "Gee, thanks, Eddie. A deputy coming along would be great." And just as quickly, the smile vanished. "Only make certain the deputy isn't the same one we met yesterday."

"Oh? And who was that?"

* * *

Shortly after dawn the next morning, Willie James halted the Keystone Cadillac in front of the police station in Santa Monica. "Is that the man who's supposed to be joining you all, Miss Normand?" Willie addressed his question to the lead actress because he understood the studio pecking order quite thoroughly.

Mabel peered through the rear passenger side window at a short man in a Stetson standing just inside the double doors of the city building. "Don't look now, Maisy, but I think that's Deputy Van Vliet waiting for us."

Maisy leaned to her right to get a better view. "Omigosh, Mabel!

You're absolutely right. It is him."

Cole squinted in the deputy's direction. "I thought you told Ed to make sure the sheriff didn't send the same deputy we met Christmas Day."

"I did."

"Then why do you think he's here?"

"I've got a hunch about that, but first let's go ask him why he's here."

The three of them emerged from the car at the same time Van Vliet opened the door to the police department and stepped outside. A smile pushed up the ends of his droopy mustache as he tipped his hat to the young women. "Good morning, Miss Normand, Miss Malone." He nodded at Milo. "And to you, Mr. Cole."

Maisy chose to be civil with the man. "What brings you here this morning, Deputy?"

Van Vliet appeared surprised by her question. "Why, Miss Malone, you requested I be assigned to escort you through the fishing village at Playa del Rey. So, here I am."

"I requested *you* specifically?"

"That's what Sheriff Hammel said. He told me Detective Sergeant Ed Browning of the Los Angeles Police Department said you asked for me to accompany you folks this morning."

Maisy glanced at Milo and then at Mabel. "My hunch was right. Eddie was behind this."

Mabel giggled. "Well, you did say his sense of humor has improved over the last few months."

Perplexity wrinkled Van Vliet's sallow face. "Is there something wrong here, Miss Normand?"

Mabel took him by the arm and laughed out loud. "No, Deputy, there's nothing wrong at all. Shall we go?"

* * *

"Over the years I've been a deputy, I've had to deal a lot with the Japanese in my area, and I've picked up some of their lingo." Van Vliet sat in the front seat of the Cadillac with Willie and addressed the moving picture people in the back seat as they rode to the fishing village at Playa del Rey. "The first expression you need to remember, Miss Malone, is '*Konnichi wa*.' It's how you greet someone in Japanese. If you know the person's name, you can add it after *konnichi wa* along with the word '*san*,' which is like saying sir or ma'am to the person. To greet me, you'd say, '*Konnichi wa, Michael-san?* Understand?"

Maisy nodded. "*Konnichi wa, Michael-san?* Is that it?"

Van Vliet smiled. "Almost as good as any Jap I've ever heard speak their gibberish, Miss Malone. Now the word for yes is *hai*. Sounds the same as our word high only with a little more harrumph in it. And no is *iie*. Say it *ee-ee-ay*, but faster. Understand?"

Maisy nodded. "*Hai!*" Then shook her head. "*Iie!*"

"You're catching on, Miss Malone. Now when you finish speaking to a Jap, you say, '*Doomo arigatoo!* That means thank you. You should probably add the man's name and *san* again."

"*Doomo arigatoo, Michael-san*. Like that?"

Van Vliet nodded. "*Hai!* Very good, Miss Malone. Now for the big one. Show the picture and say, '*Shitteimasu ka kono hito?* That means, 'Do you know this man?' It's a mouthful, I know. I'll say it slower for you. *Sheet-tay-ee-mah-soo kah koe-noe hee-toe?* When a real Jap says it, he kind of loses the *ee* between the *tay* and the *mah* in *shitteimasu*. Now you try it."

"*Shitteimasu ka kono hito?*"

The deputy chuckled. "Almost as good as a Jap, Miss Malone. Incredibly good. I think we're ready to go question those fishermen to see if they know this dead man."

"How do I introduce myself?"

"That's easy. Just tap your chest just under your neck and say your name and the word *san*. They'll catch on."

"Like this?" Maisy tapped her sternum with two fingers just below her throat. "*Maisy-san*."

"That will do it, Miss Malone. You ready to go do this now?"

"Yes, we can go now, but there is one thing more that I would ask of you, Deputy."

"And what might that be?"

"Would you please not call these people Japs? I think they find it to be very disrespectful of them."

Van Vliet gave her a patronizing smile. "Well, Miss Malone, I wouldn't call them that, if any of them were around." He waved his arms to indicate no Japanese were in their immediate vicinity.

As straight forward as she was much of the time, Maisy gazed sternly at him. "Then how about not saying it around me?"

The deputy appeared taken aback by her request. He hesitated to speak what he was really thinking. Instead, he forced himself to give her another pretentious smile. "Okay, Miss Malone. You're the boss here."

Maisy shook her head. "No, Deputy Van Vliet, I'm not the boss. It's just my belief that everybody deserves to be respected until they give me a reason not to."

An attack of humility struck Van Vliet. "Yes, of course, Miss Malone. I will do my best to watch what I say from this moment on."

"Thank you for your understanding, Deputy."

* * *

Most of the fishermen had gone out to sea with first light that morning. Only a handful of women and children remained in the village with two men who were nursing injuries from fishing accidents the week before and another man who was repairing a leak in his boat.

While Mabel and Milo stayed behind with Willie and the Cadillac on the bluff above the village, Maisy and Van Vliet approached every single adult and showed them the photograph of the dead man's face. Each time they received the same response. "*Shirimasen!*"

"Just as I thought, Miss Malone. Nobody knows nothing about this man. You're barking up the wrong tree here."

"Deputy, there are dozens of men out there on that ocean who will be coming in soon. I'm not leaving until I've shown all of them this picture."

Determined to that end, Maisy met each boat as it came ashore, showed the photo to the fisherman as he finished tying up his craft, and received the same answer as before. With only a few boats remaining on the water, she finally let her frustration get the better of her, pleading as loud as she could with every man, woman, and child within earshot of her on the beach to give her a break.

"There has to be a better way to do this. All I want to do is find out who this man is so we can tell his family and friends that he's died, so they can give him a decent burial. Is that wanting too much for him? Is that asking too much?"

Every almond eye in the vicinity turned to a single man, one of the two men who had stayed ashore that morning because he needed to give his hand time to heal. Two sets of round eyes followed their lead focusing on the man sitting in the shade of his boat and smoking a cigarette.

With no hesitation, Maisy hurried over to him. "Please, sir, can you tell me about this man? I'm not the police. I only want to see that this man gets a decent burial with a head stone with his name on it. I want to tell his family that he's dead."

An older man with graying hair and a very weathered face, he simply stared blankly at her as if he failed to comprehend a single word she'd said.

"Deputy, get Mabel down here, would you please? Maybe somebody here will tell us something if they see there's two white women who are trying to ... do ... whatever it is I'm trying to do here."

Mabel and Milo had heard Maisy shout out her aggravation at being blunted by the villagers and had already left the vicinity of the Cadillac and were coming down the path from the road along the bluff. As they approached, the man seated in front of Maisy glared past her at the newcomers. Every other eye did likewise. In seconds, little knots of people formed, all whispering in their native tongue and some pointing at Mabel.

"Maisy dear, what's wrong?"

The injured fisherman stood up, his expression no longer one of disinterest. He bowed respectfully to Mabel. The rest of the people did the same thing.

"Maisy dear, what's going on here?"

"Beats me, but if I had to guess, I'd say they must think you're somebody really important or they wouldn't be acting this way. What do you think, Deputy?"

"I've never seen anything like this before from any of these little yellow fellows."

The hurt man held out his hand toward the photograph in Maisy's hand. "Please. Me see one time more."

Maisy held it out to him. "Okay. *Doomo arigatoo*, fisherman-*san*." She shrugged, hoping she had said the words correctly and politely enough to the man.

He took the photo from her, studied it for a moment, then looked up at the people who had slowly gathered around his boat and these four *gaijin*. His head turned slowly as he appeared to be looking for a single face. When he saw the one, he wanted, a smile curled his lips and a twinkle danced in his eyes. He nodded at a boy who was too small to do the physical labor of a fisherman and said a single word. "*Oide!*"

The boy obeyed without question, racing to the man, and bowing before him. He never let his eyes meet the man's until the man spoke to him gently. The boy listened intently to every word and then turned to Mabel and bowed.

"Grandfather says you are welcome in our village."

Mabel's mouth gaped but was speechless for a few seconds. "You speak perfect English."

"I learn from the Christian lady who comes to teach us."

"Well, you've learned very well."

"Thank you, pictures lady."

Mabel smiled and let her view fall on Maisy. "So that's it. They recognize me from the movies."

"Everybody recognizes you from the movies. I'd bet more people have seen your face on a moving picture screen somewhere in this country than have seen Woodrow Wilson's mug. And they remember yours. Here's proof of that right here."

The boy translated for the old man, listened, and then repeated his words in English to Mabel. "Grandfather says we are honored by your presence, pictures lady. How can we help you?"

"First off, you tell your grandfather my name is Miss Mabel Normand, and these are my friends. Miss Maisy Malone and Mr. Milo Cole. This other gentleman is Deputy Sheriff Michael Van Vliet."

As Mabel spoke, the child translated for the village leader.

"Now you tell us your name and your grandfather's name so we may properly speak to him."

"I am Damuko Shibuta. Grandfather is Hanada Shibuta."

Maisy knelt down in front of Damuko. "Would you please ask your grandfather if he knows the man in the photograph?"

The question was asked and answered.

"Grandfather says he has seen this man fishing for tuna on the big boats when they come this way, but he does not know his name. He only knows that he must live in a village south of here because he always comes from that direction in the morning and goes in that direction in the afternoon."

Van Vliet spoke up. "Well, that narrows it down for you, Miss Malone. That fellow came from the Jap... uh, Japanese village on Terminal Island. If we go right now, you'll have just enough daylight left to get to San Pedro and catch the ferry over to the island."

"Damuko, please tell your grandfather we are grateful for his help. And tell him we have to go now to another village to find this man's people. I only wish we could take you with us. But don't tell him that. He might get the wrong idea about us."

The boy translated her words to his grandfather who made a quick reply with a wide smile.

"Grandfather says when you go to another village take Miss Normand with you into the village. They will know her there, and they will be more willing to help you."

"Good tip, Damuko." Maisy mussed the boy's hair, then bowed to Hanada. "*Doomo arigatoo, Hanada-san.*"

* * *

As soon as they were all in the Cadillac again, Maisy questioned Van Vliet. "Deputy, what kind of fishing do they do at Terminal Island?"

"Those people fish for tuna and sardines. They work for the California Fish Company. The big fishing boats are there, tied up mostly at the wharf on the inland side of the inner bay. The smaller boats are usually tied up along the wharf on the outer bay side of Terminal Island. Why do you ask, Miss Malone?"

"Deputy, didn't you hear Damuko say his grandfather would see our dead man on the *big* boats when they passed through these waters?"

"Missed that, but so what?"

"Are there any *big* boats at Playa del Rey?"

Van Vliet thought for a moment. "I don't rightly recollect ever seeing any whenever I've been down here. So what are you saying? That we should go straight to Terminal Island?"

"That's exactly what I'm saying, Deputy."

"Well, if that's the case, then you can go there on your own. Terminal Island is part of San Pedro and East San Pedro, and both towns are part of the City of Los Angeles, meaning it's out of my territory."

"But I thought you were supposed to go with us today?"

"I am as long as you're in my district or the Sheriff's Department's jurisdiction. Nothing was said to me about going into San Pedro."

"But we talked about going to Terminal Island to ask around there about this man."

Van Vliet shook his head. "No, you didn't talk to me about it. You might have talked to someone else about it, but you never said nothing to me about it."

"But you said the dead fisherman came from the village at Playa del Rey or the one on Terminal Island near San Pedro."

"Yes, ma'am, I did, but I said nothing about me going there with you, now did I?"

Chagrin dulled Maisy's face. "No, I guess you didn't." She sighed. "Well, I guess that means you're done helping us, Deputy."

Mabel appeared to be a little more than perplexed. "What does this mean, Maisy?"

She turned to Mabel. "It means we take Deputy Van Vliet here back to the police station in Santa Monica and then go downtown to see Eddie at Central Station."

* * *

Detective Sergeant Ed Browning sat at his desk in the Los Angeles Police Department's downtown station. "So, you've narrowed it down to Terminal Island or Rattlesnake Island, if you prefer. Little late to be going there today. It'll be dark in three hours or so, and it'll take you at least an hour to get there from here. That only leaves you a couple of hours at most to ask around about this man. I've still got some work to do here, so I can't go with you. But I can send a couple of officers with you. However, by the time I can get that arranged, you might only have an hour, or an hour and a half left to do any asking around about this fellow. Do you still want to do that today? Or do you want to wait until tomorrow when I can go with you?"

Maisy continued to be insistent on going to San Pedro that afternoon. "An hour and a half or even an hour is better than no time at all. At the very least, we can get a feel for the place."

Browning threw up his hands. "A feel for the place? Is that what you want?"

"Yes, it is."

"Listen, Maisy. Rattlesnake Island got its name from all the snakes that went there when bad storms struck the area. It's rather misleading as a name. It's always been a quiet place. There used to be a writers and artists colony there, and until recently, there was a resort there called Brighton Beach. Then the Japanese fishermen started settling there, and most of the white people moved away. It isn't Terminal Island that can be dangerous. It's the San Pedro and Wilmington waterfronts that can be troublesome. There are some rough and tough characters who roam the saloons and pool halls there. You don't want to get caught there after dark."

Maisy smiled. "Then we won't stay after dark. We'll leave as soon as the sun sets. I promise."

"You'll leave before the sun sets. I'm going to tell my men to get you off that island before the sun touches the ocean, even if they have to drag you off. Understand, Maisy … Miss Normand … Milo?"

Maisy frowned. "All right, we get it. Off the island before sundown. Now stop wasting our time and get those officers you want to go with us."

* * *

Browning assigned Patrolman Orville Barney and Patrolman John Fitzgerald to ride in the Cadillac with Maisy, Mabel, and Milo. They arrived at the 5th Street Landing in San Pedro shortly after three o'clock.

Looking much like an overgrown leprechaun with his brown eyes and ash brown hair, Officer Fitzgerald pointed across the inner channel to Terminal Island. "Just on the other side of there is another finger of the harbor and beyond that is what's properly known as East San Pedro, Miss Normand. Not much to look at from here. You can either hire a water taxi to take you over there or you can wait for the ferry. But I think we just missed the last ferry. Next one won't be coming back for thirty minutes or so. Only takes about ten minutes to get across, but they wait at each landing for stragglers to board."

"Thank you, Officer Fitzgerald. What do you think, Maisy? Should we wait?"

"I suppose we should wait. By the time we find a boat for hire, the ferry will be back here. What do you think, Milo?"

Before Cole could respond, an older Asian man seemingly appeared out of nowhere and approached Mabel, smiling at her with an incomplete set of tobacco-stained choppers. "You need boat take you island, picture lady?" When she didn't answer right away, he removed his conical straw hat and held it over his chest, revealing his deeply tanned and lined face. "I know you, picture lady. See you all time in moving picture. Very funny picture lady. Know not your name. Just know face. Very funny picture lady."

Maisy came forward. "Do you have a boat to take us over to the island?"

He nodded at Mabel, as if she had asked the question.

Maisy was unperturbed. "Will it hold all five of us?"

"Yes, take all. Ten cents each. Picture lady go free. Honor Tsuchin have picture lady in boat."

"Tsu-chin? Is that your name?"

The man finally acknowledged Maisy. "Yes, name Tsu-chin. My boat." He pointed to an eighteen-foot steam launch tied up fifty feet or so down the quay. "See? Big boat take all over to island. Ten cents each."

"Fair enough." Maisy dug into her purse, took out a silver dollar, and held it out to him. "This should cover it."

Tsu-chin grinned. "Bring you back here later?"

"Yes, that's exactly what I was hoping. You wait for us while we do our business on the island and then bring us back here when we're done. Okay?"

He nodded rapidly. "You come now." He waved toward his craft. "Get on boat now." He took several steps in that direction. "We go now."

The five of them followed him. Maisy and Mabel, then Milo, and the two policemen in the rear.

Cole leaned closer to the women as they walked. "Why don't you show him the photograph, Maisy? Being a boatman here, he might know our man."

"Good idea, Milo."

As soon as they boarded the little steamer, Maisy took the photo from her purse and approached Tsu-chin with it. "Do you know this man?"

The boatman looked at it for a second, and his face turned sour. "This Japanee man. All look same to Tsu-chin."

Maisy nodded. "I see. In other words, you don't know him. Is that right, Tsu-chin?"

The boatman glanced past Maisy at the two police officers prior to answering. "Tsu-chin Chinee man. Japanee man all look same to Tsu-chin. You sit now. Tsu-chin take you to island."

Maisy stared deep into the Chinese boatman's eyes for a few seconds. "Well, I guess that answers that question. Here's another. Can you take us to the Japanese fishing village on the island?"

"Japanee fishing village on north end of island. Face outer bay."

"Okay, but can you take us there?"

Tsu-chin nodded. "Yes, I take you there. Cost more."

"How much more?"

The boatman grinned. "Two time more."

Maisy clinched her teeth. "Jesse James used a gun to rob people. This guy uses a water taxi." She turned to Cole. "Pay the man, Milo. We're running out of daylight."

* * *

Once Tsu-chin had his craft underway, Mabel nudged Maisy's elbow with her own and leaned closer so only her sister sleuth could hear. "Did you notice that our boatman is carrying a knife?"

Maisy turned her head and looked directly into Mabel's eyes. "He better be carrying a knife. It's his boat, and he's the only member of the crew."

Mabel appeared puzzled. "Excuse my ignorance, but what are you talking about?"

"You haven't spent much time on the waterfront, have you, Mabes?"

"So what if I haven't?"

"Well, if you had, then you'd know that just about every man who works on a ship or on the docks carries a knife."

"Really? What on earth for?"

"For cutting things like rope or canvas or baling twine. It's a tool of the trade, Mabes. Men who crew ships carry knives, and so do longshoremen. The only problem with them carrying a knife comes when they're off work and drinking too much at some dockside saloon. Too many of them get a snoot full of booze or beer and they become a little too quick to pull a blade on another man."

"How do you know all of this stuff?"

Maisy shrugged. "I guess I pick stuff up wherever I go. Language, local customs. You know how it is."

"Not like that, I don't."

"Well, stay around me for a while and you'll pick up stuff, too."

Mabel turned her head slowly to the left, but her eyes continued to focus on Maisy. "I'm not sure I want to do that."

The farm girl in Maisy stared back at the actress. "You know what, Mabes? You're probably right about that. I'm pretty sure, if you had seen some of the horrible things, I have in the last six years, then you wouldn't be sitting here next to me right now."

"I wouldn't?"

"No, dearie, you wouldn't."

"So what sorts of horrible things have you seen?"

Maisy shook her head. "Believe me, Mabes, you don't want to know."

"But—"

"Trust me on this, Mabes. You don't want to know."

Maisy and Mabel approached several men on the dock at the north end of the island, not knowing who might be Japanese, Chinese, Korean, or even Mexican, as so many of them fit a general description of black hair, deep tan, almond-shaped eyes with brown irises, and wearing work clothes. Maisy noted many wore straw hats, some felt, a few leather. Mabel eyed each man for a knife on his belt and soon realized Maisy was right about them carrying such an item.

Milo and the two Los Angeles policemen kept within a watchful distance of the two young actresses, but any onlooker could easily see the white men were there to protect Maisy and Mabel. After trying to show the photograph of the dead fisherman to more than a dozen men and getting brushed off, the would-be detectives grimaced with frustration.

"I don't know what's going on here, Mabel. Most of these men seem to recognize you, but then they see Fitzgerald and Barney and they turn cold again. Do you think we should tell our escorts to stay farther away from us while we try to find somebody who recognizes this man's picture?"

"Probably won't hurt. I'll go tell them to keep a wider distance between us, and then let's try to find somebody in those houses over there. I thought I saw a woman looking at us from there."

"Good idea."

Mabel went to the policemen. "Look, fellas, Maisy and I are going over to those houses." She pointed to a group of unpainted wooden shacks. "We think we saw some women there, and we think they might be more willing to speak to us than these men here who seem to be afraid of you."

Being the senior of the two men in uniform, Fitzgerald did most of the talking for both of them. "We can't let you do that, Miss Normand. Our orders are to stick to you like glue."

"Yes, I know, but we're not getting anywhere with you two so close to us. You can see us from here. That should be sufficient, don't you think?"

"I don't think that's such a good idea, Miss Normand." He turned to Officer Barney. "What do you think, Orv?"

With his long nose, sharp chin, brown hair, and blank blue eyes, Barney looked more like a Congregationalist minister than a big city cop. "I know what Sergeant Browning said, but I think we can give these ladies a little more line here, Fitz. It's not that far over there, and if they get out of our sight, then we can move closer to them. Or we could send Mr. Cole with them?"

Fitz snapped his fingers. "That's a crackerjack idea, Orv. How about it, Mr. Cole?"

"Sure, I'll go with them."

Mabel took Milo by an arm. "Ever the faithful companion." She pulled him forward until he was beside Maisy who took his other arm.

Milo glanced at Mabel. "You make me sound like a cocker spaniel."

Maisy leaned against him as they walked. "And just as cute, too."

Cole rolled his eyes and let the two women guide him toward the steps of the first house in the tiny Japanese fishing village.

Maisy gave him a wink. "Smile, Milo. These people don't bite."

"I never said they did."

"Not verbally, you haven't, but the look on your face says you're scared half out of your wits. Now smile and act friendly. Mabel and I will do all the talking with these people."

Cole forced himself to grin. "As you so often say, fair enough."

Maisy knocked on the door and waited for someone to answer.

When nobody came immediately, she rapped her knuckles on the door again. Growing impatient, she knocked a third time and called out in her best Japanese. "*Konnichi wa.*" Finally, the door opened a few inches and a pair of dark eyes peered through the crack. Maisy bowed politely. "*Konnichi wa, okusama.*" Then she tapped her chest just under her throat. "Maisy-*san.*"

"*Konnichi wa, Maisy-san.*"

Mabel stepped forward, bowed, and then straightened up. "*Konnichi wa, okusama.* My name is Mabel Normand. Do you speak English?"

"*Aruteido.*"

Mabel turned to Maisy. "*Aruteido.* What does that mean?"

The woman inside answered for Maisy. "Mean a little bit in American." She opened the door a few inches wider.

The film star nodded. "*Doomo arigatoo, okusama.* My friend here has a photograph we would like to show you. Would you please look at it and tell us if you know the man in the picture?"

"*Hai!*" The woman inside opened the door wider yet.

Maisy held out the photograph to her. "We think he is a Japanese fisherman. Do you know him?"

The woman took the photo and studied it for a moment before making eye-contact with Maisy. "Name Masi Tanaka. Fisherman on tuna boat name *Blackfin.*"

A smile curled Maisy's lips. "Does he have any family in this village?"

She shook her head. "No family. Live other fishermen in big house. Koki house." She pointed toward the largest building in the village, a two-story with a one-story front that stood alone near the north tip of the island. "There." She handed the photograph back to Maisy. "You go now. Talk Koki-*san.* He tell you Masi Tanaka. You go now."

Maisy gave the woman a half-bow. "*Doomo arigatoo, okusama.*"

The woman closed the door abruptly without another word.

Mabel was taken aback. "Well, that was certainly rude."

"Just be glad she talked to us at all. I'm getting the distinct impression that we're not all that welcome here. So, we should be grateful for any bits of information we can get from these people. Now let's go see if Koki-*san* will tell us anything about Masi Tanaka."

"Yes, you're right, dear. At least now we know the poor man's name. What was it again?"

"Masi Tanaka."

* * *

Like most buildings on the island, the Koki boardinghouse was an unpainted, clapboard structure. The major difference between it and the others was the length. Toichero had built a two-story section for boarders on the rear of the original house. Besides a front entrance, it had a private entry for the family on one side and another in the rear for the lodgers to enter and exit without disturbing the owner and his wife. The dining room for the boarders separated their quarters from the Koki family's part of the residence.

Maisy and Mabel stepped onto the porch at the front of the house, leaving Milo behind a few feet from the bottom step. Before they could knock on the door, it opened, and a stern-faced, middle-aged Japanese man came out to meet them.

"I help you ladies?"

Unabashed, Maisy bowed respectfully at the man. "*Hai!*" She held out the photograph to him. "*Shitteimasu ka kono hito?*"

The man ignored the picture of Masi Tanaka. "Who tell you come here talk me?"

Mabel pointed to the house they had just left. "The nice lady who lives over there."

He looked in the direction she indicated. "Mrs. Mizuno?"

Maisy shook the photograph to draw his attention to it again. "She didn't tell us her name, but she said this man lived here in this house. The house of Koki-*san*. Are you Koki-*san*?"

He nodded. "Yes, I am Toichero Koki. This my house."

Maisy nudged Mabel. "I am honored to meet you, Koki-*san*." She bowed again. "I am Miss Maisy Malone."

Mabel also bowed. "I am also honored to meet you, Koki-*san*. I am Miss Mabel Normand."

Koki bowed to Mabel. "I know you face. You lady in moving picture show. Very funny. Make me laugh." He bowed again, and when he came erect again, his facial features had softened to a friendlier attitude. "You honor this house. You honor me."

Mabel smiled at the man. "*Doomo arigatoo, Koki-san.*"

"You say Japanese word better I say American word."

"*Doomo arigatoo, Koki-san.*"

He smiled at Mabel. "You welcome, Miss Normand."

Maisy rippled the photograph again to get his attention back to her. "Japanese is a beautiful language, Koki-*san*. I wish I could speak more of it."

"You say Japanese word good, Miss Malone." Finally, he looked at the picture of the dead fisherman. "I know him. Masi Tanaka. Fisherman. Work on tuna boat *Blackfin*. Not see him for four day now. Last see morning of big wind." He shook his head. "Not good picture of him."

"That's because he's dead, Koki-*san*."

This sudden revelation startled the man, stiffening him most noticeably. "*Tanaka-san shinda?*"

"Well, if *shinda* means dead, then ... *hai, Koki-san! Tanaka-san shinda!* He's dead."

Koki furrowed his brow as he seemed lost for words. "How he die?"

"He was found on a beach north of Santa Monica."

"Die in ocean? Not Tanaka-*san*. Tanaka-*san* swim good. Tanaka-*san* abalone fisherman in Japan. Leave there, come here. Work tuna boat more money. Save money, bring wife from Japan."

"Tanaka-*san* had a wife in Japan?"

Koki nodded. "Yes, wife in Japan. Picture bride." Seeing the confusion on the faces of the two female callers, he held up his hand. "Wait. I show you." He left Maisy and Mabel standing on the porch, while he went back into the house. A moment later he returned with his wife and a framed photograph of her. She stood politely to his side and a step back from where he stood. "I want marry. I tell marriage man here. He write marriage man in Japan. Marriage man in

Japan send pictures. I pick this one." He handed the portrait to Mabel who then shared it with Maisy. "She now my wife. Her name Hatsenke. She come here from Ehime prefecture in Japan. She work canning factory when tuna boat bring in catch. Take care my house. Cook, clean, do laundry for boarders."

Mabel and Maisy performed the customary bows and spoke the usual greeting when meeting a Japanese person. "*Konnichi wa, Hatsenke-san.*" Then each took a turn tapping herself on the chest and saying her name.

In their native language, Koki explained to his wife that Mabel was the lady they had seen in the moving pictures at the theatre in San Pedro. This brought a warm smile from Hatsenke that disappeared as soon as he said, "*Tanaka-san shinda.*" She immediately lowered her eyes to hide the emotional pain she was feeling, followed by a slight bow and the placement of her right hand on her belly. Then with a couple of muttered words in Japanese, she lowered her hand, turned away from their *gaijin* visitors, and went back into boardinghouse.

Maisy pursued the interview. "Koki-*san*, you said Tanaka-*san* had a picture bride. Is that right?"

"Tanaka-*san* tell marriage man here write letter to marriage man in Japan. Marriage man send Tanaka-*san* pictures women want marry. Tanaka-*san* pick one he like. Marriage man make marriage for Tanaka-*san* and picture bride. Tanaka-*san* save money. Tanaka-*san* send money marriage man. Marriage man send picture bride America. Tanaka-*san* go San Francisco, meet picture bride, bring here, live here, make family, become American."

Hatsenke returned, her eyes moist and red from crying. She spoke to her husband in Japanese. When she finished, he returned his attention to Maisy. "My wife want know why you ask about Tanaka-*san* if he dead."

"Miss Normand, our friend Milo behind us, and another man … Mr. Sennett, and I found Tanaka-*san*'s body on the beach two days ago and reported it to the police. They have his body at the Los Angeles County Morgue, hoping somebody will come to identify him and claim his body for burial. We volunteered to search for anybody who might have known him. That is why we are here talking to you, Koki-*san*."

Koki gave Maisy a stern look. "You not say how Tanaka-*san* die."

The actresses exchanged hesitant glances before Maisy nodded. "We have to tell them, Mabel, and we have to tell them the truth, if we expect them to be honest with us as well."

"You're right, of course. They're going to find out sooner or later, so they might as well hear it from us."

"My thoughts exactly." Maisy faced the Kokis, her focus shifting from Mrs. Koki to her husband. "Tanaka-*san* was murdered."

Koki tilted his head to the left. "What ... murdered?"

"We think someone killed him."

"Kill ... Tanaka-*san?*"

Maisy lowered her eyes. "*Hai!*"

Seeing her husband's face suddenly ashen, Hatsenke asked for an interpretation. When he explained, she gasped. "*Satsujin?*"

"*Hai! Satsujin.*"

Maisy peered at Mabel. "*Satsujin.* I guess that's the Japanese word for murdered."

Koki nodded.

As much as she wanted to see Tanaka's personal belongings in his living space in the rear of the Koki boardinghouse, Maisy knew better than to ask Toichero for permission to do so. She and Mabel had gained the trust of this Japanese immigrant and his wife, and they had no desire to risk damaging that golden bond. Instead, they asked a few simple questions about the dead man.

"Did he have any family in America?"

"*Hai!* Brother live Los Angeles."

"Do you know his brother's name?"

"Name Tokutaro Tanaka. Own candy store, Alameda Street, downtown Los Angeles. Between Fifth and Sixth street. We go there Saturday. Not often. Visit friends live there."

"When did he come to America?"

"Not know sure. Maybe eight, nine year back."

"And you said he worked on the tuna boat *Blackfin*. Is that right?"

"*Hai!*"

"Does the *Blackfin* dock on this island?"

"Yes, *Blackfin* dock on wharf. Only *Blackfin* and *Yellowfin* fishermen live here."

"Are they here now?"

"No, both at sea now. Come back tonight maybe. Not tonight, maybe tomorrow morning."

Maisy and Mabel thanked Toichero and Hatsenke for their help and bid them *sayonara*. With Milo close at hand, they rejoined Fitzgerald and Barney at the quay.

"You spoke with that Japanese couple a long time, Miss Malone," said Fitz. "I gather you learned the identity of the dead Jap fisherman."

"We did, Officer Fitzgerald."

Maisy gave the two policemen a brief report on their interview with the Kokis as they walked along the quay. "All things considered; I think we did as good a job of questioning as Detective Browning would have done if he had been here. Don't you agree, Mabel?"

"Absolutely, Maise." Mabel's expression turned quizzical. "Did you see anything odd about those people?"

"Only that he looked a lot older than his wife. But that's probably because he's spent more time in the sun than she has."

Mabel nodded. "Yes, that's it. He's been outdoors more than she has. That explains why she looks so pale."

Smoking a cigarette and sitting on a coiled mooring line piled neatly on the dock, Tsu-chin, the Chinese boatman who had brought them over to Rattlesnake Island, waited patiently for the five of them to return for the ride back to the main side quay. When he saw them approaching, he popped erect. "You find Japanee man in picture?"

"What difference is that to you?" asked Cole a bit snidely.

The boatman shrugged. "Mean nothing to Tsu-chin. Just ask friendly. No matter to me."

Sensing something suspicious in the ferryman's defensive tone, Maisy responded for Cole. "Well, if you must know, we didn't find him on the island. But we did learn his name and the name of the boat where he works. His boat is out to sea right now, so we'll have to come back again tomorrow."

"What boat he work on?"

"The *Blackfin*. Do you know it?"

Tsu-chin smiled, showing his tobacco-stained teeth. "Yes, Tsu-chin know *Blackfin*. Captain name Esteván Garrido. Mexican. He is brother to Geraldo Garrido, merchant at fish market in San Pedro. *Blackfin* come into harbor tonight sometime, I think. Unload catch for cannery. Stay in harbor till Monday or later. You come back tomorrow early to talk to Captain Garrido and other fishermen before get pay and get drunk tomorrow night and stay drunk till go back to sea."

"That's a good tip, Tsu-chin." She turned to Cole. "I think Tsu-chin deserves a little extra for his help here."

Milo frowned. "I don't have any money. Don't forget, I'm just a poor gofer at the studio. I'm not a lead player or even a featured player, am I?"

Mabel dug a five-dollar bill out of her purse and held it out to the boatman. "Here you go, Tsu-chin. Thanks for your help."

The amount of the gratuity greatly pleased the boatman. "Tsu-chin thank you, Picture Lady. You so kind. We go now before fishing boats come into harbor."

The two women boarded Tsu-chin's little steamer and sat as far away from the boatman as they could.

"You know, Mabel, I found that picture bride business rather interesting, didn't you?"

"Yes, I did. Can you imagine marrying a man you've never met?"

"I can't, but it's done all the time, even here in America. You've heard of mail order brides, haven't you?"

"Yes, I have."

"Well, this is the Japanese version of it, I guess."

The two policemen joined them. As usual, Fitzgerald did most of the talking for them. "Will you be coming back to the station with us, Miss Malone?"

"Do you think Detective Browning will still be at the station by the time we arrive back there?"

"He might be waiting for us. Can't rightly tell."

"Then can we get to a telephone and call him as soon as we reach the dock?"

"I'm certain there's a call box on Beacon Street, Miss Malone. I can call the station from there and pass them the word to have Sergeant Browning stick around until we get there."

* * *

Browning had waited at Central Station for the trio of pseudo-detectives as requested. "You never cease to astound me, Maisy. You find the body of a Japanese fisherman washed up on the beach north of Santa Monica on Christmas Day, and two days later you've not only learned his name but where he lived, where he worked, and who is relatives are. You are simply amazing, my dear Miss Malone."

"You're only saying that because you want something from me, right?" Browning glanced at the others around Maisy before focusing on her again. "And there's that about you as well. You really know how to read people, don't you?"

"Vaudeville training. Now spill it, Eddie. What do you want?"

"Well, since this is now a case for the Los Angeles Police Department, which means I will be handling the investigation, I'd like you and Miss Normand to accompany me to the candy store on Alameda and help me break this sad news to the fisherman's brother."

"I'm okay with that. How about you, Mabel?"

"Do you want to do it right now?"

Maisy turned back to Browning. "There's no time like the present, right, Eddie?"

"Right, you are, Maisy."

"Okay, we'll do it, but on one condition."

Browning sagged. "I should have known." He grimaced at Maisy. "And what is that condition?"

"I get to interview Mr. Tanaka about his late brother."

Surprise burst all over the policeman. "That's it?"

Maisy nodded. "That's it … for now."

"Done. You tell him his brother is dead, and then you can interview him all you want. I'll have Miss Sharpe come along to record everything."

"Good idea, Eddie. Glad to have Nellie along."

* * *

Because they would need a ride home after visiting with Masi Tanaka's brother, Mabel had Willie drive her, Maisy, Browning, and Miss Sharpe to the Tanaka candy store on North Alameda. Milo Cole begged off going with them, claiming he was tired and had a busy day ahead of him. The Keystone Studio's Cadillac arrived in front of the Tanaka's confectionary shop half past five o'clock to find it still open.

"Oh, look, Maisy. There's a restaurant on each side of the candy store. I've never had Japanese food before. Why don't we pick one and give it a try after we're done with Mr. Tanaka?"

"What about Eddie and Nellie? Don't you think it would be a bit rude for us to—"

Mabel blushed. "Oh, of course, you're right. I'm sorry, Eddie. Would you—and you, too, Nellie—would you like to join us for some Japanese food? My treat, of course."

The stenographer hesitated a breath before responding. "I wouldn't like to impose on you, Miss Normand."

"You wouldn't be imposing. Now I insist both of you join us."

Browning smiled politely. "Well, I've already called my wife and told her I would be late getting home this evening, so I guess I'm up for it."

Nellie Sharpe's plain face brightened with a huge smile. "If Detective Browning is all right with it, then I am, too. I can't wait to tell the girls back at the station that I had supper with Mabel Normand." She gasped and covered her mouth. "Oh, I'm sorry, Miss Normand. I meant no disrespect by that. I only—"

Maisy tapped Nellie on the forearm. "Forget it, dearie. I eat with her all the time, and I still get a thrill when she picks up the check."

The bespectacled stenographer gasped again, mouth agape.

This time Mabel tapped her arm. "She's only making a joke, Nellie. You don't mind if I call you Nellie, do you? Miss Sharpe is so formal at times like these, don't you think?" Gently, she took Nellie by an arm and guided her toward the candy store entrance.

The brown-eyed transcriptionist with mousy brown hair tied in a bun went along quite willingly.

Browning held the door open for them. "Ladies." Then he followed them inside, where a few customers, all Asian and all eating ice cream, sat at the tables along the wall to the right. The patrons glanced up at the new arrivals, saw their race, and just as quickly returned their attention to consuming the tasty dairy treats. Glass cases with bins containing all sorts of candy from lemon drops to pink sugar mints to chocolate covered raisins to striped candy canes lined the area to the left. The man behind the counter smiled at the newcomers in anticipation of serving them. Maisy went directly to him.

"*Desu ka Tanaka-san?*"

"*Hai!* May I help you?"

"You speak American very well, Mr. Tanaka."

"Thank you." He gave Maisy a half bow.

With his brow pinched tight over the bridge of his distinctive nose, Browning stepped forward and spoke softly. "Mr. Tanaka, is there a place where we can speak to you privately, sir?"

"I cannot leave the store. I am only one here."

The detective leaned against the candy counter to get as close to the proprietor as he could and spoke even softer. "Mr. Tanaka, I am Detective Sergeant Edward Browning of the Los Angeles Police Department."

The proprietor blanched with fright as he rasped out two words. "Police Department?"

Maisy intervened. "You're not in any trouble, Mr. Tanaka."

The smile and normal color returned to Tanaka's face. "That is good to hear."

Browning made a quick survey of the ice cream parlor. "I'm

sorry to tell this, sir, but you we have some very sad news for you."

Tanaka's smile vanished. "Sad news?"

Maisy pressed herself close to the counter beside Browning. "*Hai, Tanaka-san*, sad news." She took the photograph of the deceased fisherman from her purse and showed it to Tanaka. "Is this man your brother Masi?"

The confectioner stepped forward to get a better look at the picture. "That look like Masi, but something is wrong with his face. He looks fat in photograph."

"Mr. Tanaka, my friends, and I discovered this man's body on the beach north of Santa Monica two days ago. He was dead."

Shock ashened Tokutaro's face. "Masi dead?"

Browning nodded grimly. "Yes, sir, I am afraid so. We have your brother's body at the county morgue. Would you please come to the morgue as soon as possible to make a positive identification of the body? Then we can release it to you for final dispensation."

The shock of the news still paralyzed Tanaka's thinking. "Masi is dead?"

"Yes, sir, he is. I'm deeply sorry for your loss, Mr. Tanaka."

Reality struck the candy store owner. "How did Masi die? You say you found his body on a beach. Did Masi drown?"

The policeman shook his head. "No, we don't think so."

Maisy focused hard on Tanaka and spoke the single word in Japanese. "*Satsujin.*"

Tanaka choked on the word as he spoke it in English. "My brother was murdered?" His eyes welled up with tears.

With great sorrow dulling the amber flecks in her brown eyes, Maisy nodded at him. "We believe so."

Tanaka tried unsuccessfully to blink his tears away. Recognizing his failure, he turned away from the bearers of this tragic report, hurried toward the rear of the store, and disappeared through drapes covering a doorway.

"Now you know why I wanted you along with me, ladies."

Tanaka's Candy Store and Ice Cream Parlor closed exceedingly early that Friday night because Tokutaro Tanaka and his family grieved for his brother.

"Detective Browning, may I see my brother tonight?"

With Miss Sharpe seated in an armchair writing down everything that was being said, Browning sat between Mabel and Maisy on the sofa in the Tanakas' living room. The detective accompanied his verbal answer with a nod. "Yes, sir, I can arrange that."

Mabel nudged the policeman. "We can take Mr. Tanaka to the station in the studio's car, Eddie."

"You don't have to go out of your way like that, Miss Normand. I can have a department car come here and ..." He hesitated to complete the sentence, suddenly rethinking his offer. "That's very gracious of you, Miss Normand. I will have a department car sent here to pick up Miss Sharpe and me. Mr. Tanaka, do you have a telephone I can use?"

Tanaka pointed to the device on a table in the hall that led to the family's bedrooms in the rear of the apartment.

"Thank you, sir." The detective went to make the call.

The two actresses and the stenographer remained with Tanaka and his wife in their apartment above the confectionary shop. Miss Sharpe wrote furiously on her pad whenever any of them spoke, adding notes of her own about a speaker's tone or expression when time allowed.

Mabel offered the Tanakas words of consolation, while Maisy

interjected the occasional disguised question about their deceased relative.

"Mr. Tanaka, once again we are so sorry for your loss."

"Thank you, Miss Normand. You are a truly kind lady."

Maisy took her turn. "Were you and Masi very close, Tanaka-san?"

"I came to America from Kochi prefecture in Japan fourteen years ago. I worked at abalone fishing at White's Point and saved money to send for Masi. I saved money for five years. I sent money to Japan for Masi to come here in year 1903. We worked together one year at abalone fishing. We saved money together. I got new job on tuna boat. Made better money. I worked on *Blackfin* for three years. I saved more money to bring Tane to America to be my wife." He squeezed his mate's hand. "Tane came to America in year 1907. We bought this store from Chinese family named Yet. Masi came here whenever *Blackfin* in port and stayed here till he go back to tuna boat and go out fishing again."

"Did he work in the store with you those days he would come here?"

"Only on Sunday when we clean store and restock candy bins. On Saturday, Masi worked with Mr. Masemoto. He is a barber with his own shop one block north."

Maisy didn't know why, but she had a sudden inclination to ask about the deceased's love life. "Did Masi have a lady friend?"

"Not many unmarried Japanese women here in America, so Masi went to marriage broker to look at pictures of women back in Japan who want to come here, just like Tane. He saw one he liked. Her name is Teruka Watanabe. Mr. Iwaturo Oura is the marriage broker here. He made contact with a broker in Japan who informed the Watanabe family that a potential husband for their daughter was found here in America. The broker in Japan consulted our family in Japan to make certain they would be a good match. When this was done and both families gave approval, Masi gave the marriage broker money for Teruka to come to America. He did this in October. He received word that Teruka would be arriving in San Francisco on third day of January. Masi planned to meet her at the Detention Barracks on Angel Island and bring her here to live. Masi then will quit the fishing boat and work here in our store and for Mr. Masemoto in his shop. Masi and Teruka will save money and buy their own business. Masi wanted to own a flower shop. No flower shops here in this neighborhood. Good idea. We planned to help him buy store, and he will repay us."

"Mr. Tanaka, this is a rather delicate question, but I have to ask it. Do you know if your brother had any enemies?"

Tanaka grimaced at Maisy. "Masi was liked by everybody. He was always happy as a boy. Always smiling. He worked hard. He made our parents enormously proud. I am proud of my brother. Now ... he is gone." He leaned close to his wife and squeezed her hand tighter as tears filled his eyes and trickled down his face.

Browning returned, almost as if on cue. "It's all arranged. Someone will be at the morgue to show you the body, Mr. Tanaka, and a department car is on its way here now to pick up Miss Sharpe and me."

* * *

Walking out of the store, Maisy turned to Mabel. "The Tanaka's are following the right path to get ahead in this country. It's the same way immigrants have gotten ahead for years. The oldest brother comes here, works, saves his money, sends for another family member or two to join him. They live together to save money until one can move out and have his own place and family and bring over another relative and so on. That's how it's been done since colonial times. The Irish did it that way when they came here, and then the Germans did it. Then the Swedes and Norwegians after them. Russians, Poles, Jews, Italians. The Chinese did it out here in California, and now the Japanese are doing it. All immigrants do it that way. That's how they survive in the beginning and prosper later on."

On the sidewalk in front of the candy shop as they waited for Tokutaro Tanaka to join them, Mabel appeared incredulous. "How do you know so much about all this stuff?"

"I read. I talk to people. They tell me where they came from and how they got here. I listen. That's all."

"You've been around a lot of immigrants, I take it."

"Probably more than most native-born Americans." Maisy shook her head. "I don't fear immigrants. I'm glad they come here."

"You are?"

"Of course, I am. New blood in America is what keeps our country strong and free."

"How do you figure that?"

"Whereas most native-born Americans whose families have been here since before the American Revolution, those who call themselves natives, they take our freedom for granted, while new people cherish the liberty we have in this country. They came from a country where they were usually oppressed or had cultural restraints put on them, and when they get here, they discover the government doesn't try to run their lives for them. The political parties do, but not the government." Maisy shook her head. "Boy, if that ever changes, the people in this country will really be knee-deep in pig manure."

"But how did you meet so many foreigners, Maisy?"

"Vaudeville at first. Then the music halls in England. You know, the sun never sets on the British Empire. Well, a lot of people from all those places where the British flag flies come to London for one reason or another, especially those who are half-castes, the children of all those British soldiers posted all over the world to protect the Empire. They're half-English, and the other half could be Indian, Malay, Chinese, Burmese, or any one of a number of African peoples, especially those whose ancestors were dragged off from Africa to be slaves in the British possessions like Jamaica and Barbados in the West Indies.

"After London, I met hundreds of them on the boat coming back to America. Did I ever tell you that when I got to New York what a hard time I had getting off Ellis Island? The cops there heard me speaking Spanish to Eduardo, this Spanish sailor who had followed me home all the way from Spain like some kind of lovesick puppy. The authorities thought I was Spanish, so they wouldn't let me leave the immigration station until I admitted I was Spanish. You won't find me in their records under my real name or my stage name. I said I was Emilia Sigorraga, and that's what they wrote down."

"How did you come up with that name?"

"That was Eduardo's mother's name. It was the only one I could think of at the time."

"You've never told me about this Eduardo. What did you do to make him follow you all the way to America?"

Maisy gave Mabel a coy smile. "Wouldn't you like to know?"

"Yes, I would, so spill it."

Before she could reply, Maisy saw Tokutaro Tanaka exit the store and come toward them. "Another time, Mabes. Right now, I want to keep my focus on finding out who killed Masi Tanaka. *¿Comprende, amiga?*"

* * *

After Tokutaro Tanaka made a positive identification of his brother's body in the county morgue, Browning took him to the Central Police Station where they could continue the interview Maisy and Mabel had begun at the candy store.

The detective opened the conversation. "Mr. Tanaka, once again we would all like to express our most sincere condolences to you for the loss of your brother. We've all lost loved ones, and we know how hard this is on you. But if you don't mind, Miss Malone would like to ask you just a few more questions."

"Thank you, Detective Browning. Yes, I will gladly answer any questions Miss Malone would like to ask me, if it will help you catch and punish the man who killed my brother."

Maisy stepped up. "Mr. Tanaka, could you tell us about your brother's friends?"

"Yes, of course. Closest friend to Masi is Yoshi Yamaguchi. Yoshi was a diver with Masi at White's Point. He went with Masi to work on the *Blackfin* tuna boat for Mr. Geraldo Garrido. Mr. Geraldo owns several stalls at the fish market in San Pedro. Mr. Geraldo is an important man around the harbor. Very wealthy. His son Esteván is the captain of the *Blackfin* tuna boat. Mr. Geraldo owns two tuna boats in San Pedro Harbor. The *Blackfin* and the *Yellowfin*."

"Does Yoshi live at the same boardinghouse as Masi?"

"Yes, Mr. Toichero Koki's boardinghouse. Mr. Koki came to America ten years ago. He worked for Mr. Geraldo on a fishing boat, saved his money, brought his picture bride here from Japan six years ago. They bought the boardinghouse from Mr. Geraldo. I lived in the same boardinghouse before I brought my wife here from Japan. Many unmarried Japanese fishermen live at the Koki boardinghouse now. Before Toichero bought it from Mr. Geraldo, not all fishermen who lived there were Japanese. Some were Mexican, some Portuguese, some Chinese. Then Japanese like me came there to live. Chinese move out. Mexicans move out. Portuguese move out last. Japanese move in."

"Was there a reason the Chinese, Mexican, and Portuguese fishermen moved out of the boardinghouse?"

Tanaka smiled. "Oh, yes. Like me, they find a wife and go to work in a factory or for a railroad. Mr. Oura finds them jobs on railroad. Mr. Oura also arranged marriage for me and other Japanese men. He is what you call a contractor. He is a very smart man, especially important man to Japanese here in California."

Maisy nodded at Tanaka. "You mentioned Mr. Oura before." She glanced at Browning before asking the next question. "Do you know where we can find Mr. Oura?"

"Oh, yes. He lives in the hotel in the same block as my store. Mr. Masuda manages hotel. Only Japanese stay there now."

"Mr. Tanaka, you mentioned your brother worked for a barber with a shop in the next block."

"Yes, Mr. Masemoto. He came to America in year 1904. His wife's name is Kame. She came to America the same year with her family, but she did not marry Mr. Masemoto until year 1908. Kame is very pretty. Masi wanted Kame for his wife, but Mr. Atanabu, her father, said no. Mr. Oura arranged the marriage with Mr. Masemoto."

"Why did Kame's father say no to your brother marrying her?"

"Masi not have enough money yet for them to have their own

home. Mr. Masemoto has his own barber shop. Mr. Atanabu only wanted the best for his oldest daughter, and he wanted her gone from his home. Three more daughters to feed still at home after Kame married."

This last brought a polite smile to Maisy lips. "Mr. Tanaka, when was the last time you saw your brother alive?"

"Masi came to our home on Saturday, and Yoshi came with him."

"Yoshi Yamaguchi?"

"Yes, that right. Masi worked for Mr. Masemoto on Saturday, and then he and Yoshi worked in the store on Sunday so Tane and I could have time with our children. Masi and Yoshi finished working in store at seven o'clock as usual, and then they come to apartment to eat supper. After supper, Masi, Yoshi, and I played *hanafuda*, a Japanese card game. We went to bed around ten o'clock and get up next morning at four o'clock so Masi and Yoshi can eat breakfast before catching Red Car to go back to San Pedro to work. That was the last time I saw Masi alive."

"Did he seem to be all right when he left that morning?"

Tanaka's face wrinkled up. "What do you mean by all right?"

"I mean, was he his usual self that morning? Or was he acting differently than he normally did around you?"

The confectioner nodded. "Yes, I see what you mean." Then he shook his head. "No, he was not acting different than normal." He suddenly twisted to the right as an odd thought struck him. "Masi was all right when he left Monday morning, but when he came home from working at Mr. Masemoto's barber shop on Saturday night, he was not his usual self. I did not think much about it then, but now I think he was a little unhappy about something."

"Do you have any idea what might have made him a little unhappy that evening?"

"I remember he spoke with Yoshi in a low tone so that only Yoshi could hear him. I do not know what was said between them, and neither of them shared anything about it with me. Why do you ask? Do you think it might have something to do with Masi's murder?"

Again, Maisy glanced at Browning before responding to Tanaka. "It probably has nothing to do with his death, Mr. Tanaka. It's only one of those many questions that have to be asked in an investigation like this."

"I see." Suddenly, another thought came to the candy store owner. "Forgive me for asking, but why are you asking all the questions, Miss Malone, and not Detective Browning? I thought you were an actress."

"I am an actress."

Browning stepped in. "I'm afraid that's my doing, Mr. Tanaka. To be perfectly honest with you, it's been my experience that most Asian people are a little reluctant to speak freely with the police. So I thought you would be more comfortable answering these questions if Miss Malone did the asking."

"Yes, of course, Detective. You were only thinking of my feelings in this matter."

"That's pretty much it, Mr. Tanaka. That and we want to get to the bottom of this as soon as we can and find your brother's killer and place him under arrest."

"Yes, we must find Masi's killer as soon as possible so his soul may have peace and move on to the next world."

His statement brought a new line of questioning to Maisy. "Mr. Tanaka, I am unfamiliar with Japanese funeral customs. What will you do with your brother's mortal remains? I only ask because Mabel and I would like to pay our respects to your brother and to your family."

Tanaka nodded his understanding. "I will send word to Shinto priest to come and mourn with me and my family tomorrow. He will stay all day, lead our family and friends in mourning prayers for Masi, and perform other rituals for Masi and for us and his friends and relatives. Next day will be the cremation of Masi's body. More ceremonies will follow. Some ashes Tane and I will take for a shrine to Masi in our home. Yoshi may want some ashes for his own shrine to Masi. This is allowed. The rest will be placed in an urn and buried in his grave in a cemetery. I will keep our store closed for next three days to honor Masi."

"One final question, Mr. Tanaka. Would it be appropriate for us to come to your home tomorrow to pay our respects?"

Tears welled up in Tanaka's eyes. "My family and I would be honored to have you." He looked from Maisy to Browning to Mabel and to Miss Sharpe. "All of you, please come."

* * *

Mabel had Willie drive Mr. Tanaka back to his candy store, while she and Maisy remained at the station with Browning to discuss what they had learned so far and where to take the investigation from this point.

Browning spoke first. "You know, Maisy, I'm really quite impressed with how you got so much out of Mr. Tanaka. Most Asians I've had to deal with since I've been on the force aren't that open when questioned. I'm thinking I should keep you around this case, but I suppose Mr. Sennett will want you back at the studio bright and early Monday morning."

"In the first place, Eddie, thank you for the compliment, and in the second, Mack is closing down the studio next week because of the New Year holiday and because he'll be busy telling the help how he wants the Cadillac decorated for the *Tournament of Roses* parade. So, I'm free to help you all I can with this investigation for the whole week."

Mabel leaned forward slightly. "That makes two of us, Eddie."

"Well, that's wonderful news, Miss Normand."

"Eddie, you have to stop calling me Miss Normand. I'm simply Mabel to you, okay?"

"It's hard to think of you as simply Mabel, since you're such a famous moving picture actress and all."

Maisy tilted her head to the left. "You'd better do what she says, Eddie, or she'll find a way to make you do it. You should see how she handles Mack when she's alone with him or when there's only one or two other people present, and those folks are limited to people who know Mack almost as well as Mabel does."

Browning threw up his hands in surrender. "Okay, Mabel it is from now on." He focused on Maisy. "So what do you think so far?"

"I think we've got a long way to go to find out who killed poor Masi Tanaka. I think before we can figure out who did it we have to figure out where he was murdered and why."

Mabel shook a finger as if to get attention. "You know, I thought it was rather interesting that Masi is working for the man who married the first girl he wanted to marry. What was her name again?"

Miss Sharpe flipped through her notepad. "*Kah-may.*"

"Yes, Kame. And then Mr. Tanaka said Masi was a little out of sorts when he came home Saturday evening from working at the barber shop. I wonder if that had anything to do with Mrs. ... what was the barber's last name again, Nellie?"

Miss Sharpe checked her notes again. "*Mah-say-moto.*"

"Yes, Masemoto. Like I was saying, I wonder if Masi's mood had anything to do with Mrs. Masemoto."

Maisy titled her head. "I guess we'll find that out when we talk to Mr. and Mrs. Masemoto, won't we?"

Browning held up a finger. "Going back to what you said a minute ago, Maisy, I think you're right about finding out where it was that Masi Tanaka was murdered. Since he washed up on the beach north of Santa Monica, it makes me wonder where he went into the water. Most likely not at San Pedro because he would have had to float all the way around Point Fermin and then west to Point Vicente and from there north and on up to where Mr. Sennett found him. I don't know how long that would take, but it seems to me it would have taken several days for a body to float that far."

Maisy nodded. "I agree with you there, Eddie. I don't believe he went into the water in San Pedro Harbor. So, it seems logical that he had to be out on the ocean somewhere when he went into the water. If that's true, then the question is, was he on board the *Blackfin* when he went into the water? Do you know if there were any reports about the tuna boat losing a man?"

Miss Sharpe flipped back another page. "Mr. Koki said the

Blackfin was still out to sea and wouldn't be back into port until around sundown."

Maisy snapped her fingers. "That's right he did say that." She pinpointed her gaze on Browning. "It's after sundown, Eddie. Is there any way you can find out if the *Blackfin* lost a man overboard?"

Browning scratched the nape of his neck. "We've got a couple choices to get an answer to your question. I can call the San Pedro precinct and ask if they've received any reports about it. Or ..."

"Or we can get in the Cadillac as soon as Willie returns and go down to San Pedro and ask Captain Garrido in person."

Browning's call to the San Pedro precinct proved fruitless. Nothing had been reported about a fisherman missing from the *Blackfin* or any other tuna boat.

"You might save yourself a trip down here, Sergeant, if you call the harbormaster to see if the *Blackfin* has returned to port yet."

"Thank you, Sergeant Willett. I'll do just that."

A call to the harbormaster's office produced one positive result and one negative. Yes, the *Blackfin* had returned and was tied up at its slip on Terminal Island offloading its catch that week; and no, nobody had reported the loss of a crew member to that office yet.

"Looks like I'll have to go down to San Pedro after all."

"Wait, Eddie. I thought I said *we* would have to go down to San Pedro. That's we as in Nellie, Mabel, you, and me."

Browning shook his head. "Absolutely not." He checked the time on his pocket watch. "It's almost eight o'clock, and the San Pedro waterfront after dark is no place for ladies."

Maisy smiled at him. "Who said I was a lady? Nellie and Mabel might fit that description, but I was born in the Choctaw Nation where the only ladies were women dressed in fancy clothes passing through on the Katy express."

Mabel broke out in a big smile. "I didn't know you were an Indian."

"Only by citizenship, Mabel, although my mother claims there's an Indian in the woodpile somewhere in our family's past. She said it's most likely Grandma Sally was either a Cherokee or a Choctaw because she was born in the Cherokee Nation and raised in the Choctaw Nation. But who knows for certain? It was for certain that Grandpa Jake was white man."

Miss Sharpe blushed at the suggestion of infidelity, even if it had nothing to do with her family.

Browning ignored Maisy's quip. "I still say I'm going down there alone."

"It's our car, Eddie."

Mabel fell in behind Maisy. "She's right, Eddie. Willie works for the studio, and he's our driver, not yours."

The detective groaned. "Fine. I'll take a department vehicle then."

Maisy became quite conspiratorial. "Well, I'll tell you what, ladies. We don't need old Mr. Fuddy-Duddy here to go with us to San Pedro. We'll have Willie along, if we need a man to protect us, and we can get a head start on Mr. Fuddy-Duddy, if we leave right now."

Browning straightened like a ramrod as he took more offense at Maisy's plan than he took at her mocking him. Then a thought to foil her plot occurred to him. "Miss Sharpe, as your superior here, I forbid you to go with Miss Malone and Miss Normand."

The stenographer stiffened with resolve. "Detective Sergeant Edward Browning, I am off duty now and on my own time, if you please, and I will make my own decisions about where and with whom I choose to spend my hours of leisure." She turned to Maisy and Mabel. "If you will allow me, Miss Normand, Miss Malone, I would like very much to join you in this adventure to the San Pedro waterfront after dark."

Mabel turned to Maisy, both smiling with eyebrows rolled up. "What do you think, Miss Malone? Shall we accept Miss Sharpe's offer to accompany us on our *adventure* to the San Pedro waterfront this dark and dreary night?"

"Well, I'll tell you, Miss Normand. Any woman who's willing to stand up to a stiff-necked copper like Eddie is aces in my book." She hooked her arm around Nellie's. "Let's take her along."

Mabel took Nellie by the other arm. "Yes, Miss Malone. Let's take her along."

Browning put his fists on his hips and glared at the three women. "All right enough is enough. You're not going anywhere. I'm placing all three of you under arrest for interfering with an official police investigation."

Miss Sharpe's nose tipped high into the air with indignity. "Under arrest, sir? If you dare, I will go straight to Chief of Police Sebastian and express my complaint to him about your heavy-handed ways with myself and these two ladies who have done nothing except *aid* you in your investigation. In fact, I believe Chief Sebastian would be quite interested in knowing that Miss Malone and Miss Normand have been more than just a little involved in *your* so-called investigation, sir." She waved her notepad at him. "And I have all the proof of their involvement right here."

Realizing defeat stood directly before him, Browning's head dropped into a droop, and he heaved a sigh of surrender. "All right, you win. All three of you can come along with me." He came to attention again. "But we're taking your boss's Cadillac, Miss Normand."

Mabel and Maisy leaned forward slightly to look past Miss Sharpe at each other. They shared a wink of an eye before standing straight and focusing on Browning. "Fair enough," they said simultaneously. Both then said, "Jinx!" and laughed together with Nellie joining them in the moment.

"Okay. Stay right here, while I get my hat." He left the room.

As soon as he was out of sight, Mabel squeezed the stenographer's arm tighter. "Nellie, you were wonderful just now."

Maisy did likewise. "That's right, kiddo. You were great."

"I don't know about that, ladies. I've never stood up to Detective Browning like that before. I've always obeyed orders around here without making a single protest. I don't know what got into me. I mean—" She swooned and would have dropped to the floor if not for Mabel and Maisy holding onto her arms.

Mabel gasped. "Nellie!"

Maisy snickered. "Well, what do you make of that?"

"You don't think the excitement of the moment was too much for her, do you?"

"I hope not. Because I've got a feeling things are soon to get a lot more exciting with this case."

* * *

The crew of the *Blackfin* had just finished unloading their week's catch into the chute at the California Fish Company on Terminal Island when Willie James brought the Keystone Studio Cadillac to a halt at the quay across the Inner Harbor from the cannery. His four passengers exited the car and walked along the wharf to the landing where the ferry would take them over to the island.

Suddenly, the shrill blast of a steam whistle shattered the relative peace and quiet of the evening, startling the investigation team.

Mabel reacted first. "Oh my god! What was that?"

Browning explained. "I know what it is. It's the cannery whistle calling their workers to come in to work. I was down here once before when it sounded. I was as shocked then as you all are now."

Maisy offered her opinion. "Louder than a locomotive whistle just before it leaves the station. Frizzes my hair every time I hear one close up."

Mabel expressed her complaint. "Feels like it frizzes my hair, too." She patted her coiffure back into place, even if it didn't need it. "There, that's better."

Nellie followed Mabel's example but said nothing.

Maisy looked over her companions. "I guess we're done here. Let's get to that ferry before we miss it."

* * *

Browning paid the ferryman the twenty cents for the four of them to be taken to the ferry landing at the foot of the Los Angeles & Salt Lake Railroad terminal across the harbor. They arrived on the island just as the crew of the *Blackfin* began debarking from the troller.

Browning and the three women approached the fishermen. Only a few electric lights illuminated the immediate area, making it difficult for all to make out the faces of anybody else until they came very close to another person. Still in the lead of his little group, the detective stopped the first man he encountered and presented his policeman's badge to him.

"I'm with the Los Angeles Police Department. Where can I find the captain of this boat?"

The man before him was a bewhiskered Japanese. "Captain Garrido on boat. You find there."

Browning nodded. "Thank you." He took one step toward the tuna boat before Maisy stopped him.

"What's that all about?"

"What's what all about?"

Maisy nodded in the direction of California Fish Cannery. "All those women wearing white aprons walking toward the cannery. And what are they carrying?"

"I suppose those are the women going into work. We just heard the cannery whistle that calls them to report to work. As for what they're carrying with them, they look like lunch pails to me."

Maisy noticed the fishermen were starting to walk away. "Excuse me, Detective Browning. I would like to speak to these men before you let them go on their way."

The detective's head bobbed in mockery. "Yes, how silly of me! Go right ahead, Miss Malone. Be my guest."

Maisy ignored Browning's scorn, stepped forward, and smiled at the fisherman in front of her, the man who had spoken with Browning. "Excuse me, sir. Are you a crewmember on the *Blackfin*?"

The fisherman nodded. "Yes."

"What's your name?"

Other men came up to them cautiously, forming a casual half-circle behind their shipmate.

"Name Enji Nakamura."

"*Doomo aroogatoo, Nakamura-san.* Do you live at Mr. Toichero Koki's boardinghouse on Rattlesnake Island?"

The fisherman appeared taken aback by the courtesy spoken in his native tongue and her question in English. Even so, he answered. "Why you want know that?"

Browning leaned in and gave Nakamura a stern look. "Just answer the lady's question."

Nakamura flinched before obeying the detective's order. "Yes, I live at boardinghouse on Rattlesnake Island."

"Do you know Masi Tanaka?"

"Yes."

"Is Tanaka-*san* still on board the *Blackfin*?" She asked the question, although she already knew the answer.

"No, Masi not on board boat."

"Do you know where he is?"

"No one see Masi since we leave Rattlesnake Island Monday morning. He not aboard boat when we reach open sea."

Maisy nodded, noting his statement mentally. Then she looked over the other crew members. Nearly all were Japanese with smooth, nearly hairless faces like his. Two had rough, week-old beards and appeared to be Hispanics. She made eye-contact with one man in particular. "Which one of you is Yoshi Yamaguchi?"

Nakamura spoke up. "He still aboard *Blackfin*."

Feeling the man was lying to her, Maisy followed Nakamura's gaze to its target. She saw fear in the man's face he was pinpointing and immediately thought of easing his distress. "Yamaguchi-*san*, my name is Maisy Malone." She waved a hand toward her companions. "We would like to speak to you about Masi Tanaka."

Yamaguchi focused on Maisy for a moment and leaned away from her, evidently thinking of fleeing the scene.

Browning recognized the panic in the fisherman's face. "Don't run, Mr. Yamaguchi. We're not here to arrest you. We only wish to talk to you about Masi Tanaka."

"Yes, Yamaguchi-*san*. We only want to talk to you."

The fisherman relaxed, then nodded his acceptance of her words.

"We understand from Masi's brother Tokutaro that you and Masi were very close friends."

The man stiffened again but remained in place. "Yes, very close."

One of the two unshaven men stepped forward. An officer's hat distinguished him from the crew. "Wait a minute. Did you say Yoshi and Masi *were* close friends?"

Maisy nodded. "Yes, that's right." She looked him over for a few seconds. "You must be Captain Estevàn Garrido, right?"

"That's right, lady." He focused on Browning. "Did I hear right? You're a cop?"

Browning presented his badge. "Detective Sergeant Ed Browning, Los Angeles Police Department."

"So what's this business about Masi? Is he in trouble or something?"

Browning answered him point blank. "He's dead."

A collective gasp came from the crew surrounding them, followed by a jabber of muffled discordance, mostly in Japanese.

Garrido spoke for the crew. "Dead? How?"

Although the captain's questions were directed to Browning, Maisy answered him. "That's what we're hoping to find out, sir. With some friendly co-operation from you and your men, that is."

Garrido allowed himself a moment to survey the faces of the other two women. Seeing Nellie taking notes, he dismissed her for what she was. But when he came to Mabel, he squinted hard at her. "You look like some actress I've seen in the moving pictures." He gazed skyward for a second of deep contemplation before answering. "Now what was that flicker called? Mabel's something or other?"

"That's because *I am* that actress you've seen in the moving pictures. I'm Mabel Normand."

The captain twisted his head to one side in disbelief.

Maisy noted his reaction and smiled. "She really is Mabel Normand, Captain Garrido. The darling first lady of comedy in moving pictures."

A huge smile burst over Garrido's face. "You are a very funny lady, Miss Normand. You make me laugh out loud when I see you in the moving pictures. You make me laugh a lot."

Mabel gave him a charming little grin. "Thank you, Captain Garrido. I'm so very glad I could make you laugh out loud. My boss will be delighted to hear it."

"Your boss is a lucky fellow to work with a young woman as pretty as you, Miss Normand."

Mabel intentionally feigned being demur, batting her eyes at him and twisting herself like a corkscrew. "Oh, Captain, you're so sweet to say that."

Maisy frowned, rolled her eyes, and shook her head. "Okay, Mabes, enough Mary Pickford. Let's get back to the point of our being here."

Mabel straightened up and put her hands on her hips. "Mary got that from me, I'll have you know."

"I'm sure she did." Maisy focused on the troller's commanding officer. "Now, Captain Garrido, when was the last time you saw Masi Tanaka?"

The smile vanished from Garrido's countenance, and along with it went his pleasant demeanor. "What is your name, lady?"

"My name is unimportant here, Captain. Just answer my question."

"Are you a cop or something?" He turned to Browning. "Is she a cop, Detective?"

"No, she isn't."

"Then why the hell is she asking all the questions?"

"Because she's working with me on this investigation. She and Miss Normand are both working with me on this case."

"A couple of frails working with the Los Angeles Police Department on a case? Now I've heard everything. The next thing you'll know the cops will have women walking a beat and directing traffic."

Before Browning could take up the argument, Maisy pressed her authority of the moment. "*No importa todo eso, Garrido capitán. Responder a mi pregunta. ¿Cuando fue la última vez que vi Masi Tanaka ... vivo?*"

The shock of hearing Maisy rattle off so much Spanish put a twitch in Garrido's mustache, which was two weeks longer than his beard. He withheld his reply for several seconds, then glared at her for several more heartbeats as he tried to think of some other way of avoiding a response. He failed.

Browning asserted his authority. "Answer the lady's question, Captain."

Garrido sneered at the policeman before turning back to Maisy. "The last time any of us saw him was Monday morning before we went to sea. Isn't that right, boys?" He waited a moment for the crew to confirm his reply with affirmations that ranged from nods to various forms of yes in English and Japanese. "He came on board just like everybody else that morning, and as soon as the whole crew was aboard, we shoved off."

"So how long was the *Blackfin* underway before you realized Mr. Tanaka was missing?"

Garrido squinted at Maisy. "You sound like you know your way around ships, Miss Malone."

Maisy frowned. "Please answer the question, Captain. How long was the *Blackfin* underway before you realized Mr. Tanaka was missing?"

The skipper shifted his view to Browning as if pleading for help.

"Answer Miss Malone's question, Captain Garrido."

"We were three, maybe four miles past Point Fermin before Yoshi came up to the bridge to tell me Masi was missing. I sent Rodrigo to look for him."

"Who is Rodrigo?"

The other man with a week-old beard stepped forward. "I am Rodrigo, *Senhorita*. Rodrigo Manuelo."

Garrido spoke for his man. "Rodrigo is my first mate on the *Blackfin*."

Maisy surprised everybody again by asking her next question in broken Portuguese. "*Você é português, sim?*"

Manuelo smiled at her. "*Sim, sou. Você diz português?*"

Maisy nodded. "*Só um pouco, mas prefiro falar em inglês, muito bem?*"

The first mate nodded, almost bowed, in deference to her request. "Yes, of course, Miss Malone. We should speak in English."

Mabel leaned close to Maisy. "What did he say to you?"

"I asked him if he spoke Portuguese, and he said he did and asked me if I could speak Portuguese. I said I could speak it a little, but I wanted to converse in English."

"That only makes sense because we have a stenographer here to record everything we say."

Maisy blushed as she looked at Miss Sharpe with apologetic eyes.

Nellie smiled sweetly. "It's okay, Maisy. I'm supposed to be seen and not heard. It comes with the job."

Maisy nodded reflexively, then focused on Manuelo again. "Did you find Masi when you went to look for him?"

Rodrigo shook his head. "We looked all over the boat. We could not find him. We figured he went back on shore for some reason."

Maisy nodded at the first mate. Then she stared at her feet for a few seconds in contemplation before leaning closer to Browning who bent an ear to her because she whispered to him. "Eddie, I think we would be wise to question these men individually from this point forward. I don't think any of them will give us a straight story with their captain and first mate around."

"I see what you mean, Maisy. Yes, let's take the lot of them to the station and question them there."

"I think it would serve us better if we questioned them on the *Blackfin*. One man at a time, starting with Yoshi Yamaguchi and finishing with the captain."

Browning nodded in agreement. "All right, we'll do it your way." He straightened up and faced Garrido. "Captain, we'd like to borrow your boat for a while, if we may."

"Borrow my boat? For what purpose?"

"We would like to speak to you and your crew one man at a time to get a statement from you and each of them in private. Where would be the best place for us to do that, sir?"

Garrido objected. "I have other things to do right now. Can't this wait until tomorrow?"

"No, sir, it can't."

The captain continued to argue. "I don't have time for this right now. I have to go to the cannery office and pick up our pay for our catch. Then I have to pay the crew. After that, Rodrigo and I have to take the *Blackfin* to the main side dock."

Browning's brow furrowed. "Why there?"

"We both live in San Pedro, so we tie up the *Blackfin* there until we're ready to go out again."

"Then you bring it back here to pick up your crew?"

"That's right. We send them word the day before that we're going out the next morning. Masi and Yoshi usually meet us at the main side dock in Wilmington just like they did this past Monday. We bring them over to the island with us, and we pick up the rest of crew from the boardinghouse."

"I see."

Maisy interrupted. "We'd still like to use your boat to question you and your crew, Captain."

Garrido sighed. "If you really must use the *Blackfin*, then I suggest you use the mess deck. It is the only place where you can sit comfortably. Will this take a long time, Detective Browning? We've been at sea for five days, and the boys are all anxious to get their pay and blow off a little steam."

The policeman turned to Maisy. "What do you think, Miss Malone? Will we be long at this?"

Maisy counted the crew again with her eyes before replying. "No more than an hour, I should think."

Garrido's head bobbed with approval. "That is good enough for me. I will go first."

Maisy shook her head. "No, Captain. I would prefer that you go last. I want to speak some more with Yoshi Yamaguchi first."

* * *

The *Blackfin*'s mess deck consisted of two tables, one to each side of the compartment. Four benches provided the seating, one built into the hull on each side and one each nailed to the deck and facing outward from amidships. Kerosene lanterns hanging from the overhead above the tables afforded ample lighting.

Maisy and Nellie Sharpe sat on a bulkhead bench, while Yoshi Yamaguchi faced them from the starboard inner bench. Browning and Mabel sat on the port inner bench listening to the interview.

"Yoshi, we spoke to Masi's brother Tokutaro earlier this evening, and he told us you and Masi were extremely close, almost like brothers. Is that true?"

"*Hai!* Yes. Masi ... me ... very close. Yes, like brothers."

"Then you might say you knew him best of all the men on the *Blackfin*, is that right?"

Yoshi nodded.

"Tokutaro-*san* said you and Masi went to his candy store as usual last Saturday and stayed the weekend with him and his family. Is that so?"

Yoshi shook his head. "No, not Saturday. We go there Friday night."

Maisy tried not to show her surprise at Yoshi's answer. She cleared her throat and continued interrogating the fisherman. "Tokutaro-*san* said Masi worked for Mr. Masemoto at his barber shop as usual and you worked in the candy store on Saturday. Is that so?"

"Yes."

"Tokutaro-*san* said Masi was not his usual happy, smiling self when he came home from the barber shop. Is that true, Yoshi?"

Yamaguchi lowered his eyes, wishing to avoid giving her an answer. Finally, he nodded. "Yes, that so. Masi tell me Masemoto-*san* wife not happy with him."

"Did he say why she was unhappy with him?"

"He say she not happy he be married soon. She no want him marry."

"Why would she object to him getting married?"

Yoshi shrugged. "Not know."

"Did it have something to do with Masi courting Kame before she married Masemoto-*san*?"

Again Yoshi hunched his shoulders. "Not know. Maybe. Masi want marry Kame very much, but Kame father say no marriage. She marry Masemoto-*san*. He much older. Old like Kame father. Still, Kame obey Atanabu-*san*. Marry Masemoto-*san*."

"I see. Okay, let's change the pace here. You and Masi returned to San Pedro on Monday morning. Is that right?"

"Yes, we eat at Tokutaro home before we catch Red Car to San Pedro. Get here before first light. Go aboard *Blackfin*. Stow our gear. Masi go on deck. I get coffee. Not see Masi again."

"Masi went on deck, and that was the last you saw of him?"

Yamaguchi shook his head. "No, not on deck. Last see Masi in crew quarters stowing gear. I go mess deck. He go topside. Not see him again."

"I see. Okay, when did you realize Masi was *not* aboard the *Blackfin* that morning?"

"Not till boat far out to sea. Maybe two hour. Maybe only one. After sunrise for sure."

"Why that long?"

"Think Masi go below to crew quarters, take nap till captain say time fish for tuna. Drink coffee. Then go to crew quarters. Not see Masi there. Think he on deck. Go topside. Masi not there. Tell captain then."

"Thank you, Yoshi. I have one last question for you. Did Masi have any enemies on the *Blackfin* or anywhere else in San Pedro?"

Yoshi scrunched up his face. "Enemies?"

"People who didn't like him or who might want to harm him?"

The light of understanding shone on the fisherman's face. "Masi not have enemies. People like him. Shipmates like him. Masi good fisherman. Like everybody. Other people at boardinghouse like him."

"Let me put it a different way. Did Masi have any trouble with anybody in San Pedro or on Rattlesnake Island?"

Yamaguchi took a moment to consider his answer. "One time I see Mr. Garrido tell Masi not be so friendly with his daughter. She get wrong idea, not good."

"What is the daughter's name?"

"Her name Belinda."

"Was there anything between Masi and Belinda? Any romance?"

The fisherman's eyes widened just a little at the question. "Masi nice to all women." He sounded a tiny bit defensive of his friend. "Same to all women. Nice."

"I see." She pursed her lips for a second before deciding to change her tack. "Did Masi have trouble with anybody else you might know about?"

Yoshi lowered his eyes for a moment. "First mate on *Blackfin*."

"Rodrigo?"

Yamaguchi nodded fiercely.

"What kind of trouble?"

"First mate make Masi do more work other men on boat. Him say Masi not work hard like other men on boat. Push Masi round. Captain tell first mate leave Masi lone. When Captain not look, first mate push Masi more hard."

"And how did Masi react to this bad treatment?"

"Masi just laugh. Say he be off boat soon. Make no difference then."

Maisy nodded. "I see." She thought for a second. "Well, that's all the questions I have for you, Yoshi." She looked past him to Browning. "How about you, Detective Browning? Do you have any questions for Yoshi?"

The fisherman turned to face the policeman.

"No, I believe you covered everything, Miss Malone."

Yamaguchi turned back to Maisy.

"You can go now, Yoshi. Thank you for your help."

"Have question for you, Miss Malone."

"Certainly. Go ahead and ask it."

"How Masi die?"

"I can't tell you that, Yoshi, but I can tell you that Miss Normand and I were there when his body was found washed up on a beach."

"When you find Masi body?"

"It was Christmas Day. Two days ago."

Yoshi shook his head slowly. "Masi dead on beach two days ago." A deep sadness came over him. "How? Why? Masi good man. Masi have wife from Japan soon. Move into Los Angeles with brother family and open flower store. We buy land together to grow flower for store." He could no longer hold back his tears. To hide them, he bowed his head. "My friend gone now. Not right."

Suddenly, he spun around and faced Browning. "You find Masi killer. Find killer, make him pay with own life. Killer need die. You find killer." His head drooped as he wept openly.

Browning patted Yamaguchi on the shoulder. "Don't worry, Yoshi. We'll find this killer, and we'll see that he's punished for Masi's murder. We promise, don't we, Miss Malone?"

Maisy bit her lower lip lightly before answering a bit reluctantly. "Sure, Detective Browning. Whatever you say."

The other seven crew members confirmed Yoshi Yamaguchi's statement that Rodrigo, the troller's first mate, had been particularly hard on Masi Tanaka when they were aboard the *Blackfin*. Only one man had anything to add to that.

Enji Nakamura expressed himself with great care. "I see Masi in town one night not long ago. He walking with Mr. Geraldo's daughter ... Belinda. Rodrigo see Masi with Belinda. He go up behind Masi ... push him to ground. Masi jump up into *jujitsu* stand. Rodrigo attack him again. Masi throw Rodrigo to ground, hold him there till Rodrigo promise no more fight. Masi let him stand. Rodrigo shake finger at Masi ... tell him stay away from Belinda ... she his woman. Belinda tell Rodrigo she not his woman ... leave with Masi.

"Next day Mr. Geraldo come down to boat ... tell Masi stay away from daughter. Masi tell boss man ... he marry already. Wife coming from Japan. Name Teruka Watanabe. Very pretty girl. All Japanese man in San Pedro not marry ... wish be Masi, even Yoshi Yamaguchi. He have own picture of Teruka. He keep secret, but Enji see ... Enji know. Yoshi Yamaguchi wish he marry Teruka."

Maisy delved deeper. "What about you, Enji? Do you wish you could marry Teruka Watanabe?"

"Enji not different from other Japanese man. Yes, Enji wish marry Teruka. But not have secret picture of Teruka like Yoshi. One day Enji have money save ... marry picture bride from Japan."

Maisy nodded. "That's all tremendously interesting, Enji. Thank you for helping us." She looked at Browning. "Do you have any questions for Enji?"

Browning shook his head. "Not at this time, Miss Malone." He focused on Nakamura. "But thank you for your co-operation, Enji."

"Enji, would you like to ask us anything?"

He shook his head at Maisy, then turned to face the policeman. "No. Only want you find Masi killer … make pay for killing Masi."

Just like he had done with Yoshi, Browning patted the fisherman on the shoulder. "We will find his killer. Be assured of that, Enji. You can go now."

Nakamura bowed to Browning and then to Maisy and Mabel before leaving the mess deck and going topside.

Curiosity had the best of Mabel. "Did either of you notice that Enji didn't ask anything about how Masi died or where he was found?"

Browning nodded. "Come to think of it, you're right. He didn't say anything about Tanaka's death. All the others asked how he was killed and where his body was found. Why didn't Nakamura say anything about either one? What do you think, Maisy? Do you think he already knows how Tanaka was murdered or where his body was found?"

"We've told all the others the same thing. We can't tell them how Masi was murdered, and we told them all that we found his body on a beach. Probably one of the others we've already questioned told everybody we found his body on a beach."

Mabel snapped her fingers. "That's right, but none of them asked which beach. There are a lot of beaches up and down the coast. You would have thought at least one of them would have been curious enough to ask about which one we found his body on."

A big sigh rushed out of Maisy. "You've got a good point there, Mabes. It is rather odd that none of them asked a thing about the beach where we found Masi's body." She looked up at Browning. "I don't know about you, Eddie, but I'm dog-tired. What do you say we call it a night and resume this questioning business tomorrow?"

"But we've only got two more men to question."

"Actually, only one. We've already gotten everything out of

Captain Garrido that we're going to get. As for Rodrigo, I think we'll have more success with him at the police station. Seeing all those cops at once might put a real fright into him, enough so that he'll spill the beans to us there."

"What about Geraldo Garrido and his daughter? Don't you want to talk to them as well?"

"Yes, but a man like that needs to be shown some respect. Why don't we call on them tomorrow while a couple of your boys are taking Rodrigo to the station for us?" Maisy turned to the stenographer. "What do you say, Nellie? You up for this again tomorrow?"

"Oh, yes, of course, I am." She seemed to shiver all over as a big grin blossomed on her face. "Oo-oo-ooh! This is so exciting. I've never been part of a murder investigation before. Well, not like this, anyway. I can't wait for tomorrow."

* * *

A few blocks from the San Pedro waterfront Keystone Studio driver Willie James did something he rarely did when he was behind the wheel of the Cadillac. He spoke in the usual drawl he had learned growing up.

"I ain't sure who I should be addressing here. Miss Normand, you be the most important person here from the studio. Detective Browning, you be the most important person here from the law. Miss Malone, you be just downright important because you be so smart and can talk that foreign lingo like Spanish and German. Miss Sharpe, you be important because you be such an educated lady and all. So who do I address betwixt the four of you?"

Browning glanced over his shoulder at the three women in the back seat before giving his full attention to the driver. "Well, Willie, I suppose it depends on the subject you have in mind. Does it have anything to do with the investigation we're conducting?"

"Now that be just the point, Detective Browning, sir. I ain't rightly sure, seeing as how I be with the car on the wharf when you and the ladies be over on that island talking to all them fishermen about that poor Japanese fellow who been killed and washed up on the beach."

Maisy leaned forward. "Willie, did you hear or see something while we were questioning the captain and crew of the *Blackfin*? If you did, whatever it was, I would certainly appreciate you sharing it with us."

"Well, Miss Malone, it be like this. While I be waiting for you-all to get done, that Chinese boatman come by the car and started talking to me."

"Do you mean Tsu-chin? That Chinese boatman?"

"Yes, ma'am, that be him. He be asking me all sorts of questions about what you-all be doing on the island talking to all them Japanese fishermen and their Mexican captain. He sure be some curious cat, him asking me all them questions."

Maisy nudged Nellie, indicating she should get her pad and pencil ready. "What did you tell him, Willie?"

Miss Sharpe understood the gesture and did as requested.

"I tell him nothing, Miss Malone. I don't know nothing, so I can't tell him nothing. He ain't believing me though. He say I must know something about what be going on with you-all on that island. I tell him I ain't there with you-all, so how I be knowing what be going on with you-all? Before he can ask me again, I ask him a question. I ask him what he be doing snooping around like he be doing asking me all them questions I ain't got no answers for. He say the harbor be his business and he be knowing everything that be going on around the harbor all the time. I tell him he be nothing more than a little Chinese boatman and he don't know nothing about nothing what be going on around the harbor." Willie chuckled at his own words. "Now that made him mad as a wet hen. He shake his fist at me and tell me I be nothing but a no-account darky driving white folks around and getting paid nothing for my time. Fat lot that little Chinese boatman be knowing about me and my job with the studio." He went silent for the moment as he concentrated on his driving.

Browning's brow bunched up over his nose. "Is that all you wanted to tell us, Willie?"

"Oh, no, sir. There be more. I just shut up because there be two

Red Cars crossing in front of us. Wouldn't be good for me to be running into no Red Cars. Wouldn't be good for you-all neither."

Maisy pressed the driver for more information. "So what did you say to Tsu-chin when he shook his fist at you, Willie?"

"I tell him again he don't know nothing about what be going on around that harbor. He get mad again, and this time he say he know things most other folks around the harbor don't know."

"Did he say anything in particular that he knew that other people didn't know?"

"He sure did, Miss Malone. He say he saw that poor dead Japanese fisherman that morning before the tuna boat go out to sea fishing for the tuna. He say he saw the Japanese fisherman get on the boat with them other fishermen and then he say he saw him get off the boat and run off to a alley where they ain't no lights. He say that be the last time he see that poor Japanese fisherman till you-all show him a picture of him dead."

Although the street lights and the lights from the buildings they drove past barely made them visible to each other, Browning and the three women could still discern the surprise on the faces of their fellow passengers. Several seconds ticked by before the policeman could speak again.

"Willie, are you certain that's what the Chinese boatman said?"

"Yes, sir. I be sure as the sun be coming up in the east again tomorrow and be going down in the west when the day is through."

"Thank you, Willie."

Maisy reached out and grabbed Browning's shoulder. "Eddie, we have to go back and talk to Tsu-chin right now."

"No, Maisy, it's too late tonight. We're all tired, and tomorrow is another day. You said yourself that you were dead tired. Besides, we're coming back here in the morning to question Geraldo Garrido. We can question the boatman then. I'm sure he'll be around the harbor somewhere."

Mabel pressed Maisy's hand. "Eddie's right, dear. It's late, and we should get some rest. It's been a really long day ... for all of us."

Maisy resigned herself to accepting their pleas. "Of course, you're right. Tomorrow is another day. Take us all home, Willie."

* * *

Maisy pounded on the Cole's apartment door. "Wake up, Milo! We've got work to do." She banged on it harder. "Milo! Wake up!"

An unhappy neighbor. "Knock it off, lady!"

Another sour apple down the hall. "Pipe down, lady! Or I'm calling the cops and have you thrown out of here!"

An irate woman. "Don't you know what time it is? People are trying to sleep here!"

From the floor below. "It's almost midnight! How about all you loudmouths up there knocking it off and going back to sleep?"

From above, not the voice of an angel. "Shut the hell up, you jerks!"

The door opened wide. Cole stood there in his red, white, and blue striped pajamas. Hair tousled. Face puffy. Chin resting on his chest. Eyes half open. His mouth so dry he could only rasp out a few very choice words. "I thought you were a dream. I was wrong. You're a nightmare from Hell."

Maisy barged past him. "Hurry and get dressed. I've got a taxi waiting for us downstairs. We've got to hurry before it's too late."

Cole gently closed the door, as if that would silence his neighbors on the second, third, and fourth floors. "Hurry? Where to?"

"San Pedro."

"San Pedro? We were already there once today. Or yesterday." He brushed back his hair with his left hand. "What time is it anyway?"

"It's almost midnight." She saw his trousers draped on the dresser and made a beeline for them. "Yes, we were there in the afternoon, and the rest of us went back there tonight, too." She threw his pants at him.

Milo caught the trousers. "So why do we have to go back there tonight? Or why do I have to go?"

"I need a man to escort me. I can't be walking around the waterfront in the dark all by myself, you know."

"But why me? What about your pal ... Detective Browning? Why can't he go with you?" He snapped his fingers. "Oh, yes, that's right. He's married, and he wants to be with his wife at this time of night."

"Get dressed, Milo. Our taxi is waiting."

"What if I don't want to go out at this time of night?"

Maisy smirked at him. "Really, Milo? You're always complaining about not getting to spend enough time with me. Well, this is your chance to spend some time with me."

"I was thinking more along the lines of an early evening or a Sunday afternoon or a Saturday night."

"Milo, remember the other day when I told Mack we were just friends when he said something about me being your girlfriend?"

"How could I forget?"

"Well, if you ever want to get any further than the 'just friends' stage of our relationship, then get your clothes on and come with me to San Pedro."

Cole slumped with his chin coming to rest on his chest. "I'm not a man. I'm a mouse. No, worse! I'm a trained seal. Throw me a fish and I'll do anything." Without thinking about modesty, he dropped his pajama bottoms and slipped on his pants.

Maisy paid him no mind as she opened the door. "I'll be waiting for you in the taxi."

* * *

Maisy used the taxi ride to San Pedro to bring Cole up to date on the investigation into the murder of Masi Tanaka. "So when Willie told us that Tsu-chin said he had seen Masi go into an alley near the *Blackfin*, I decided we needed to talk to Tsu-chin as soon as possible."

"I still don't see why you couldn't wait till morning to talk to him."

"Tsu-chin either lied to us or he withheld information from us. Or he lied to Willie. I need to know which one before we confront Geraldo Garrido and his family as well as Rodrigo the first mate of the *Blackfin*. Do you understand now?"

"I think so."

"Well, it makes no difference now. We're here." Maisy leaned over the back of the front seat. "Driver, there's an extra five dollars in it for you, if you hang around until we're done here."

"Are you kidding, lady?"

Maisy opened her purse and pulled out a money clip filled with bills. "Does this look like I'm kidding?"

"I guess not. I'll be here. Just be sure you come back."

She nodded toward Cole. "I've got my good luck charm with me. We'll be back."

Milo followed Maisy out of the car. "Where are we going?"

"That's the *Blackfin* tied up over there." She pointed to the troller that was tied up behind another, the *Yellowfin*, on the San Pedro side of the inner harbor. "Tsu-chin said he saw Masi go into an alley over there."

"It's pretty dark around here, Maisy. I don't see how he could have seen much at that time of the morning, even on this side of the harbor."

"Milo, don't you ever look up at the sky at night?"

"Not very often. Why?"

"If you did, you might see the moon, and if you had seen the moon on the morning of Monday, December twenty-third, you would have seen it was a waxing moon that was almost a full moon. Also, if you could recall that morning, you would remember the sky was free of clouds. So the moon would have given off a lot of light around the time the crew of the *Blackfin* was reporting for work that day. Therefore, Tsu-chin just might have been telling Willie the truth about seeing Masi on the dock after everybody else had gone aboard the tuna boat."

Maisy pointed to their left. "Now if you'll look off to the east, you'll see the moon is in its waning phase and is about thirty degrees above the horizon. Pretty soon it will be lighting up this area almost as much as it did Monday morning just before the sun started to light up the eastern horizon."

"Waning phase? That means it's getting smaller?"

"Yes, and waxing means it's getting bigger."

"How do you know all this stuff?"

"I read books, and I remember most of what I read." She stopped him at a spot directly across the inner harbor from the *Blackfin* and the buildings on the dock. "Do you see an alley between any of the buildings?"

"No, I don't. How about you?"

"No, I don't either. At least nothing that I would call an alley. Maybe Willie or Tsu-chin meant the walkway between the buildings. If he did, I still don't see one that would be wide enough for two people to stand in side by side. I guess we'll have to confront Tsu-chin about what he meant."

"So where do we find him at this time of night?"

"Let's take a walk along the wharf and see if we can find his boat. He might live on it."

The wharf on the San Pedro side of the harbor extended only a half mile between the water and the Southern Pacific Railroad tracks. Although the quay ended at the city's edge, the rails culminated at the breakwater that protected the entire harbor from the force of the ocean whenever it decided to throw its weight around.

Maisy and Milo walked the length of the dock in search of the Chinese boatman's craft and finally located it a few hundred feet south of where they had originally seen it earlier that afternoon. With the tide ebbing, they had to climb down a ladder to board the water taxi.

As soon as her feet touched the deck, Maisy made their presence known. "Tsu-chin, are you here?"

No answer.

She pointed toward the bow. "I remember a cabin door beneath the helm. Let's see if he's sleeping in there." She led the way as usual. "Are you in there, Tsu-chin?" She knocked as hard as she could.

Still no answer.

Maisy turned the door handle, opened the door, and looked inside. "Tsu-chin, are you in here?"

Silence as black as the compartment.

"Milo, do you have a match or a lighter?"

"You know I don't smoke."

"Yes, but I also know you usually carry something to light cigars or cigarettes for those people you know who do smoke because they're either too forgetful or too cheap to carry their own."

Cole felt his coat and trouser pockets until he found a tin of matches. "Here you go." He handed the box to Maisy.

She took one from the tin, struck it on the door frame once to ignite the sulfur tip, watched it flare alive, then held it out as she looked for a lamp, found one hanging from the middle of the overhead, and lighted it.

"Now what?" asked Cole.

"Now we have a look around. Just don't make a mess of things or he'll know somebody was here going through his things."

After fifteen minutes of searching through every nook and cranny they could find in the cabin, Maisy gave up and went topside. "Blow out the lamp before you come up, Milo."

Cole obeyed her command and joined Maisy on deck. "Now what?"

"We wait for him."

"Wait for him? What if he doesn't live on the boat? What if he lives somewhere in town or in one of those shacks along the wharf? We could be waiting here until dawn. Besides that, we have a taxi waiting for us. What about him?"

Maisy nodded. "You're right. We shouldn't wait here for him. Let's go into town and see if he might be enjoying a night out."

"Better idea. Let's just call it a night and go home. How about that?"

She heaved a sigh. "I really wanted to talk to him tonight before we interview the Garridos and Rodrigo tomorrow. But ... if he's not here, I suppose we'll have to wait until morning. So let's go."

As the pair returned to the taxi, Maisy stared ahead at the *Blackfin* tied up to the wharf. Then she looked at the buildings across the railroad tracks from it. Suddenly, she grabbed Cole's arm and stopped him as well as herself.

"Milo, I just now had a thought. The tuna boat docked there

because it had to unload its catch right away and get it into one of those buildings over there. That makes sense, doesn't it?"

"Yes. And?"

"So why would the crew come all the way from the north end of Rattlesnake Island so early in the morning to board the boat here? I mean, wouldn't it be easier to *take the boat* around to the north end of Rattlesnake Island and pick up the crew before going out to sea?"

"I guess that makes sense. Why is that important?"

"Yoshi Yamaguchi said he and Masi Tanaka took the Red Car from the candy store to San Pedro and got here before first light. They went aboard and stored their gear. Yoshi then went to the mess deck for coffee, while Masi went topside. He didn't say why Masi went up on deck, only that he did. And I didn't ask him why, either. But you'd better believe I will when I see Yoshi tomorrow."

"Good. I'm glad that's settled. Can we go now?"

"Not yet. Yoshi never mentioned how they got across the harbor to the *Blackfin*."

"Beats me, Maise."

They took three steps before Maisy stopped them again. "You know, if Masi and Yoshi boarded the *Blackfin* here and then went from here to Rattlesnake Island to pick up the rest of the crew, why was Tsu-chin over there?" Before she could postulate an answer, she recalled the interviews with the other crew members. "You know, none of the other men mentioned coming over here that morning to board the boat. They all simply said they boarded the *Blackfin* and went below to stow their gear and get some coffee before going to work. None of them mentioned seeing Masi on deck." She wobbled her head from side-to-side twice. "But then again, silly me, I didn't ask them if they had seen Masi on deck before going below. I just assumed they did." She pulled Milo forward toward the taxi. "Come on, let's go home. All this stuff is beginning to make me a little nutty. I really do need a good night's sleep."

All the extra hours the night before spent with Maisy Malone and Mabel Normand investigating the murder of Japanese fisherman Masi Tanaka showed on Detective Sergeant Ed Browning's face when he arrived for duty Saturday morning at the Los Angeles Police Department's Central Station. Every officer he met from the moment he approached the building from the corner Red Car stop greeted him with a polite, "Good morning, sir," and those that knew him on a more personal level felt compelled to add a remark on his facial appearance.

"Tie one on last night, Sarge?"

"Geez, Sarge, you look like crap."

"Not feeling too well today, Sarge?"

"You look like you could stand a little hair of the dog, Ed."

"Didn't your mama warn you about the evils of alcohol, Sarge?"

By the time he reached his desk, Browning had heard them all more times than he liked, especially the one that disturbed him the most.

"That's what you get for running around town behind your wife's back with three women at the same time, Ed."

Never having been a sporting man, Browning ignored the snide asides that only poked fun at him alone, but he took great exception to the implications behind the latter comment. He prided himself on his love for and loyalty to his wife Nealy. They had been married for nine blissful years, and not once in that time did, he ever consider straying from the trust his wife placed in him. Therefore, he picked up the telephone on his desk and called his home.

"Darling, would you please come to the station this morning?"

"Whatever for, Edward?"

"I'll be going by the Tanaka's home to show my respects to them, and I would like you to accompany me in order to show them my presence there is more than a police matter."

"Well, if you really think it would help you, then I'll be there as soon as I can get properly dressed. Should I wear mourning clothes?"

"Yes, you should. The Japanese are much the same as we Americans when it comes to honoring our dearly departed."

"Will Miss Normand and Maisy be there as well?"

"Yes, I'm sure of it, although neither of them has arrived here yet. Actually, I'm rather surprised that Maisy wasn't already here waiting for me this morning. But I'm certain they will both be a long before much longer. See you soon."

* * *

Mabel's departure for the police station was delayed by a telephone call from Mack Sennett. "Good morning, Sweetheart. Did I wake you?"

"No, Nappy, I've been up for some time already. In fact, I was just about to call Maisy and see if she's ready to go yet."

"So, the two of you are still snooping around that Jap fisherman's murder, are you?"

Mabel sighed with a touch of impatience. "Nappy, his name was Masi Tanaka, and he was Jap-*anese*, if you don't mind."

"My-my, aren't we a little touchy this morning? Since when did you get so culturally sensitive?"

"Since I met his brother and his brother's family and several of his friends who are very nice people."

"Okay, I get it." Sennett pause to change his attitude. "So, you found out his name and who he was?"

"Actually, we learned a great deal about Mr. Tanaka." She proceeded to give Sennett a report on what Maisy, Milo, and she had done together the past two days. "And then Willie dropped Maisy and me here not much before midnight, I think. I would have called you last night, but I was simply too tired to talk. You understand, don't you?"

"Of course, I do, dear." Another pause. "Well, it sounds like you and Maisy are making some headway in this murder investigation. I'm surprised that Detective Browning is letting you two do so much."

"Maisy talked him into it. He's been rather reluctant to investigate right from the start. Apparently, if a crime doesn't involve white people, the Los Angeles Police Department doesn't bother to get involved."

"It's the same way back in New York. The police there keep their noses out of the various ethnic neighborhoods. As long as it's something between their own people, the cops leave them alone. The Jews, the Italians, the Irish, the Puerto Ricans, they all settle their own affairs among themselves. Not until one bunch has a problem with another do the cops get involved. I suppose it's pretty much the same thing out here."

"Maisy says that's not right, and I tend to agree with her. It doesn't make any difference who murdered poor Mr. Tanaka. The police should be investigating to find out who did it and arrest them just the same as they would if the victim was a white person."

"Yes, I suppose you're right. So, what are you doing today?"

"I'm not sure exactly what we'll be doing today, except paying our respects to Mr. Tanaka's family. Today is their first day of mourning. We'll go by their home, I suppose, and ..." Her voice drifted off as an idea came to her. "You know, Mack honey, since you're the one who found Mr. Tanaka among the rocks, I think you should go with us to his brother's home and pay your respects as well. I'm sure his brother would like to thank you for finding Mr. Tanaka."

"Oh, no. You can just leave me out of this. I've done all I'm going to do with this murder business. I'm not getting involved any further."

"Mack dear, why don't you join us after you close down the studio this afternoon? I mean, what else do you have to do?"

"I've got lots to do. I have plenty of film to watch and edit before it goes off to New York. You know that's my routine on Saturdays."

"I know you can skip doing that today for this one time."

"This one time? I closed down the studio for a whole day and a half because of Leslie Clover's wake and funeral. Or have you forgotten about that business? Not one foot of film was shot, and no editing was done that night either. No, sir. I'm not going, and that's that."

Mabel was not pleased. "Nappy, if you ever want to spend another evening with me, then I suggest you join us when we visit the Tanaka family to pay our respects to their late brother's memory."

Sennett knew when she started calling him by her insulting pet nickname for him that she had made up her mind about something and nothing on earth would change it. He sighed. "Okay. Just call me later after you and crazy Maisy decide when we're going, and I'll meet you there."

Mabel giggled. "Now that's the proper spirit, Mack darling."

* * *

The wake for Masi Tanaka began at noon on Saturday.

Toichero Koki received mourners at the Alameda Street entrance of Tanaka's Candy Store and Ice Cream Parlor. He had rehearsed two welcoming greetings; one for fellow Japanese and the other in English for the few *gaijin* who were expected. Recognizing two of the people who had brought him the sad news of Masi's death, he bowed respectfully to them.

"Thank you for honoring our friend, Masi Tanaka, with your presence here, Miss Malone, Mr. Cole."

Among the first to arrive, Maisy bowed back. "You are most welcome, Koki-*san*."

Toichero motioned toward his wife Hatsenke who sat a table to his left. "Would you please sign the registry book? Hatsenke will accept your *koden*."

"I'm sorry, Koki-*san*, but I don't know what *koden* is."

"*Koden* is gift of money for departed one's family. Gift help them pay funeral expenses. Customary all mourners give set amount according to relation to departed." He turned and picked up two small envelopes, each with a black and white ribbon attached to it. "You put your gift in here and write amount on outside. Seal envelope and tie ribbon around it. You sign registry and give gift to Hatsenke. She write amount you give beside your name in registry."

"How much would be customary for us to give?"

"One dollar each."

"We can do that, can't we, Milo?"

"Certainly."

The Browning's and Nellie Sharpe were next in line to be greeted by Koki. Mack Sennett and Mabel Normand followed them. Maisy quickly explained the meaning of *koden*, and both couples and the stenographer gave the same gift as Maisy and Milo.

Yoshi Yamaguchi and Enji Nakamura took turns escorting mourners to the Tanaka residence located above their business, where they could pay their respects to the bereaved family.

Maisy and Milo brought incense sticks to be burned at a later time as tokens to the memory of Masi Tanaka. Mabel and Mack placed a bouquet of yellow chrysanthemums on the empty casket. The Browning's and Miss Sharpe paid their respects with a potted pink tea rose to be planted in honor of the family's late brother.

One-by-one the mourners passed by the Tanaka family who were sitting cross-legged on the floor cushions to the right of the coffin. Each of them expressed his or her condolences with sympathetic words and a courteous bow.

When her turn came, Mabel took Sennett by the hand, and they bowed together just like Maisy and Milo and the Browning's had done.

"Mr. Tanaka, this gentleman is Mr. Mack Sennett, my employer and dear friend. Mr. Sennett is the man who first discovered your brother's ... your late brother on the beach."

"Ah, thank you, Mr. Sennett. I thank you for Masi as well. Having his body found is a great weight lifted from his soul. Now we must learn the identity of his killer and let the retribution happen."

"Well, you're welcome, Mr. Tanaka. But it really wasn't a big deal. I mean anybody could have come along and seen him lying there. It was just my dumb luck to be the one to find him."

Mabel wanted to kick Sennett for his seemingly inappropriate and very insensitive words. Instead she twisted her foot closest to him and dug the heel of her shoe into his toes.

"No, Mr. Sennett, it was not dumb luck. My brother's spirit guided you there for that very purpose, to find him. You and Miss Normand and Miss Malone and Mr. Cole. He recognized you as the good people that you are and knew you would be the ones to see that his body was returned to his family and that you would seek out his killer and see that Masi receives justice."

"Well, gee, Mr. Tanaka—"

The increased intense pressure of Mabel's heel on his toes cut him short. "What Mr. Sennett means, Mr. Tanaka, is he's sorry for your loss and he hopes your brother will rest in peace once his killer is brought to justice. Isn't that right, Mack darling?"

"Oh, yes … yes, that's right, Mr. Tanaka. May your brother rest in peace once his killer is found and brought to justice."

When they finished offering their sympathies to the Tanaka's, a Japanese man approached the group of *gaijin*.

"I am Nakaturo Masemoto. Please come this way." He led them into another room that was bereft of furniture except for an exceptionally low table with several dishes of food, a large teapot, teacups, a stack of plates, an assortment of chopsticks and forks, and napkins. Mats and cushions lined each side of the chamber. "My wife Kame will serve you food and tea."

After giving each mourner a large bowl with a sparing portion of *oyako-donburi*, a small bowl of *miso* soup, and chopsticks, Kame Masemoto motioned toward the mats and cushions. "Sit please. Eat."

Deftly and agilely, Maisy and Mabel crossed their legs while still standing and then lowered themselves gracefully onto the side-by-side mats like a pair of ballerinas. Seeing how much trouble Cole was having with his awkward attempt to follow their lead, Maisy offered to hold his plate and bowl for him while he sat down stiffly next to her. Mabel did likewise with Sennett who appeared to be even more ungainly than Milo. Nealy Browning squatted easily, then leaned forward onto her knees to place her plate and bowl on the floor before sitting backward on a cushion. Ed Browning and Nellie Sharpe followed Nealy's example. As soon as the seven of them were seated, Kame came around with a teapot of steaming hot tea and a stack of teacups. Each of them took a cup, and Kame filled it three-quarters full. As soon as she finished the task, she returned to the table to await the next mourners to be brought into the room by her husband.

Maisy leaned close to Mabel. "So that's the barber and his much younger wife. He does look old enough to be her father."

"I was thinking the exact same thing."

Sennett nudged Mabel. "What's this stuff in the bigger bowl?"

"You don't know?"

"I wouldn't have asked, if I knew what it was."

"We've been out here in California for four months, Nappy, and we were out here last winter, and you still haven't eaten anything exotic yet. You need to get out and about more."

"Okay, I need to get out and about more. So what is this stuff?"

"It's a dish with fish and vegetables and mushrooms. Those are slices of carrots, a little Oriental cabbage, onions, and bamboo shoots over some white rice."

"Okay, now how do I eat it? There's no forks."

Mabel heaved an impatient sigh. "You hold the bowl up to your mouth and you scrape the food into it with your chopsticks. The idea is not to spill anything."

Maisy leaned in front of Mabel. "And you can't let any of it go uneaten. Not even a single grain of rice. If you don't eat it all, our host will consider it an insult."

"That's right, Nappy. From what you said to Mr. Tanaka, I'd say you've already insulted these people enough for one day."

"Okay, okay." He stared down at his food again. "So how do I eat the soup? There's no spoon."

Maisy explained the method to him. "You drink it and scrape the noodles and vegetables into your mouth with your chopsticks. Oh, and be sure to slurp the soup a little. That's considered good manners, too."

"You're kidding."

Mabel shook her head. "She's not kidding, Mack. Slurp your soup but not too loud."

Sennett shook his head in disbelief. "Well, if that's the way they do it, then I don't want to be rude." He picked up the bowl, slurped a little broth into his mouth, and gave it a good taste before swallowing. "Hey, this stuff is pretty good. What is it?"

"It's called *miso* soup. That leafy green stuff is a Japanese version of spinach, and the round white and green things are slices of green onions. The white chunks are *tofu*. That's bean curd."

"Bean curd?"

"Yes, bean curd. It comes from soybean milk."

"Never heard of it."

"Nappy, will you just shut up and eat it? It's good. You'll see."

Gradually, the room filled up with mourners, all of the additional people being Japanese.

Browning surveyed the faces around them. "I think we should leave as soon as we finish eating."

"I think you're right, Eddie."

Just then, Nakaturo Masemoto returned with another pair of bereaved friends of Masi Tanaka. Before he could leave the room, Maisy got his attention.

"Masemoto-*san* excuse me for asking, but we don't want to insult anyone by not following your customs correctly. What do we do now that we're through eating?"

"Go out the back door and down the steps to the backyard. Some people are already down there. More will be coming. Mr. Masuda is serving *sake* to mourners."

"Thank you, Masemoto-*san*."

On their way out, Sennett had to ask. "What's *sake*?"

Mabel grimaced. "It's rice wine."

Maisy giggled. "Don't drink too much of it, Mack. Drink too much and you won't know what month it is until after New Year's

Day."

Genkichi Masuda owned the hotel two doors down from the candy store. He greeted the *gaijin* when they reached the bottom step and directed them to his much younger wife Koito who served them *sake* in cups a little smaller than the ones they had used to drink tea upstairs.

"Sip it slowly, Nappy. A little of this stuff goes a long way."

More mourners soon joined them.

Mabel nudged Maisy. "Isn't that the captain of the *Blackfin* over there with that other swarthy gentleman?"

"It sure looks like him. And that looks like Rodrigo, the first mate, coming up behind them with that Mexican woman."

"You don't suppose that woman is Captain Garrido's sister Belinda, do you?"

"I certainly do." Maisy stepped closer to Browning. "Eddie, it looks like we won't have to go San Pedro this afternoon after all. Look who came to the wake." She indicated the Garridos and Manuelo with a nod of her head. "Do you think the older gentleman with Captain Garrido is his father Geraldo and the lady with the first mate is Geraldo's daughter Belinda?"

Browning nodded. "It would appear to be so, Maisy."

"Nice of them to come here so we can question them about Masi Tanaka's murder."

A frown shaded Browning's face. "Maisy, I believe this is neither the proper place nor time to be questioning folks about a murder."

"Maybe not, but since we're so close to downtown, maybe you can ask them politely to come over to Central Station after they leave here."

Browning nodded. "I do believe that would be the more polite thing to do. Wait here while I go speak to them."

Mabel came close to Maisy. "Where's Eddie going?"

"He's going to invite the Garridos and the first mate to stop by the police station after they leave here so we can have a little talk with them."

"Oh, good idea! Then we won't have to go back to San Pedro

this afternoon."

"That was my thought exactly, dear." An idea popped into Maisy's thinking processes. "You know, I wish I could talk with Yoshi for just one minute before we leave here."

"Well, why don't you?"

"You know, you're right. I should go ahead and talk to him for a minute before we leave."

Mabel appeared perplexed. "How are you going to do that? It would be rude for us go back upstairs and then through the dining room and living room and downstairs to the store again."

"Yes, you're right about that, so I'll simply take a short cut."

"A short cut?"

"Yes, through the store by way of the back door. You take Mack and Milo back to the street through the lane between the buildings, and I'll meet you out front after I've spoken to Yoshi."

"What about Eddie, Nealy, and Miss Sharpe?"

Before Maisy could answer, Browning returned to their little group. "It's done. The lady is Belinda Garrido. She, her father, her brother, and the first mate will come over to the station as soon as they leave here. I said we'd be waiting for them."

"Then we'd better get going, don't you think?"

Browning nodded. "Yes, you're right, Maisy." He turned to his wife and Nellie Sharpe. "Ladies, we're leaving now. I have some business at the station that will require your presence, Miss Sharpe. Nealy darling, you can wait for me at the station, but I might be a few hours."

Mabel tapped Browning on an arm. "You don't have to do that, Eddie. Since the four of us will be joining you at the station, Willie can take Nealy home in the studio's car. Isn't that right, Mack dear?"

"Sure. Willie can take her home for you, Detective."

"That's very generous of you, Mr. Sennett."

Mabel smiled. "Then I suppose we'd better be going." She led the others toward the walkway between the candy store and the building next door with Maisy bringing up the rear. Mabel entered the narrow space first, followed by Sennett. The Browning's walked behind the studio head, and Nellie Sharpe trailed them closely. Cole hesitated, thinking the polite thing would be for Maisy to be next in line. Instead, Maisy stopped and jabbed her left thumb toward the lane, silently indicating Cole should walk ahead of her. When his lips moved in protest, she quickly covered his mouth with her right hand, gritted her teeth, and aimed her left thumb toward the others with more vehemence. Not immediately understanding her intent, his brow furrowed with confusion for a second. Maisy's jaw jutted out in anger at his slow reaction, and this expression finally made her point. Cole shrugged and headed off after the others, looking back over his shoulder just in time to see Maisy shaking her head at him. When his feet stuttered, she instantly thrust out her right arm and pointed with her index finger to reiterate he should keep up with the others. He rolled his eyes and faced forward again. Near exasperation, Maisy watched her friends continue toward the street for a few seconds before turning and dashing up the back porch steps and into the rear of the candy store.

Now inside the store Maisy marched through the hall, moving past the kitchen and then the stairway to the apartment above, until she reached the curtained doorway to the ice cream parlor. She peeked through the drapes to see the Kokis greeting another pair of mourners and Enji Yamaguchi standing off to one side waiting to escort them upstairs. In the next instant, she heard footsteps on the stairs behind her and determined that Yoshi must be coming downstairs again to resume his place in the store. Quickly, she turned and went to meet him at the bottom step.

"Miss Malone!"

Maisy grabbed his hand and pulled him toward the kitchen. "Yoshi, I need to talk to you for a moment."

He followed her reluctantly. "Talk to me?"

"Yes. Right now." She drew him into the kitchen, stopped, and faced him. "Yoshi, on the morning you and Masi returned to the tuna boat, did you board the boat at the wharf in San Pedro or the one on Rattlesnake Island?"

Yamaguchi stared at her for a few heartbeats as he replayed her question in his head and dug into his memory bank for an answer. "We board *Blackfin* from San Pedro wharf."

"And then what?" When he appeared to be mystified by her next question, she decided to rephrase it. "After you and Masi boarded the *Blackfin* in San Pedro, what happened next?"

"We cast off lines, and Captain Garrido take boat to Rattlesnake Island to get other men of crew."

"And what did you and Masi do then?"

"We go below and stow gear."

"And after that, what?"

"I say before. I go to mess deck for coffee. Masi go topside."

"And what happened when you got to Rattlesnake Island?"

"Other men of crew come aboard."

"Did the boat tie up to the dock on the island and stay there for a while?"

Yamaguchi thought for a few seconds before replying. "Yes, we always tie up and stay for few minutes. Captain Garrido always want make sure all crew aboard before getting underway for sea."

"When did you realize that Masi was not on the boat?"

"Captain call for all men to set their lines when we pass Castle Rock. Masi missing then."

Maisy squeezed his arm. "Thank you, Yoshi. You've been a big help."

As promised, the Garridos and Rodrigo Manuelo presented themselves as promised at the Los Angeles Police Department's Central Station later that afternoon. Sergeant Johnson escorted the older man into Browning's office, while the others waited on a bench in the outer area for their turn to be interviewed.

The detective proffered his hand to the fishing magnate. "Thank you for coming into the station, Mr. Garrido. You saved us a trip to your home in San Pedro."

With an olive complexion, jet black hair graying at the temples, bushy eyebrows, thick black mustache neatly trimmed at each corner of his mouth, and piercing brown eyes, Geraldo Garrido shook hands firmly with Browning like a man of authority and confidence, his gaze: eye-to-eye with the police detective. "My family and I only wish to help you find the man who did this terrible thing to Masi."

When they released their grip, Browning waved toward the chair in front of his desk. "Please be seated, sir."

Before sitting, Geraldo shifted his view from Browning, bypassing Nellie Sharpe, to Maisy and Mabel, a casual smile spreading over his face as his head dipped toward the leading lady of cinematic comedy. "I recognize Miss Normand here from the moving pictures." He tilted his head toward Maisy. "But this young woman? Her face is familiar to me, but I am unacquainted with her."

"Then allow me to introduce you, sir. This is Miss Maisy Malone. She is also an actress and works with Miss Normand at the Keystone

Film Company in Edendale. You may have seen her in a few films with Miss Normand."

Garrido smiled broadly. "Yes, of course. Now I remember you. You usually play the friend or the sister or someone else close to Miss Normand in her films."

"That's me all right. Mabel's shadow."

Mabel waved off Maisy's attempt at self-deprecation. "Don't be silly, dear. You're a fine actress, and you know it."

With her eyes fixed on Garrido's, Maisy smiled brazenly and nudged her friend gently. "Tell Mack that, will you? Maybe you can get me a raise."

Browning cleared his throat. "Miss Malone and Miss Normand were two of the people who found Masi Tanaka's body on the beach north of Santa Monica. I have asked them to assist me in my investigation of Mr. Tanaka's death because they have an innate ability to communicate with folks like the Tanaka's and the Japanese men you employ on your boats. Miss Malone also speaks a modicum of Spanish and is more familiar with your people than I am, sir. So, she will be conducting the interviews with you and your daughter and brother and the first officer of the *Blackfin* Rodrigo Manuelo."

Garrido focused a warm smile on Maisy. "*¡Muy bueno para mí, Señorita Malone! Por lo que se habla a español.*"

"*Sí, un poco, Señor Garrido.*"

"*Por favor llámeme Geraldo.*"

"*Mucho gracias, Geraldo. Por favor llámeme Maisy. Pero por favor, dejemos hablar a inglés.*"

Still smiling at Maisy, Garrido nodded. "Yes, of course. As you wish, Maisy." He sat.

"I only ask so Detective Browning and Miss Normand can follow our conversation, and so Miss Sharpe can transcribe it for the record."

"Miss Sharpe?"

With a wave of her hand, Maisy indicated the transcriptionist sitting in the corner with a notepad in her lap. "Yes, Miss Sharpe is one of the police department's stenographers. Her Spanish isn't as good as mine, which is why I would like us to converse in English."

Garrido nodded with understanding. "Yes, I understand completely." He turned to Browning. "I want you to know, Detective Browning, that my family and I offer you our full co-operation in helping you find the man who did this terrible thing to Masi. He was the best employee I have ever had."

"Thank you again, sir."

The San Pedro businessman returned his attention to Maisy. "Now I am ready for your questions, Maisy. Please begin."

"Well, first off, Geraldo, I am a little surprised to hear you say Masi Tanaka was the best employee you ever had."

"And why is that Maisy?"

"Well ... one of your other employees told us you told Masi to stay away from your daughter. Apparently, Masi was good enough to catch tuna for you, but he wasn't good enough to be in the company of your daughter. Is that right?"

Garrido's face darkened. "Absolutely! We are Mexicans, and he is ... he *was* ... Japanese. The blood of Spanish nobles runs in our veins. We are descended from *los Californios, los Rancheros, los Conquistadores,* the men and women who conquered and settled this land before the coming of the Americans."

"And now you and your family are Americans."

Garrido's face pinched around his nose, as if he had just bitten into a very dill pickle. His reply came out slowly, measured, failing to disguise his disdain for the fact that the term American applied to him. "Yes, we are, but the Japanese are not. They are still Japanese, foreigners just like the Chinese. We do not mix our blood with theirs."

"Would you say Rodrigo Manuelo is also an American?"

The question took Garrido by surprise. "Why do you ask that?"

"I ask because Rodrigo assaulted Masi Tanaka while he was walking one evening with your daughter not too long ago. Apparently, Rodrigo has his eye on your daughter, Geraldo."

"Who told you that?"

"One of your fishermen."

"Yes, but which one?"

Browning intervened. "I'm sorry, Mr. Garrido, but the statements of witnesses remain confidential with the police department until after a trial and a verdict has been handed down by a jury. You understand how important that is, don't you?"

Garrido's jaw tightened. "Yes, of course, I understand the importance of confidentiality."

Maisy resumed her questioning. "So, Geraldo, did you know about the spat between Masi Tanaka and Rodrigo Manuelo?"

"Spat?"

"Yes, spat. I call it that because of the way our witness described their confrontation it wasn't much of a fight. Rodrigo pushed Masi from behind and knocked him down, and Masi retaliated swiftly and firmly by throwing Rodrigo to the ground and holding him there until he promised to stop fighting and go away and leave him alone with your daughter. So, to rephrase my question, did you know about this little tussle between Masi and Rodrigo?"

"No, this is news to me."

"So, neither your daughter nor your first officer on the *Blackfin* told you about it?"

"No, neither one. Why would they tell me about it? Belinda was already told to stay away from Masi. She would not want me to know she was still having contact with him. And if the fight happened the way you were told, then Rodrigo would be too embarrassed by the result to tell anybody else about it … especially me."

"What do you mean she was *already* told to stay away from Masi?"

Confusion cast its shadow on Garrido's face. "What do I mean …? I mean nothing by that. What are you trying to get at with that question?"

"You said, 'Belinda was already told to stay away from Masi.'" Maisy shifted her view to the stenographer. "Isn't that correct, Miss Sharpe?"

Nellie nodded. "Yes, it is, Miss Malone. The witness's exact words were, 'No, neither one. Why would they tell me about it?

122

Belinda was already told to stay away from Masi. She would not want me—"

Garrido threw up his hands. "All right, I said that, but that's not what I meant to say."

Browning leaned forward on his desk and pressed the point. "Then what did you mean to say, Mr. Garrido?"

After a few seconds of silence, the fishing magnate retreated. "All right, I don't know what I meant. Are you satisfied now, Miss Maisy Malone?"

"Not really. So, let me rephrase the question again. Did you tell your daughter to stay away from Masi before this incident … or after it?"

Garrido saw an opening. "If I don't know when Masi and Rodrigo got into their fight, how am I to know whether I told him to stay away from Belinda before or after they fought?"

Maisy persisted with this line of questioning. "Then let me ask you this, Geraldo. Did you tell Masi to stay away from your daughter *before* … or … *after* he tangled with Rodrigo?"

Garrido looked to Browning for some kind of help, but none was forthcoming. "Please answer Miss Malone, Mr. Garrido."

The fishing boat owner refused to surrender. "I came here to help you with your investigation into Masi Tanaka's murder, but you have turned this into an inquisition aimed at me. Why have you done this? You don't think I had anything to do with Masi's death, now do you? I mean, if you do think that, then—"

Without blinking an eye, Maisy cut him off. "You can only help us by telling the truth, Geraldo. By answering my questions honestly and directly. Anything less is unacceptable. Am I right, Detective Browning?"

"Absolutely, Miss Malone."

Recognizing his cause was lost, Garrido appeared to surrender. "All right then, I'll tell you. When I first saw Masi showing interest in Belinda, I told him to stay away from her."

"When was this?"

"Two weeks ago. Maybe three weeks. Esteván and my other

captain, Victorio Dominguez, they came into port early because the fishing was so good that their holds were filled in two and a half days. They unloaded the boats that afternoon and celebrated their catch that evening in San Pedro. That is when I saw Masi talking to Belinda. I sent her home and told him to stay away from her."

"How did Masi take your order to stay away from your daughter? I mean, how did he react to it?"

Garrido grinned. "He acted like he always did. He smiled and said, 'Okay, boss.' Then he just walked away and took the water taxi home to Rattlesnake Island."

Maisy nodded. "I see." She paused before asking another question. "Did anybody hear you tell Masi to stay away from your daughter?"

"I cannot rightly say. I don't recall anybody being close to us at the time I was talking to him. Of course, somebody could have been listening nearby and I did not see them."

"Did you tell anybody later that you had told Masi to stay away from your daughter?"

Geraldo shook his head. "No, I told no one. Perhaps Masi said something to one of his friends, someone like Yoshi Yamaguchi or Enji Nakamura, but I did not say anything to anybody about it."

Maisy shook her head. "Geraldo, I am terribly disappointed in you. Nothing you've said matches up with what your fisherman told us."

"What do you mean by that? What did he tell you?"

"He told us the day after Masi and Rodrigo had their little spat you came down to the dock and told Masi to stay away from your daughter. That tells me you didn't see him with your daughter at all. That tells me Rodrigo told you he saw Masi with your daughter. Was that the correct sequence of events, Geraldo?"

Garrido grimaced. "Yes, now that I think of it, it was. Rodrigo came to my home to tell me he had seen Masi walking with Belinda. When she came home that evening, I confronted her about it. She told me about Rodrigo pushing Masi from behind and how Masi quickly turned the tables on him. I could see in her eyes how much this excited her. I feared she was taken with Masi, so I told her to stay away from him. The next morning I went down to the boat and told him to stay away from her, and like I said before, he said he would."

"Thank you, Geraldo, for finally telling us the truth. Now we can move on to another line of questions."

The businessman waggled a finger at Maisy. "You know, young lady, you are very clever with your words and your ability to get the truth from me. I am very much impressed."

"Thank you for the flattery, Geraldo, but we have no time for it. We still have a killer to catch."

"Yes, please proceed with your questions, Maisy. I promise you nothing less than the truth from this moment forward."

Maisy wanted to roll her eyes, but she restrained the desire. "Where were you this past Monday morning when the *Blackfin* went to sea?"

"I was at the same place I always am on weekday mornings. I was at the fish market in San Pedro."

"Can anybody corroborate that, Geraldo?"

"I would think everybody else who was there that morning could."

Maisy nodded. "Yes, of course. What about your daughter? Where was she that morning?"

Garrido appeared offended, then angry. "My daughter? Why would you ask me that? Belinda has nothing to do with Masi's death."

Browning rejoined the interview. "That remains to be seen, Mr. Garrido. Right now, everybody from you to that Chinese boatman to every man on the *Blackfin* is a suspect, including your daughter. So please answer Miss Malone's question. Where was your daughter this past Monday morning when the *Blackfin* left port?"

"My daughter is a lady like her mother was, may she rest in peace." He crossed himself in respect for his departed mate. "Belinda does not have to rise with the men in our household. She was home asleep."

"Can you verify that, sir?"

"You only need to ask our housekeeper Ming Yet."

The detective's brow pinched together. "Why does that name ring a bell with me?"

Maisy had the answer. "That's the name of the family that sold the candy store to Mr. Tanaka."

Browning nodded. "Oh, yes, that's right. Now I remember."

Garrido snickered. "I could have told you that. Ming Yet has been working for us since before my wife passed away, God grant her peace." He crossed himself again. "Her husband Ah-loo used to own a store in Chinatown, but he sold it about five years ago and came to work for me as my bookkeeper."

Maisy nodded at Browning. "That's when Mr. Tanaka bought his store."

The fishing magnate shrugged. "I suppose Ah-loo and Ming could be the same family. I don't know for sure. You'll have to ask them."

"We will." Maisy looked up at the policeman. "Do you think you could have your officers bring them in for questioning right away, Detective?"

"I'll get on that immediately."

* * *

After Geraldo Garrido supplied Browning with the Yets' address in San Pedro, Maisy finished questioning the fishing magnate and he was taken to another office temporarily to keep him separated from the other family members and Rodrigo Manuelo. At the same time, Belinda Garrido was led into the detective's office, where Browning made the introductions.

"Miss Malone will be asking the questions, Miss Garrido, because we thought you would feel more comfortable talking with her than with me."

Belinda smiled with nearly perfect white teeth made even brighter in appearance by her golden brown complexion and silky black hair. "That was very considerate of you, Detective Browning, but quite unnecessary. I am much accustomed to being around men of authority like *mí padre* and Uncle Esteván. Although *mí padre* insists on treating me like a schoolgirl, I can assure you that I am a woman who can think for herself just as much as Miss Normand and Miss Malone here."

Browning suddenly became speechless, but not Maisy Malone. "I'm glad you spoke up like that, Belinda. Most of the Mexican women I've met here in California and in Spain behave rather timidly in the presence of men."

A sparkle danced magically in Belinda's agate brown eyes. "You have been to Spain?"

"Well, a small part of it. It's a long story. Let's just say I spent a little time there this past spring before returning to America."

"You are so lucky, Miss Malone. I have dreamt of visiting Spain all my life. *Mí madre* used to tell me stories of castles and knights and beautiful ladies being rescued from the horrible Moors." A veil of sadness dropped over her lovely face. "*Mí madre* is no longer living, may God rest her soul." She crossed herself. "So I have to read about Spain in books now."

"I'm so sorry to hear that, Belinda. Your mother's passing, I mean."

"Thank you. That is very kind of you, Miss Malone."

"*Por favor llámeme Maisy.*"

The joy returned to Belinda's expression. "*¿Hablas español?*"

Maisy held up her hand to indicate how much Spanish she spoke with her index finger and thumb. "*Un poco.* But we should speak English so Miss Sharpe can record what we say."

"Oh, yes, of course."

"Belinda, you do know why you and your father and uncle are here, don't you?"

A hint of grief dimmed the shine in Belinda's eyes. "Yes, you want to ask us things about Masi Tanaka. May God rest his soul." Sorrow toned her voice. Again, she crossed herself. "I know he was killed by someone, but how was it done? Was he shot with a *pistola*?"

"I'm sorry, Belinda, but I can't tell you how he died. I can only tell you that his body was found on a beach on Christmas day."

"Oh, yes, now I remember. *Mí padre* said he read in the newspaper yesterday morning that a Japanese man was found on the beach north of Santa Monica and he had drowned."

Maisy took a deep breath before resuming the interview. "Well, I can tell you this much. The newspaper got it wrong. He didn't drown, but we are fairly sure he was murdered."

Belinda lowered her eyes from Maisy's view. "That is so terrible. Masi was such a nice man." She looked up again, her eyes welling with tears, her joy now forced. "He was always smiling and spoke softly and kindly about … everything and everybody."

"Did you know Masi very well?"

A new glow shone in Belinda's eyes after she blinked away the tears. "I knew him as well as most people, I suppose. Maybe a little better. He told me some things that I don't believe he told to very many other people."

Maisy nodded. "Can you give me an example of those things he shared with you? So we can get a better picture of him in our minds, which will help us find the person who killed him."

"Oh, yes. He told me a great deal about his life back in Japan and how he missed his homeland very much. At the same time, he was also glad he came to America like his brother Tokutaro. Did you know that he was planning to leave the tuna boats and open up a flower shop in Los Angeles?"

"Yes, Tokutaro told us about it. Did Masi tell you that he had married a picture bride and she was on her way to America?"

Belinda looked down again, avoiding eye-contact with Maisy for the moment. "Yes, he mentioned it to me." She lifted her head and stared hard at the actress. "It's sad, isn't it? Teruka is on a boat right now on her way to America, and he won't be there to meet her when it arrives in San Francisco next Friday."

"Yes, it is sad, Belinda." Maisy paused for a few heartbeats. "Look, Belinda, I'm sorry this is taking so long, but I only have a few more questions for you, if you don't mind."

"No, not at all. Ask me anything."

"One of Masi shipmates told us about an incident involving you and Masi and Rodrigo Manuelo." Maisy studied Belinda's face for a reaction and saw exactly what she expected to see: surprise followed by fear. "Do you know the incident I'm talking about?"

"I'm ... I'm not sure what you are talking about, Maisy."

"Well, your father confirmed there was an incident involving Masi, Rodrigo, and you. I'd like to hear your version of what happened that evening, if you don't mind telling us about it."

Belinda shrugged her shoulders and feigned innocence of any misbehavior. "There's not really much to tell. Masi and I were walking along Beacon Street when Rodrigo ran up from behind us and knocked Masi to the ground. Rodrigo was screaming something about Masi staying away from me because I was promised to him."

Browning interrupted. "Are you promised to Rodrigo?"

"No, of course not. Rodrigo is an employee of *mí padre*. He would never allow me to marry anybody like him."

Maisy frowned at the detective for a second before returning her attention to Belinda. "So why would Rodrigo say something like that? That you were promised to him?"

Again Belinda shrugged and feigned innocence. "I don't know. That Rodrigo, he is Portuguese, and he can be wild and crazy sometimes. He says he likes to live dangerously. So he does wild and crazy things to impress people."

"Meaning you?"

"Yes, I suppose he does."

"Do you like these wild and crazy things he does to impress you?"

Belinda's head bobbed. "Yes, I suppose I do. What of it?"

Maisy shook her head. "Nothing. It's not important." She pursed her lips for a few seconds. "So, what happened next between Masi and Rodrigo after Masi was knocked down?"

"Masi sprang to his feet and faced Rodrigo. Rodrigo then charged Masi, and Masi moved out of his way like a bullfighter. Rodrigo tried again, and this time Masi tripped him. Rodrigo got up and walked up to Masi and tried to hit him with his fist. Masi deflected the punch, and Rodrigo threw another one that Masi deflected again. This made Rodrigo even angrier. He tried to kick Masi, but Masi grabbed his foot and flipped Rodrigo on his back ...

extremely hard. Rodrigo tried to get up, but Masi put his foot on Rodrigo's throat and told him to stop fighting. Rodrigo cursed Masi, so Masi pressed his foot a little harder on Rodrigo's throat to quiet him. Masi told him again to stop fighting and said he would let him up if he stopped fighting and went away. Masi lifted his foot to let Rodrigo speak, and Rodrigo promised he would stop fighting and go away. Masi let him up. When Rodrigo got to his feet again, he cursed Masi and then went away."

"Rodrigo cursed Masi? Exactly what did he say?"

"He said he would tell *mi padre* about Masi being with me and then he said, 'I will get you for this, Jap boy. I will make you pay. I promise you that, Jap boy.' And then he went away."

"Then what happened?"

"Masi said he must go back to the boardinghouse on Rattlesnake Island and go to sleep. He walked me home, and then he left. I suppose he went back to the boardinghouse like he said."

"Okay, thank you, Belinda. I only have one more question for you. Why did you ask if Masi was killed with a *pistola*?"

The color faded from Belinda's face. "I don't know why I asked that. Since so many men are killed with guns, I suppose I only wished to know if Masi was, too."

Maisy shook her head. "Belinda, I don't think that's quite right. I think you had a definite reason for asking if Masi had been killed with a gun."

"No, I—"

"You promised to be truthful with me, Belinda. Now tell me why you really asked if Masi was killed with a gun."

Belinda appeared shaken as what little color remained in her faced drained away completely. "I can't tell you that, Maisy. It would be bad if I tell you that." Suddenly, a new thought entered her thinking. "Besides, I don't think it would make any difference for helping you find Masi's killer."

Browning leaned forward. "I'll be the judge of that, Miss Garrido. Now please answer Miss Malone's question."

Belinda glared at the policeman with anger but seeing

intimidation in his eyes she balked at arguing with him. Instead she faced Maisy. "When I went into the house that same night, I saw Rodrigo talking to *mí padre*. *Mí padre* was angry. He went to the cabinet and took out his *pistola* and began loading it. Rodrigo went to him and asked to let him do it."

"Do what, Belinda?"

She heaved a sigh and then sat silently.

Browning loomed over the fishing magnate's daughter. "Answer the question, Belinda."

She heaved another sigh as her eyes pleaded with Maisy not to make her answer.

Maisy also pressed the issue. "Do what, Belinda? What did Rodrigo want to do instead of your father doing it?" Maisy leaned across the desk and spoke in the lowest, most threatening tone she could summon. "Belinda, you have to answer the question or Detective Browning will place your father under arrest for the murder of Masi Tanaka."

Terror struck Belinda. "No, he can't do that. Not *mí padre*. No, he simply can't do that. He mustn't. Not *mí padre*." She shifted her view to the detective bending ominously over her. "No, I beg of you, sir. Please do not arrest *mí padre*. I know he didn't kill Masi. He couldn't do something so terrible. I just know it. Not *mí padre*."

"Then tell us what Rodrigo wanted to do instead of your father doing it, Miss Garrido."

Belinda buried her face in her hands and wept copious tears. But nobody could tell whether she was really crying or not.

Browning thought so. He stood to go around his desk to comfort Belinda.

Maisy thought otherwise. She said nothing, but she did hold out her hand to wave off Browning.

The detective saw Maisy's gesture and returned to his chair.

Belinda's feigned weeping subsided. She removed a white handkerchief from her handbag and dabbed away the few tears she had managed to force her eyes to secrete.

Still quite perfunctory, Maisy asked another question. "Are you ready to continue, Miss Garrido?"

"Yes, I ... think so." She nodded. "Yes ... yes, I am."

"Now would you please tell us what Rodrigo said he would do instead of your father doing it?"

"He didn't actually say what he planned to do."

"Then what exactly did he say?"

"He took the *pistola* from *mi padre* and said he would do it for him. Rodrigo did not say exactly what he would do for *mi padre*. He just took the *pistola* from him and stuck it inside his waistband and covered it with his coat."

"And then what happened?"

"Rodrigo left."

"Do you know where he went?"

Belinda shook her head. "No. He just left the house."

"And when did all this happen, Belinda? I mean, the incident between Masi Tanaka and Rodrigo and when Rodrigo took the gun from your father. Did those two things happen on the same night?"

"Yes, they did."

"And what night was that?"

"Last Thursday a week ago after the *Blackfin* returned to San Pedro."

Maisy focused on Browning. "That's all the questions I have for Miss Garrido. What about you, Ed? Any questions?"

"None that I can think of at this time."

Now looking at Mabel, Maisy asked her the same question. Mabel shook her head in response.

"In that case, you can go, Belinda."

Browning stood. "I'll show you out, Miss Garrido. Who do want next, Maisy? Rodrigo?"

"Absolutely, Ed."

* * *

Rodrigo Manuelo sat in the same chair as the Garridos had. He seemed to be a bit nervous and at the same time presented an air of arrogance.

Maisy charged in with her interrogation. "Rodrigo, do you still have the gun you took from Mr. Garrido last Thursday night a week ago?"

The man's entire demeanor changed. "How do you know about that?"

"That's for me to know and for you to find out. Do you still have the gun you took from Mr. Garrido last Thursday night?"

"Yes, I still have it."

"Do you have it right now?

Rodrigo shook his head. "No, I left it at my home in San Pedro."

"Have you fired the gun since you've had it?"

Manuelo straightened up in the chair, totally shocked by the question. "If you mean, did I shoot Masi Tanaka, then my answer is no." He cleared his throat. "If Masi was shot to death, it wasn't me who did it."

"I didn't say he was shot. I only want to know if you have fired the gun since it's been in your possession."

"In that case, yes, I fired the gun. I took it to the beach below the bluff at Point Fermin for some target practice."

"Why did you do that? Were you planning on shooting someone?"

Again, Manuelo was taken aback. "Yes, I was."

A big smile spread Maisy's lips.

Mabel gasped.

Browning's mouth dried up instantly.

Maisy shook her head with astonishment. "An honest answer. I can hardly believe it, Rodrigo."

Mabel burst out. "Me, too."

Browning rasped. "That makes three of us."

"So, who were you planning to shoot?"

"Masi Tanaka."

Maisy threw up her arms and looked to the heaven above. "Well glory halleluiah! Two straight honest answers from a man I was sure would lie through his teeth to us." She refocused on Manuelo. "So, when were you planning to shoot Masi?"

Manuelo appeared chagrinned. "I was still trying to figure that out when I heard from you that he was dead."

"Still trying to figure out when you were going to shoot him? Why?"

"Well, I thought about going after him that same night I took the gun from *Señor* Garrido, but once I left his house, I realized I had no idea where Masi might be at that time of night. And even if I had known where he was, I couldn't shoot him and nobody knowing about it. I mean, surely someone would hear the shot and see me with the gun." He shook his head. "So, I went home and tried to figure out a plan to kill him. I couldn't think of how to do it. So, I went to the beach for some target practice. When I used up all the bullets in the gun, I realized I would have to go to a store and buy some more. That made me realize that committing a murder with a gun was not an easy thing to plan. So, I put the gun away in my house and put that notion out of my head for good."

"So, if you didn't shoot Masi, how did you kill him?"

Manuelo's brow pinched together in protest. "I didn't kill him. I wanted to kill him, but I didn't do it. I swear on my mother's soul, I did not kill him." He crossed himself to reiterate his oath.

Maisy was incredulous as she looked at Browning. "You know what, Ed? I believe him. But what do you think?"

"Sounds like he's telling the truth, Maisy."

Mabel's head bobbed in agreement. "I do, too, Maise."

"Then you can go, Rodigo. Detective Browning will show you out."

Browning stood. "Who do you want next, Maisy?"

"The *Blackfin*'s captain. Esteván Garrido."

* * *

"Captain Garrido, would you please tell us exactly everything you can recall that happened last Monday morning? Start with the time you left your home to go down to the harbor."

Garrido sighed. "On days when we are going out to fish, I rise three hours before sunrise. My wife has my breakfast ready. I eat, then I leave my house. Rodrigo meets me at the front door, and we walk down to the harbor together. Usually, when we arrive at the boat, Masi Tanaka"—he crossed himself— "may he rest in peace … and Yoshi Yamaguchi are often there waiting for us. Often but not always. Like last Monday morning. Rodrigo and I arrived at the boat first. I went below and made the coffee, while Rodrigo went to the engine room and started the boat's engine. When we finished, we went back on deck and saw Masi and Yoshi just then coming aboard the boat."

"Did either of them say anything to you that seemed out of the ordinary that morning?"

The captain pursed his lips and shook his head. "No, I don't remember them saying anything other than good morning." His brow furrowed. "But now that you mention it, I did think something was bothering Masi. He wasn't his usual happy-go-lucky self that morning. I didn't think anything about it at the time as the four of us went about our business of getting the *Blackfin* underway. The *Yellowfin*'s crew had already untied its lines from the wharf and were preparing to back out into the harbor to go around Terminal Island to pick up the rest of their crew who lived at the boardinghouse or in some shack. Masi and Yoshi released our lines, and Rodrigo manned the engine, while I went up to the bridge to man the helm."

"Do you know where Masi and Yoshi went after they secured the lines aboard the *Blackfin*?"

"No, I don't. I was too busy steering the boat through the harbor to the dock near the cannery."

Maisy nodded. "So what happened when you reached the dock near the cannery?"

"Nothing out of the usual. The men who live on the island were waiting for us. A couple of them helped to secure the lines to the dock. They came aboard. I went down to the main deck to do a head count, you know, to make certain I had the whole crew aboard."

"Were Masi Tanaka and Yoshi Yamaguchi present at this head count?"

Estevàn scratched his head as if the motion would prompt his memory to recall the moment in question. "You know, I don't recall either of them being there then, but I know for certain they were aboard the boat. As I said before, they were waiting on the dock, and they were there when we docked at the island. I know that because they threw the lines to the men waiting on the dock."

"But you didn't see them after that?"

The captain scratched his head again. "I don't recall seeing Masi again that morning."

"What about Yoshi Yamaguchi? When did you see him again?"

"Not until we were out to sea. He brought me a fresh cup of coffee."

"And when was that?"

"Just about the time we were passing Castle Rock."

Maisy paused for thought before asking her next question. "Captain, was this your usual course when you left San Pedro

Harbor?"

"No, we hardly ever go the same way two times in a row."

"And why not?"

"Our experience tells us to follow the direction the wind is blowing, so that's the course we take."

Mabel interjected a question of her own. "Why do you do that?"

"Because the wind pushes the water, and the water pushes the food the tuna eat. Although more people don't know it, the ocean has currents somewhat like rivers do. The fish follow the currents. That morning the wind was blowing north-by-northeast, making the ocean a little choppy, which is why we stayed so close the shore."

Mabel smiled at him. "I didn't know that about the ocean. The winds and the currents, I mean. Thank you, Captain. That was highly informative."

"*De nada*, Miss Normand."

Maisy resumed her line of questioning. "Captain, since you've had time to think about Masi Tanaka's death, do you have any thoughts about how his body wound up on the beach at Castle Rock?"

"Yes, I have, Miss Malone. If Masi was still on the boat when we were sailing north, I think it was quite possible that he either fell overboard or he was thrown overboard. I don't think he was thrown overboard because that would have meant there was a struggle between him and someone else in my crew. The only man on the *Blackfin* who might want to do Masi any harm would be Rodrigo Manuelo. But I don't think Rodrigo would try to throw Masi overboard because everybody knows how Masi handled Rodrigo with such ease last Thursday evening in San Pedro. Rodrigo is something of a fool, but I don't think he's such a fool that he would attack Masi a second time."

Browning interjected a question. "You said the ocean was choppy that morning. Do you think Masi could have fallen overboard?"

Garrido shook his head. "My crew are all good sailors besides being the most excellent fishermen in the harbor. Masi wouldn't have fallen overboard. He could only have been thrown overboard, and knowing Masi as I did, that would have taken at least two men to do it." He shook his head again. "The only way Masi would have wound up in the water would be if he was unconscious from being hit on his head with something."

Maisy and Browning exchanged glances.

Garrido saw how they looked at each other. "Is that it? Is that how Masi was killed? Someone hit him in his head and threw him overboard?'

Browning took charge. "I'm afraid we can't tell you how he was killed, Captain Garrido."

Maisy jumped in again. "The police have to keep certain details about Masi's death confidential until they find the killer. You do understand that don't you, Captain?"

"Yes, of course."

Maisy gave him a respectful smile. "Very good, Captain. Now let's get back to the day the *Blackfin* went to sea. If Masi was thrown overboard, how do you think his body ended up at Castle Rock by Christmas Day?"

"That's a very good question, Miss Malone. I've been asking myself that ever since you told us about Masi's body being found on the beach at Castle Rock. To be perfectly honest with you, I can't really say how his body ended up on the beach at Castle Rock without knowing exactly where it entered the water."

Maisy nodded. "Fair enough. So let's theorize about how Masi wound up dead on the beach at Castle Rock. Let's say Masi was still alive when your boat passed Castle Rock and he was killed and thrown overboard. Would the current of the ocean there wash him up on the beach by Christmas Day?"

"That wouldn't have happened."

"Why not?"

"Because the sun was up when we passed Castle Rock. One of the lookouts or even I would have seen him being thrown overboard. So you see, he had to have been killed at least an hour before we reached Castle Rock and thrown overboard. That would be at least ten to fifteen miles south of Castle Rock. Maybe farther. For all we know, Miss Malone, Masi could have been killed while we were still tied up at Rattlesnake Island and taking on the crew. He could even have been killed on the island and thrown into the harbor and gradually washed out to sea by the flow of the Los Angeles River. I recall the weather was rather stormy in the mountains with rain and snow at the higher elevations. The river was running fairly high with a stronger current than usual."

Maisy appeared impressed by Garrido's conjecture. "You really have been thinking about this, Captain. I would never have considered the Los Angeles River's current would wash Masi's body out to sea." She turned to Browning. "This really changes things, Eddie. I think we might have to start all over with this investigation."

"I was thinking the same thing, Maisy." Browning looked directly at the *Blackfin*'s captain. "Thank you, Captain Garrido. You've been most helpful, sir." He stood. "Come on. I'll show you out to where the others are waiting for you."

* * *

When he returned to his office, Browning scanned the faces of the three women before speaking. "Did I miss anything?"

Maisy shook her head. "No, we decided to wait for you before we discuss anything about the investigation."

Browning lifted his left eyebrow. "That was considerate of you."

Maisy shifted in her chair. "You are the investigating officer, Eddie. We haven't forgotten that have we, Mabel?"

"No, of course not. You're still in charge, Eddie."

The detective burped a sarcastic laugh. "Well, isn't that nice to know?"

Maisy showed her serious side to Browning. "I may be doing most of the questioning, Eddie, but you're still the boss here."

Browning hesitated to answer her immediately, but when he did, he nodded. "Well, thank you for that."

Maisy smiled politely. "So … what do you think about the case so far, Eddie?"

The policeman shrugged and shook his head slightly. "I have to admit I really don't know what to think about it so far. We don't have an exact time of death, no murder weapon, and no plausible cause for the murder. We don't even have a coroner's report yet, which I'm sure we won't have until Monday at the earliest. Until then, I don't see where we go from here. What do you think, Maisy? Any thoughts on where we go from here?"

"I agree with you, Eddie. We don't have all the facts yet, which makes it impossible to put any suspicion on any one suspect."

Mabel spoke up. "There's the rub, isn't it? Not all the facts are in yet, so we can't start narrowing down our list of suspects."

Maisy grinned Mabel. "Omigosh, Mabel! You're starting to catch on to this sleuthing business, aren't you?"

The actress feigned modesty. "Well, I can only blame that on you, kid."

Browning cleared his throat. "So what do you plan to do next, Maisy? As for me, tomorrow is Sunday and my day off. I'd like to spend it with Nealy, so I hope you aren't planning anything that will include me."

Maisy shook her head. "No, Eddie, I'm not. After four straight days of trying to get somewhere on this case, I have to admit I'm a little stumped and in need of some time to myself and my friends. What do you think, Mabel?"

"I agree with you totally. So why don't we go home and get some rest tomorrow and talk about it Monday morning?"

"Good idea. Let's do that."

Not being much of a church-goer since leaving her native home in the Choctaw Nation, Maisy Malone became quite accustomed to sleeping in on Sundays. This Sabbath should have been no different, but outside forces had other ideas for her.

The telephone rang incessantly much to Maisy's chagrin. She let it ring and ring, hoping all the while that whoever had the audacity to call her before noon would give up and let her go back to sleep. On the twentieth-something jangle of her phone, she finally surrendered, rolled to the side of her single bed, threw back the blanket covering her, slid off the mattress to stand as erect as she could, straightened her dhinty lace-trimmed pale blue nainsook chemise, inserted her feet into her knit slippers, and grumbled her way from her bedroom to the living room of her latest apartment where she flopped down on the end of the sofa near the telephone stand. Another ring of the annoying bell, and she reached for it like a cobra attacking a mongoose, grabbing the device by its candlestick stand and bringing the whole mechanism up to her face. She jerked the receiver from its hook and in a single motion pulled the speaker to her lips and put the receiver to her ear.

"This better be important or I swear I will hunt you down and throttle you into next week."

"Maisy? It's Mabel."

"Like I said, this better be important or—"

"Yes, dear, I know. You'll throttle me into next week."

"I'm not kidding, Mabel."

"Yes, dear. I know you sleep in on Sundays, so I wouldn't have called you this early if it wasn't really important."

Maisy yawned. "How early is it anyway?"

"It's almost ten o'clock."

"Like I said before—"

"Mack told me to call you and tell you we need you to help us with decorating the Cadillac for the *Tournament of Roses* Parade."

Maisy's face soured. "You're kidding, right?"

"I wish I was, Maise, but that's simply not the case. D.W. wants you here. Not Mack. And you know who the real boss is around here, don't you?"

Maisy had to do a mental translation of "D.W." before she could reply to Mabel's question. "Griffith ... wants ... me ... there? How does that happen?"

Mabel hesitated to answer immediately—and for good reason. "I really shouldn't be telling you this, Maise, but D.W. is considering using you in a full-length feature he has in mind. But before he puts you in one, he wants to put you in a couple of two-reelers and see how the audiences like you and whether you can do serious acting. But before that, he wants to get to know you better, which is why he wants you to come to Keystone and help with the decoration of the Cadillac."

"And how do you know all this, Mabel?"

"Mack often lets me sit in whenever D.W. visits the Tower, or he takes me with him when he meets D.W. for dinner or drinks. Mack is no dummy. He thinks I can direct some films and maybe write one or two. He says I can learn a lot just from listening to him and D.W. chat about the business. Same goes for you."

As it so often happens with Maisy, her mind leaped ahead to another universe. "Wouldn't that be a hoot? Me behind a camera giving orders to other actors. That'll be the day. You ... I can see directing. You've got so much experience on a set you'd be a natural at directing."

Mabel joined Maisy on the other plane of existence. "Listen, Maise. Have you ever heard of Alice Guy Blaché?"

"Can't say that I have. Sounds French."

"She is, but now she lives back east and has her own studio called the Solax Company at Fort Lee, New Jersey. She started out in the business over in France in her early twenties. She directed her first film in 1896 for Léon Gaumont in Paris."

"Sounds like you know her."

"I do … a little. I met her last year at her studio. She's a brilliant woman. She does it all as well as any man. Writes, directs, produces. All of it." Mabel burped a chuckle. "She scares the bejesus out of Mack. D.W. respects her, but he'll never admit it."

"Sure, but what about you? Are you thinking of directing?"

"I already have done some directing. And some writing."

"Really?"

"Yes, really! Mack let me co-direct with him in *Mabel's Lovers*. We made that one back east before you joined us out here."

Maisy came back to her home planet. "Okay, Mabes. Enough of the history lecture. I'll get dressed and round up Milo and—"

"Milo's already here."

"Figures. Mack's gofer." Maisy sighed. "Okay, I'll get dressed and get there as soon as I can. See you there."

* * *

Maisy left her flat at the Roosevelt Apartments on South Figueroa Street at 10:30 that morning, walked two blocks north to the corner with 2nd Street, and waited there for the next northbound Pacific Electric Railroad streetcar to come along. Catching the 10:48, Maisy rode the Red Car all the way to the Keystone Studio in Edendale. She thanked the conductor for going the extra distance up the hill to the movie lot's entrance before stopping to let her off.

The weekend guard at the gate greeted Maisy warmly, speaking with a slightly Mexican accent. "Good morning, Miss Malone."

"How do you know my name?"

"Miss Normand came out and told me to expect you."

"Fair enough, but how did you know who I am? I mean, anybody about my age could walk up here and say she was me. Then what?"

"Oh, I asked Miss Normand about that. She said not to worry because I could recognize you by the look on your face."

"The look on my face? How's that?"

"Miss Normand said I'd know you were Miss Malone because you'd be in a snit and looking stern with an attitude."

The guard's remarks caught her completely off her guard. "Mabel said that, did she?"

"Yes, ma'am."

"*¿Cómo se llama, señor?*"

The swarthy gentleman smiled. "*Me llamo* Alejandro Arguello."

"You're Mexican?"

"My father was. I'm an American. I was born here in Los Angeles."

"Is this your only job?"

Arguello shook his head. "No, Miss Malone. I'm a mounted policeman during the week. I only work here on Sundays."

"You must be an honest flatfoot."

"What makes you say that?"

"A copper on the take doesn't need to work an extra job."

Arguello chuckled. "I guess you're right there, Miss Malone."

"Glad to know you, Alejandro."

"Same here, Miss Malone."

* * *

Milo Cole was the first person to see Maisy walking toward the Tower. "Here comes Maisy now." With him were Mack, Mabel, D.W. Griffith, Fred Mace, Ford Sterling, Henry Lehrman, and Sennett's Cadillac. Everyone except the car turned to look at Maisy coming toward them.

Maisy forced herself to smile and wave at them. Beneath her breath, she cursed the lot of them. But from her lips, she spoke only loud enough for herself to hear. "This better be worth it." For their consumption, she added a simple greeting. "Hello, everybody."

The group greeted her in near unison.

Then Sennett took charge. "Good morning, Maisy. Nice of you to join us. I'd like you to meet the man who got me into this business. Mr. D.W. Griffith." Mack gave a wisp of a wave toward his mentor.

"I'd know Mr. Griffith anywhere, Mack. Who in this business wouldn't recognize Mr. D.W. Griffith on sight?" Maisy moved closer to the top man at Biograph and held out her right hand to him. "I'm honored to meet you, Mr. Griffith."

He accepted her handshake and spoke with a Virginia drawl. "Same here, Miss Malone." When he released his grip from her hand, he stepped back a pace. "So how is it you would know me anywhere, Miss Malone?"

"Everybody in the motion picture business here in southern California knows you by your Stetson, sir. And I'm no exception."

Griffith chuckled softly. "Well, it is sort of a trademark, isn't it?"

"And a dandy one as well."

"I'm told your people also hail from the South, Miss Malone. Is this true?"

The actress added a touch of southern to her voice. "Oh, please, Mr. Griffith, call me Maisy."

"And so I will, Maisy."

"Yes, my people do come from the South. North Carolina to Alabama to Mississippi to Arkansas to the Choctaw Nation, which is now part and parcel of Oklahoma."

"Oklahoma? Really? Are you part Indian?"

"By the laws of the Choctaw Nation, I'm all Indian."

"How does work?"

"I was born there, and my parents were married there. By the laws of the Nations, that makes us Choctaw."

Griffith grinned. "Now isn't that interesting?"

Maisy smiled. "Well, it makes for good conversation at parties."

"I'll bet it does." Griffith turned to Sennett. "I like this girl, Mack. Can she do drama?"

"Believe me, D.W., this girl is full of drama."

"Oh, yes, that's right." Griffith turned back to Maisy. "I remember now. You're the girl who solved that murder a few months back."

"I had help. Mabel worked with me, and we figured out who did it."

Mabel stepped forward. "She's being modest, D.W. It was all Maisy. I had very little to do with figuring out who did it."

Sennett stuck his two cents into the conversation. "These two sleuths are working on another murder now. They're trying to figure out who murdered some poor Japanese fisherman whose body we stumbled upon on Christmas Day on the beach north of Santa Monica. They tried to drag me into it, but I told them I had work to do here, like the preparations for turning this Cadillac into a float for *Tournament of Roses* parade New Year's Day in Pasadena."

Griffith's head bobbed. "Oh, yes, the float for the parade. I'm going to have my camera crews filming the parade from different angles. I understand several other studios will be there as well. Good footage can be made filming these public events. Of course, who am I telling this to? You send Henry Lehrman out to film all sorts of public events, don't you, Mack?"

"You can never have enough stock footage. Besides filming the parade, we'll be shooting scenes for a film. I'm calling it *The Sleuths at the Floral Parade*. Fred Mace and I will be playing two sleuths dressed like Sherlock Holmes. Mabel will be in it as well."

Griffith patted Mabel on her left arm and smiled. "Makes sense. Every float in a parade should have a pretty girl riding on it."

"We still need a driver. Seems that none of our regular extras know how to drive an automobile like my Cadillac."

Maisy had an idea. "What's wrong with Willie being the driver?"

Sennett cleared his throat. "Willie has a family and wants to be with them on New Year's Day." He glanced sideways and made a slight tilt of his head at Griffith to show Maisy what he really meant.

She understood without batting an eye.

While Maisy and her ancestors might have come from below the Mason-Dixon Line, D.W. Griffith was from the real South. The look on Sennett's face couldn't have made that any clearer.

Griffith took a turn at clearing his throat. "Well, Mack, I was unaware that you were planning to shoot a film during this parade. Since that's the case, I believe I will have to bow out of riding in your car at the *Tournament of Roses*."

"Well, that's rather disappointing D.W. Perhaps we can collaborate again some other time."

"Yes, perhaps." Griffith turned to the others. "I suppose that makes my presence here unnecessary. You-all enjoy dressing up Mack's automobile. I'll be going now." He walked toward his own car, also a Cadillac, where his driver had been waiting for the last hour. The driver opened the door for his employer, closed it, scurried around to his side, climbed in, started the motor, and drove away through the gate to the studio.

Sennett turned to Cole. "Milo, who do you know who would be good at playing the driver?"

A grin spread over Cole's face. "I think I know exactly who would fit that bill, boss. His name is Beverly Griffith, and he works as an assistant in the prop department. And no, he's not related to D.W."

"Well, get him over here as fast as you can. The rest of us are going for lunch."

* * *

Inevitably, the lunch-time conversation of the movie people turned to the investigation of the murder of Masi Tanaka. Sennett raised the subject as they ate sandwiches and drank a variety of beverages from beer to soft drinks to milk, while seated on the benches where the extras sat when waiting for a call to perform in a scene.

"So, Maisy, I hear you're having trouble solving the murder of that Japanese fisherman we found on the beach. What's holding you up?"

Maisy swallowed a bite of her ham and cheese sandwich before answering. "Well, we don't have a murder or and a motive."

"A motive?"

"Yes, a reason to murder the man who was apparently liked by everybody. So far, none of the people we've interviewed has given us a clue as to why someone would want to murder him."

Fred Mace offered a suggestion. "Perhaps that's your motive right there, Maisy. Everybody liked the man, and that just might have made someone jealous of him."

"I hadn't thought about that, Fred. What do you think, Mabel?"

Mabel took on a serious face. "The green-eyed monster does cause a lot of people to do some pretty bad things to the object of their resentment. I mean, it's a possibility that we should consider, don't you think?"

"I agree, Mabes. We should consider that possibility."

Sennett asked a question. "Is there a woman involved somewhere?"

Maisy answered. "Two or three. One is the daughter of the man who owns the tuna boat, the *Blackfin*. She has a suitor who's Portuguese, and the father doesn't want his daughter involved with him, but she was involved Masi Tanaka. How involved is hard to say at this point. She says they were just friends. I'm thinking they might have been closer than that."

Mabel nodded. "I got the same impression from her. Masi meant more to her than just a friend. I think she had romantic feelings for him."

"That makes two of us, Mabes. Besides Belinda Garrido, there's also the wife of the barber and the wife of the boardinghouse owner. I think there might have been a little hanky-panky between Masi and one of them or even all three of them."

Sennett voiced his opinion. "I don't know a whole heck of a lot about the Japanese, but the way they keep to themselves here in Los Angeles, it seems to me they're pretty strait-laced. Even if this fellow was popular among his people, I find it hard to believe he was the kind to ... go ... uh, fishing in another man's pond, so to speak."

Maisy nodded. "I hear what you're saying, Mack. The Japanese do seem like they live by some pretty high morals. As a people, I mean. But you didn't see the looks on the faces of those three women when we told them Masi was dead. They weren't only shaken by the news, they looked heart-broken to me. What do you think, Mabes? You saw the looks on their faces. Did you think there was more there than just sorrow over losing a friend?"

"I have to admit you're right, Maise. They did have that lost love look in their eyes when you broke the news to them. Maybe Masi was a better friend to them than most people knew."

Mace defended Tanaka. "Have you got any other evidence to back up your suspicions of these women fraternizing with this fisherman?"

Maisy shook her head. "That's just it. We don't have a single shred of evidence as to how Masi was killed. Or where he was killed. We don't even know for sure who the last person was to see him alive. The Chinese water taxi owner said he saw Masi leave the *Blackfin* and go between two buildings toward the outer harbor, but he didn't say anything about seeing him come back to the tuna boat after that."

Mabel added a memory of her own. "Then there's Mr. Koki who said Masi came to the boardinghouse to get something and then he left for the boat right away."

Maisy pinched her lower lip between her right index finger and thumb. She released the hold, then held the finger upright, slowly wagging it at Mabel. "Wait a minute, Mabes. I don't think that's quite right. Let me think for a second."

Before Maisy could continue, Milo arrived with the prop-man's assistant. "Most of you have seen Bev here and there around the lot, haven't you?"

Everyone voiced some sort of confirmation that he or she had seen him except for Sennett. "You haven't been with us very long, have you?"

Bev drawled; his Georgia accent slightly different from that of D.W. Griffith. "No, sir, Mr. Sennett, I haven't. I only started a few weeks before Christmas."

Mack's head drooped. "Damn, another southern gentleman in our midst, ladies and gentlemen."

Near to being six feet tall, the handsome newcomer grinned with a buoyance that made his blue eyes stand out like sapphires. "Yes, sir, Mr. Sennett. I'm from Georgia. I was born in Butler, a small town about 100 miles south of Atlanta. I grew to manhood in Atlanta before attending Georgia Military School in Milledgeville, another small town in southeastern Georgia about 100 miles from Atlanta."

"So what brought you out here to California?"

"My brother William and I came out here in 1905 for a short time. I worked in shoe store in San Francisco until the Great Earthquake struck the following year. I went back to Atlanta after that, but I always wanted to return to California because the climate was so agreeable. I was told there was a particularly good chance of owning my own store in a town in the Arizona Territory, so I returned to the West in 1910. The town was Parker. It lies on the banks of the Colorado River. The only opportunity to come my way there was meeting the legendary lawman Wyatt Earp who was living across the river in a settlement named for him. He was prospecting for gold there. I don't know that he ever found any, though.

"Then I came on to Los Angeles and got a job at the New Broadway Hotel as a bellboy. I worked my way up to steward, and then to engineer of the hotel. My studies at Georgia Military School came in handy for that post. Then I was made assistant manager until I was named acting general manager of the entire hotel. Recently, I left the Broadway to come here to work in your prop department.

"Most folks call me Speed, Mr. Sennett, because I have a big interest in racing automobiles."

"Racing them or just watching them race?"

"Both, sir."

"So, Milo told you why I wanted you to come here today?"

"Yes, sir, he did. He said you needed a chauffeur to drive your Cadillac in the *Tournament of Roses* Parade in Pasadena on New Year's Day."

"That's exactly right. You interested?"

"Well, sir, I wouldn't have come here today if I wasn't."

Sennett grinned. "I think I'm going to like this young man." He focused on Griffith. "I think you'll go far in this business, Speed."

* * *

With lunch behind them, the Keystone crew began deliberating how to decorate Sennett's Cadillac for the upcoming parade, which was only three days away.

Maisy started the discussion. "So who signed us up for this parade over in Pasadena? I'll bet it was you, Mack."

"Wrong there, Miss Malone."

Mabel raised her right hand. "It was my idea, Maise. I thought it would be a good way to advertise the studio. We're new out here, and not everybody knows we're here just yet. The *Tournament of Roses* is a very big deal here in southern California. People come from nearly all the surrounding counties to watch the parade on New Year's Day. They run special trains to Pasadena from as far away as San Bernadino and San Diego, and then they take their riders back in the afternoon and early evening when all the festivities have finished for the day. I hear the parade is expecting nearly a hundred thousand people to show up this year."

"That is impressive. So what are we supposed to do to Mack's Cadillac to get it in the parade?"

"We have to decorate it with flowers."

Maisy's brow rolled up her forehead in disbelief. "With flowers? Real flowers?"

Mabel nodded. "That's right. Real flowers."

"Okay, and where do we get these real flowers? Help ourselves to people's gardens."

"No, silly. They're shipped in from all over southern California. Some even come from Arizona, I'm told, and Mexico, too. We get what we need from the *Tournament* committee. Of course, we have to pay for them."

"Of course."

"Mabel assures me it will be money well spent. She's never let me down before, so I don't expect her to let me down now."

"It's like this, Maise. We have to decorate the Cadillac to look like ... a ship."

"Like a ship? What kind of a ship? Sailing or steam?"

Sennett answered the question. "It doesn't make any difference which kind, Maisy. It just has to look like a ship when we're done with it."

Maisy gave Mack a dark stare. "Have you got any ideas on just how we're going to make this automobile look like a ship by stringing flowers all over it?"

Sennett shook his head. "Not a one. That's why you're here. Mabel tells me you're one of the most imaginative people she knows, so it's all up to you, Miss Malone."

"Just tell me one thing, Mr. Sennett. Why in the world did you sign up to be in this parade?"

The master of comedy grinned quite precociously. "To make a film of us in the parade as part of a two-reeler I'm calling *The Sleuths at the Floral Parade*."

"Where did you get a cockamamie idea like that?"

His grin went from being precocious to resembling the smile of a Cheshire Cat. "From you, Maisy Malone."

"From me?"

"Quite right, from you."

"I don't recall ever suggesting to you that you should make a film at the *Tournament of Roses*. In fact, I don't recall ever hearing about the *Tournament of Roses* until you mentioned it on Christmas Day."

"Well, that's when I got the idea for *The Sleuths at the Floral Parade*. I wrote the script that night, and I had Pathé read it to see if he wants to direct it. He agreed to do it, so he'll be working with Mabel, Fred, Ford, and me as the cast. Both of our cameras will be there as well as one from D.W. You can't have too much stock footage, you know."

Mabel patted Mack on the shoulder. "That's our boss. Always thinking ahead." She turned to Maisy. "So what do you think, Maise? How should we decorate the Cadillac for the parade?"

"Well, what colors do you suggest, Mabes?"

"I like purple and pink together."

"Hm! And green. Flowers have green leaves, you know."

"Yes, of course."

Maisy waggled her right index finger upward. "I'm thinking violets and pink roses."

Sennett made an insertion into the process. "And don't forget this. We'll need something to identify the company. Maybe a big letter K for Keystone. Make it so it really stands out for everybody at the parade to see right off."

Maisy added a thought. "We'll mount it on the radiator. How's that suit you, Mack?"

"Sounds like a good place for it. Why don't you and Mabel draw up a plan, so we'll have some idea on what flowers we'll need?"

Mabel nodded. "We can do that, can't we, Maise?"

"Easy as one, two, three. Your place or mine?"

The telephone ringing awakened Maisy Monday morning, much to her annoyance. She rolled over in bed and pulled her pillow over her head hoping to deaden the jangling of the bell. The ploy failed to work; she could still hear it. Now well-past being just a little annoyed she threw the pillow through the bedroom doorway, hoping to knock the little beast off its stand to the floor. She missed. The cushion fell short of the phone, but it did strike the tripod platform just hard enough to cause the candlestick to tip over and free the receiver from its cradle. Both parts remained precariously atop the stand. The ringing ceased, only to be replaced by the faint sound of a man's voice.

Maisy's fury could be felt in the volume of her voice. "That better not be you, Milo Cole. Because if it is, you'll be dead before the sun goes down, and I swear no one will ever find your body."

The caller spoke louder. "Maisy, it's Ed Browning."

Recognizing the detective's voice, Maisy rolled out of bed and staggered from the bedroom into the living room.

"Maisy, it's Ed Browning. Are you there?"

She picked up both parts of the telephone, one in each hand, putting the receiver to her ear and holding the speaker to her mouth. "I'm here, Eddie. What's up?"

"I just now heard the coroner is writing his report on what he found out in his examination of Masi Tanaka's body this morning. Would you like to come to the station and read it for yourself? Or would you like me to call you when I get it from him?"

This news activated Maisy's adrenal glands. "What time is it?"

"A little past ten. Why?"

"Would you mind if I call Mabel before I decide whether to come down there or not?" She spoke again before he could answer her question. "Never mind. I'll call Mabel right now, and one or both of us will be there before lunch. Is that okay by you?"

"Sure. I'm not going anywhere this morning. I'll alert the desk sergeant that you're coming in. See you when you get here."

Maisy wasted no time calling Mabel's apartment. No answer.

"Where else would she be today?"

She searched for an answer for a few seconds, then she called Mack Sennett's personal number at the Keystone studio.

"Mr. Sennett's office. Milo Cole speaking."

"Milo, it's Maisy."

"Oh, hiya, Doll Face. What's cooking today?"

"Never mind all now, Milo. Is Mabel there?"

"Do you mean here in the Tower?"

"Yes, there or anywhere on the lot. Do you know where she is?"

"Sure, I do."

Frustrated, Maisy growled at Milo. "Well, where is she, meat head?"

Cole felt a bit hurt by the name she called him. "You don't have to get all huffy about it, Maise. I'll tell you. She's down on the set with Mack, Fred, Ford, and Pathé. They're all going over the script for the movie they're shooting at the parade on New Year's Day."

"Well, go tell her to call me right away. It's extremely important. Tell her Ed Browning called me this morning to tell me the coroner is writing his report on Masi Tanaka's murder today and Ed wants to know if we want to read it. Now hurry and tell her that."

"Sure thing, Maise. Right away."

"And tell her to call me immediately."

"Sure thing. I'm on my way."

* * *

Cole knew better than to interrupt rehearsals or filming on the set. Doing so was a good way to get yourself fired. He waited quietly until the actors and director stopped for a break or to be recognized by Sennett; whichever came first.

Director Pathé Lehrman made the first move. "Let's take five for now, and when we resume, I want the camera rolling."

Sennett saw his assistant. "What's up, Milo? I thought I told you to stay in the Tower unless it was an emergency."

"Maisy called for Mabel."

"How is that an emergency?"

Mabel joined them. "What did she want, Milo?"

"She said to tell you that Detective Browning called her to tell her that the coroner is writing his report on Masi Tanaka this morning and he wanted to know if the two of you wanted to come down to the police station to read it with him."

"You bet I do."

Sennett interrupted. "Now wait a minute, Mabel. I know I made a deal with you and Maisy about time off to do your sleuthing, but you came in today voluntarily, which is why we decided to shoot the scenes that you're in now instead of waiting until after the parade to shoot them. Now we've only got one more scene to shoot here that has you in it, so—."

Mabel raised her hand to stop Sennett from going any further. "You're right, Mack. There's only one more scene with me in it." She turned to Cole. "Milo, go call Maisy and tell her I'll meet her at the police station right away. But don't tell her I'm working here today. Just tell I'll catch the next Red Car downtown and I'll meet her at Detective Browning's office. Understand?"

"Sure, Mabel. I get it."

She turned back to Sennett. "Okay, let's shoot my scene."

* * *

Maisy had been sitting beside the telephone stand in her apartment for several minutes when Milo finally returned her call. "What took you so long?"

"Sorry, Maise. I was up in the Tower when you called, and I had to go down to the set where the boss and the others are shooting some scenes for the movie their going to shoot at the parade on Wednesday."

"I suppose Mabel is working as well."

"Well ..."

"Don't fib to me, Milo."

"She told me not to tell."

Maisy smile to herself. "That's our Mabel. Work first, play second." She got back on track. "So what did she say about coming downtown to see Ed Browning?"

"She said she was going to shoot the last scene she was in and then catch the next Red Car downtown to the police station."

"The last scene? How many more does she have to be in?"

"Just the one."

Maisy gave that a quick thought. "That shouldn't take long. You go back and tell her I'll meet her at Ed's office. You coming with her?"

"Probably not. The boss wants me to stay by the telephone just in case somebody important should call."

"And I'm not important?"

"Aw, Maisy, you know better than that."

She giggled. "Just pulling your leg, Milo. Just pulling your leg."

* * *

The two movie actresses turned would-be sleuths arrived at the Los Angeles Police Department's Central Station just seconds apart: Maisy coming from 3rd Street and Mabel debarking her Red Car on 2nd Street right in front of the building. Amidst a gaggle of pedestrians navigating their way to or from somewhere to someplace, Mabel saw Maisy in a similar gathering of humanity coming around the corner with Main Street. Mabel had just raised her left foot to take the first step to the entrance. The film star took a second step up and turned to face the direction of Maisy's approach. When the two friends made eye-contact, each raised her right hand to wave a greeting. Mabel stayed in place now, while Maisy increased her pace until halting within embracing distance of Mabel.

"As always, Mabes, your timing is impeccable."

"Yours, too, Maise."

They giggled, then locked arms to ascend the remaining steps together.

Mabel spoke. "I hope that nice Sergeant Willett is on duty this morning."

"So do I. And I agree with you, Mabes. He is a nice man."

Up they went to the landing before the main entrance. Maisy pushed the door open and allowed Mabel to precede her inside. Moving from the bright sunshine into the artificial light of the station made them hesitate a moment in the foyer.

A woman's voice from further inside caught their attention. "I'll take charge of this rascal, Sergeant Willett."

Curiosity drew the two actresses into the main room before their eyes could completely adjust to the dimmer light. They blinked several times, hoping to see who had spoken.

Just in time, they saw a woman in an ankle-length dress and waist-length jacket, both articles being the same dark blue material of a police officer's uniform. She was leading a teenage girl by an arm toward the hall leading to the detention areas of the station. As she turned the corner into the corridor, Mabel caught a glimpse of a police officer's badge pinned to the left side of her jacket. Then the pair were gone.

The desk sergeant's voice returned their attention to the purpose of their visit to the police station. "Ah, good morning, Miss Normand."

Maisy had become quite accustomed to being ignored whenever she and Mabel were out and about together. She understood perfectly that Mabel was a film star, while she was merely a face many people had seen but just could not place in their conscious thought processes.

As almost always, Mabel smiled sweetly as she spoke. "Good morning to you, too, Sergeant Willett."

Maisy was more businesslike in her address to Willett. "Good morning, Sergeant."

"Good morning, Miss Malone. Detective Sergeant Browning told me you ladies would be coming by to see him this morning and that I was to send you right up to see him."

Maisy nodded politely. "Thank you, Sergeant, but before we go up, would you mind telling us who that woman was who just left here?"

Willett grinned with pride. "That was Officer Alice Stebbins Wells."

"Officer?"

"Yes, Miss, officer." The sergeant bucked up with pride. "Officer Wells was sworn in two years ago as the very first official female police officer in America. She's Policewoman Badge Number One. She was assigned to the department's newly formed Juvenile Division. The police board then passed a new rule that only female officers could question young women. She's been doing that for the past two years until the chief decided it was too much of a workload for one officer, so he hired two more women to serve under Officer Wells. She's a college-educated woman. I could be mistaken about this, but I was told that she attended Oberlin College back in Ohio and graduated from there and then went to another college in Connecticut. Would you like to meet her, Miss Malone?"

"I certainly would, Sergeant Willett, but perhaps another time. Right now, Miss Normand and I have to see Detective Sergeant Browning."

"Of course, Miss Malone. You know the way, so go right on up."

The actresses headed for the stairs to the second floor.

Mabel shook her head ever so slowly as they walked. "A woman police officer. Can you believe that Maise?"

"Do you think this might mean getting the vote is coming closer?"

"We can only hope so, Maise. We can only hope so."

* * *

Browning appeared to be more than his usual friendly self when Mabel and Maisy entered his office. "Come in, ladies, and have a seat." The detective held a sheaf of papers upright in front of him. Seeing the two women staring at them, he chuckled. "Sorry to disappoint, but these aren't the autopsy report from Coroner Hartwell." He placed the papers in a box on the corner of the desk and picked up a single sheet lying conspicuously in front of him. "But this is." He held it up for his visitors to see.

Leaning forward, Mabel couldn't control her curiosity. "So what did he find out?"

Resting against the back of her chair, Maisy looked Browning in the eyes. "Let me guess, Eddie. Masi Tanaka didn't die from that curved wound on the back of his head, did he?"

Browning flinched. "What makes you say that Maisy?"

"Simple. The wound wasn't very deep, so he didn't bleed to death from it. And it wasn't in an area of his head where it would definitely kill him."

"So you think he drowned?"

"Eddie, you know better than that. I'm betting the coroner discovered another cause of death."

"Really?"

Mabel turned toward Maisy. "So how do you think he was killed?"

Browning leaned forward. "Yes, Maisy, how do you think Tanaka was killed? I'm dying to hear this, you know."

"We weren't allowed to see beneath his clothes, but I did see a cut in his shirt just below the bottom of his sternum. Am I right so far, Eddie?"

"You are, but didn't you say something about this before?"

"Don't you read Sherlock Holmes, Eddie?"

"No."

"Well, maybe you should. If you did, then you'd know a good detective keeps things he sees to himself until he needs them to snare the perpetrator of the crime."

Browning leaned back in his chair. "I'll keep that in mind in future investigations. But for now, what do you think that cut in his shirt means?"

"My deduction is it was made with a knife."

Mabel gasped. "Do you think he was stabbed?"

"Not only stabbed. The cut was at an angle, wasn't it, Eddie?"

Browning showed surprise. "Right again, Maisy. And what else?"

"The killer knew exactly where to stab Masi in order to get an instant kill. That's the sign of a professional assassin. Don't you agree, Eddie?"

"I certainly do, Maisy. Last February we had a case of burglary where a Japanese thief named Tani had slipped into the apartment of another fellow and made off with $70. My partner and I picked him up at 1st and Alameda and brought him in for questioning. When he wouldn't talk, we brought in Tom White, who had been with the department before this. Tom speaks Japanese fluently, so we asked him to question Tani. When Tani continued to avoid answering any questions, Tom threatened him by saying we should use the same method of questioning as the Japanese police use back in Japan. That put the fear of God into Tani, and he sang like a canary, confessing to stealing the money and giving us all the details of how he did it."

Mabel appeared puzzled. "What is it the Japanese police do to get their criminals to talk?"

"I'm not sure, but I do know it comes from the *Book of Jiu-Jitsu*. I'm not exactly sure what that is, but I do know that *jiu-jitsu* is a kind of wrestling in Japan that's meant to be a way of defending yourself should you be attacked by an assailant. It teaches you a way to use your attacker's weight and size against him. That's putting it rather simply, but I understand it's quite effective."

Mabel tilted her head to the right. "*Jiu-jitsu* sounds like something every woman should learn in order to protect herself from every man who comes at her with evil intent."

Maisy waggled her right index finger in front of her. "We're getting off the point, Eddie. We were talking about Masi Tanaka being murdered by a professional assassin, and you went off on a tangent about this *jiu-jitsu* stuff. What has one got to do with the other?"

"*Jiu-jitsu* is just one martial art from the Orient. It's Japanese. There are other martial arts around the world. The French have a defensive art called *savate*, where feet and hands are used as weapons. I've also heard of a Chinese art called *karate*, a martial art that combatants use both defensively and offensively. There are a lot more whose names I don't know, but they are all basically defensive arts. Then we have martial arts that use weapons, such as knives and daggers. This is where I think an assassin comes into the Tanaka murder case. Now we have to consider the distinct possibility of his killer being a trained assassin."

Mabel nodded. "And you think the fact that he was killed with a knife could mean his killer was a professional killer?"

Maisy voiced an opinion. "A trained assassin would use a dagger for that kind of kill, not a knife. Am I right, Eddie?"

"You certainly know a lot about how to kill a person, don't you, Maisy?"

"Like I said before, I read a lot."

Mabel shook her head slowly. "Ain't that the truth?"

Browning patted the coroner's report. "Well, you got it right again, Miss Malone. The coroner states that the murder weapon had to be a dagger of some kind because the entry wound was V-shaped on both ends and wide in the middle. Most knives are thick on the dull side of the blade and thin on the sharp side. Furthermore, the wound was deeper than a knife would usually make."

"How deep did he say?"

The detective read from the report. "The blade passed through the heart at an upward angle and through the left lung; leaving a wound that measured approximately seven inches in depth, an inch in width, and a half inch thick; and causing death instantly. Dr. Hartwell said he was no expert in knife blades, but the wound in Tanaka looked to him to have been made by a spearhead."

Mabel looked a bit perplexed. "A spearhead wound a half inch thick? What does that mean?"

Browning held up his right hand with his index finger and thumb spread to indicate a measurement of a half inch. "It means the blade was this thick." He increased the distance between the two digits. "And this wide." He repeated the first distance. "A half inch thick." He showed her the second again. "An inch wide."

Maisy held up her left hand. "You do know what this means, don't you, Eddie?"

"I'm not sure what you mean."

"It means we have to go back to the *Blackfin* and look at every knife owned by every crew member."

Browning shook his head in disbelief. "Maisy, you are one remarkable woman. You've got to give me a list of the books you've read."

Mabel shuddered. "Not me. I don't want to know all this stuff you know about crime, Maisy Malone. Some of it just gives me the creeps."

After leaving the police station, Maisy and Mabel decided to have lunch downtown and talk over what they had just learned from Ed Browning. They chose the upscale Café Richelieu, formerly the not-so-elegant Levy's Café, just a block away on the southwest corner of Main and 3rd Street.

As soon as they were seated by a uniformed waiter who appeared to be no older than either of the two actresses and they had their menus in front of them, the server cleared his throat. "Would you ladies like a glass of water with your meal?"

Maisy answered for them. "That would be nice."

The fellow offered a polite smile. "I'll give you ladies a moment to decide what you'd like to order. In the meantime, I'll get your water."

Mabel leaned forward and softly asked the one question that had been on her mind since they left Browning's office. "Does this new information from the coroner change anything for us?"

Maisy frowned. "More than I'd like it to change. The way I see it now we might have to question everybody all over again."

"Really? I thought we'd only have to question the couple who own the boardinghouse on Rattlesnake Island. Remember what the husband said about the last time he saw Masi Tanaka?"

"He said he hadn't seen Masi since the morning of the big wind."

Triumph sparkled in Mabel's eyes. "And that was all he said."

"You're right, Mabes. That was the only important thing he said during the entire conversation." Maisy paused for thought. "I think we need to pay Mr. Koki and his wife another visit."

"I think you're right, Maise."

The waiter returned with two glasses of water and set them on the table to the right of his customers. "Would you ladies like something else to drink with your meal? Perhaps some wine or a soft drink?"

Mabel smiled at the waiter. "Do you have Coca-Cola?"

"Yes, we do. Miss."

Maisy stared quizzically at her friend. "No wine for you, Mabes?"

"I have to go back to work, so I'd better not. The Coca-Cola will suit me simply fine."

Maisy looked up at the waiter. "Same for me. In a glass over ice."

"Oh, yes, for me, too. In a glass and over ice."

The server wrote their order on a paper pad in his left hand. "Have you decided what you would like to eat?"

Mabel ignored the menu. "I'll have a club sandwich. Make it with bacon instead of ham, chicken instead of turkey, and French Dijon mustard instead of mayonnaise. Oh, and a thin slice of Swiss cheese. Slice the tomato to less than a quarter inch and go easy on the lettuce. I'm a person, not a rabbit."

While writing her order on the pad, the waiter couldn't help smiling. "And the gherkins, Miss? Sliced thin or whole on the side?"

"Are they dill?"

"Sweet, Miss, but you can have dill, if you like."

Mabel didn't miss a beat. "Dill, whole, and on the side. Just one."

"Very good, Miss." He turned to Maisy. "And for you, Miss?"

"I'll have the same except instead of mustard make it mayonnaise, two slices of Swiss but not together, and two regular slices of tomato just inside the cheese, and no lettuce. And forget the pickle. I really love cucumbers, but they don't always agree with me."

"Very good, Miss. Two club sandwiches for the ladies. Will this be on separate checks?"

Mabel spoke before Maisy could. "Just one." She turned to Maisy. "Old Nappy pays me more than you get from the old tightwad."

"That's a given, Mabes."

"So! What's next in your investigation of Masi Tanaka's murder?"

Before Maisy could answer, the waiter brought them their Coca-Colas in eight-ounce bottles with the caps already removed and glasses filled halfway with crushed ice. "Would you ladies like me to pour your sodas for you?"

Maisy looked up at him and smiled. "No thank you. We can do it."

"Very well, Miss. I'll be back with your sandwiches in a jiffy."

"There's no hurry."

He nodded. "Yes, Miss." And he promptly left them alone again.

"Where was I? Oh, yes, you asked me what I plan to do next. Well, I'm not sure. You have to go back to work. Milo is already at work. Willie is off work for the week." Maisy paused a second. "I suppose I'll go back to the police station and see if Eddie's too busy to go with me to Rattlesnake Island this afternoon. If he can't go, I'll ask him for the loan of one of their officers to join me."

"Why are you going back there?"

"Do you remember Willie telling us he had a chat with the Chinese water taxi fellow?"

"Yes, I do. His name was Tsu-chin."

"Well, I'd like to talk to him again and ask him about what he was doing that morning."

Mabel's eyes widened with surprise. "Of course, Tsu-chin! Why didn't he tell us about seeing them that morning?"

"Exactly! Was he just forgetful? Or was he trying to hide something from us? Either way, I intend to find out this afternoon … providing I can find someone to go with me."

The waiter brought their sandwiches, and the two actresses ate in silence.

* * *

Detective Browning was walking through the police station lobby just as Maisy entered the building. He wasn't alone.

"Oh, Maisy, you're back so soon. I didn't expect to see you until … well, tomorrow at the earliest." He noticed she was looking at the man beside him. "Bill, this is Maisy Malone, the young woman who helped solve the murder of that actor last fall. Maisy, this is my partner, Detective Sergeant Bill Ingram."

Maisy extended her right hand in greeting. "How do you do, Detective Ingram? I'm pleased to meet you."

"Likewise, Miss Malone." He doffed his bowler with his left hand, took her hand with his right, and squeezed it gently as he smiled and gave her a slight bow of his head. "Eddie has told me a lot about you. So much so, that I feel like I already know you. But he failed to mention how young and how attractive you are."

"Flattery will get you any place you want to go, Detective Ingram. Well, almost any place."

"Eddie said you had a quick wit about you. Being from Iowa, I find that quite charming."

"Easy, Bill. You're old enough to be her father. And you were married the last time I checked."

Maisy touched Browning's left arm above the wrist. "Leave the man alone, Eddie. What's the harm in being friendly?"

The detective countered. "Cops aren't supposed to flirt when they're on the job."

A coy smile flickered across Maisy's face. "Is that a written rule? Or did you just make that up?"

Browning sighed. "Let's change the subject, Maisy. So, what brings you back here this afternoon?"

"Well, I'm planning to visit Rattlesnake Island again to talk to a couple people we interviewed the other day, and I thought a police escort and Nellie Sharpe along to record everything might be a good idea."

The policeman smiled back at her. "Well, it would be if we weren't just now headed out to make the rounds of some local joints to see if anybody is up to any mischief this afternoon."

"Oh, Eddie. Don't be such a spoilsport."

Ingram nudged his partner's right arm. "You know, Ed, we don't have to make the rounds this afternoon, do we? I mean, wouldn't it be better to escort Miss Malone to San Pedro?"

Browning frowned at his partner. "You want to go with Maisy, don't you, Bill?"

"I would. I'd like to see her in action if you don't mind. I mean, from all that you've told me about Miss Malone here, I think I might be able to pick up a tip or two on how to be a better interrogator. Seems you've gotten sharper at it since you worked with her last fall. So why not me, too?"

Browning drooped. "All right, we'll go with her. But you run back up to the office and get Miss Sharpe to come along with us."

Ingram grinned. "Deal!" And off he raced.

* * *

Instead of taking a Red Car to San Pedro, which would make several more stops along the way, Browning, Ingram, Maisy, and Nellie Sharpe took a taxi to the Southern Pacific Depot on Central Avenue and 5th Street, where they caught a nearly non-stop local train to Wilmington, arriving at the waterfront station at 2:20 p.m. From there, they had a short walk to the dock where they soon found their first goal: the water taxi and its owner Tsu-shin.

The boatman smiled his best tobacco-stained grin at the sight of Maisy coming his way, but as soon as he realized she was accompanied by two men in suits and Nellie Sharpe, his genuine joy vanished and turned into a feigned expression of delight. He made a polite bow to them but said nothing.

Maisy spoke first. "Hello, Tsu-chin. Are you available to take us over to the island?"

"Oh, yes. Tsu-chin very available. These men and lady with you?"

"Yes, they are. This is Detective Sergeant Browning, Detective Ingram, and my friend Miss Sharpe. We're going over to the island to interview some more people about Masi Tanaka."

"Pleased to take you there. Fare is five cents each."

Browning and Ingram exchanged glances before Ingram grimaced and slid his right hand into his right trouser pocket. "I'll pay him, Miss Malone." In the next instant, he withdrew a few coins, fingered through them, and produced two nickels and a dime. "Here you go." He handed the money to Tsu-chin who accepted it with a slight bow of thanks.

"You go aboard now."

The four passengers followed the boatman's instruction and seated themselves in the aft section of the craft. Tsu-chin united the mooring two lines and jumped over the rail onto the water taxi. He nodded in the direction of his customers, eying Maisy in particular, who met his gaze straight on with a polite smile until he turned to go toward the helm. Now with his back to her, she focused on the knife handle protruding from the sheath stuck inside his waistband on his left hip. The grip looked to be four-to-five inches long from the guard to the hilt, a normal length. Next, she eyed the leather sheath, which in her estimation, was only an inch or two longer than the handle. She concluded this knife could not be the weapon used to murder Masi Tanaka, but she did not rule out Tsu-chin as a possible suspect. An assassin would never use his weapon as a tool for anything other than its designed purpose. Nor would he carry it in plain sight. This much Maisy knew for certain. Thus, she studied the boatman closely as they made their way across the inner harbor.

* * *

The taxi boatman delivered his passengers to the north end of the island, which brought them as close as possible to the Koki boardinghouse without going around to the outer bay. "I wait here for you when you wish return to main side dock."

Maisy smiled at him. "That's very thoughtful of you, Tsu-chin, but we might be here for an hour or more."

"Make no difference, Picture Lady. Business not much today. You go. I wait here."

"We'll try not to be too long."

From this point on the island, the boardinghouse was in clear view and only a short walk of about sixty yards for the newly arrived party of four. They approached the north face of the building.

Maisy glanced at Browning. "Let's go around the west end instead of the east. I've seen the front entrance. Now I'd like to have a look at the back just to orient myself to the boardinghouse better."

"Fine by me. Just lead the way, and we'll follow."

Instead of heading for the front door of the boardinghouse, Maisy chose to venture around the rear of the building. Her first observation was the distance between the house and the sandy shoreline of the outer harbor; in her estimation a good hundred feet, maybe a little more. Six 4X4 wooden posts, each standing four feet high, lined the beach, five of the pilings having a rowboat moored to their steel eye-bolts protruding from them three feet above the sand. Closer to the house stood two taller posts, each with a four-foot crossbar six feet above the ground and three steel wires connecting these T-posts for hanging laundry out to dry. The rear entrance to the domicile was a porch twelve feet in length and four feet in width with four wooden steps with handrails on each side leading up to it and a screen door over a wooden door. Two straight-back chairs occupied each side of the doorway. Hanging on hooks to the east side of the door were a white apron, a metal pail, and a knife in its sheath. The latter item caught Maisy's attention as they passed around the building to reach the front door. She mentally noted the blade was no longer than six inches; thus, ruling it out as the possible weapon used to murder Masi Tanaka.

Now at the front entrance, Maisy stepped onto the landing and knocked on the door, rapping her knuckles on it three times with authority. The rest of her party remained a respectful distance away on the sand. They waited for someone to answer with the same patience as Maisy. In less than a minute, they were rewarded with the door opening slowly at first only a foot or so, then wider as the person within recognized the actress.

Hatsenke Koki smiled with genuine delight. "Ah, Miss Malone, you come again." She leaned to her right to scan the others behind Maisy. "Miss Normand not come with you this time?"

"No, I'm sorry, Hatsenke-*san*. Miss Normand could not come with me this time. She had to stay at the studio to work on a new motion picture."

"I see. So why you come this time, Miss Malone?"

"Well, Hatsenke-*san*, we'd like to speak with your boarders who work on the tuna boat *Blackfin*, if any of them are here at this time."

"*Hai!* Some here. They resting upstairs or playing cards in living room downstairs. You wish come through here to go to them?"

Before Maisy could answer, Toichero Koki came up behind his wife and aimed a piercing glare at Maisy. "You here again?" He looked beyond his wife at the others. "Where Picture Lady? She not come with you this time?"

"No, Toichero-*san*, Miss Normand is filming today."

Koki waved his left hand rather casually at the other three visitors. "So who these people? More friends of you?"

"Why, yes, they are my friends." She turned halfway around to introduce them. "I believe you've already met Miss Nellie Sharpe. She was with us at the candy store when we attended the memorial service for Masi Tanaka."

The landlord forced a smile. "Ah, yes. Now I remember." He pointed to Browning. "And you police detective. I remember you."

"Yes, sir. I'm Detective Sergeant Edward Browning, and this gentleman is my partner Detective Sergeant William Ingram."

Ingram took a half-step forward and tipped his bowler. "How do you do, Mr. Koki?"

Toichero returned the gesture with a slight bow. "So why you policemen come to my house?"

Maisy turned back to face the husband and wife. "Like I told Hatsenke, we'd like to speak to the crew members of the *Blackfin* that are here today. Is that agreeable to you, Toichero-*san*?"

His reply was quick. "Yes, of course. Follow me. I take you to them."

* * *

Missing from the *Blackfin* crew that afternoon at the Koki boardinghouse were Yoshi Yamaguchi and Enji Nakamura. Both were still in Los Angeles helping Tokutaro Tanaka with the candy store. This was quite understandable to Maisy and the two police detectives as they interviewed the remainder of the crew.

Each man was asked to bring his knife to the interview; the explanation for this being that they were looking for a certain kind of blade that might have been used to cut Masi Tanaka's clothing. The fishermen accepted this as a perfectly logical reason for the request, and each man co-operated fully by handing over his blade as he sat down at the communal table where Maisy and the detectives conducted their brief interrogations. Not surprising to them, the knives were remarkably similar in length and design; all about six inches from guard to point; their ricassos flat, square-edged, and stamped with the makers name; some with a fuller in the spine and some without; everyone with a cutting edge honed nearly razor sharp; none of them fitting the lethal description noted by the coroner in his report. Each man called his knife a *kiridashi*.

After the final interview, Maisy voiced her frustration over the absence of Yamaguchi and Nakamura. "I really wanted to question them again." She heaved a sigh. "Well, I guess that only leaves Mr. and Mrs. Koki to interview again."

Browning straightened up. "Mr. and Mrs. Koki? Why them?"

"Oh, that's right. I didn't tell you about Mabel and me having lunch today. She reminded me of something Mr. Koki told us the last time we were here."

"And what was that, if I may ask."

"Let's go see him and his wife, and then I won't have to repeat myself."

* * *

"Koki-*san*, the last time we spoke you said the last time you saw Masi Tanaka was the morning of the big wind, the last time the *Blackfin* went out to sea. Is that right?"

Toichero stiffened. "Yes, that right."

"Okay. Where did you see him?"

"Here at boardinghouse."

Maisy continued to press him for a detailed answer. "But where in the boardinghouse?"

"Not in boardinghouse. Outside."

"Outside? You were outside when you saw him?"

Koki shook his head. "No, I was inside. Masi outside. He walk by our bedroom window when I go to bed."

Maisy turned to Koki's wife. "Did you see him, too?"

"Oh, no, I not see him. I clean up fishermen room when Toichero go to bed. Not see Masi."

"He didn't come into the boardinghouse?"

Hatsenke shrugged. "Not know. I not see him."

Toichero interrupted. "Maybe Masi go upstairs … use back stairs to go to fishermen sleep room."

Maisy nodded. "I suppose he could have done that." She sighed, frustrated as she realized she was getting nowhere fast with these two.

Browning interjected a question of his own. "Did either of you see Masi leave that morning?"

Both man and wife shook their heads and simultaneously said, "No."

"Neither of you heard him go up the back stairs or come down again?"

The couple responded in the exact same way; heads shaking and saying no in unison.

Maisy had one more question to ask. "Toichero-*san*, do you own a knife like the fishermen use when they work on the tuna boat?"

"Yes."

"May we see it?"

Koki rose from the table and went to the bedroom. He returned in little more than a minute carrying two knives; both sheathed; one, a *kiridashi* with a wooden handle in a plain leather scabbard like those of all the fishermen; the other very ornate with an ivory handle and a wooden sheath intricately carved and painted with cherry blossoms. Proudly, he placed the knives on the table in front of Maisy.

"This *kiridashi* mine." Toichero pointed to the other. "This *tantō* belong Hatsenke."

Koki's announcement caught Maisy, Nellie, and both policeman by total surprise.

"Hatsenke bring *tantō* to America from Japan. Mother give to her. Keep her safe on long journey across ocean. Some sailor man not nice to Japanese girl on big boat." He picked up the knife and drew the blade with one hand while the other held the scabbard. "She keep in sleeve so can pull out quick when need to defend against bad man." He puffed out his chest. "Bring to bed first night with me. Japanese custom. Wife put under pillow as warning to husband to be gentle lover."

Nellie and the two detectives blushed at the slight suggestion of marital intimacy.

Still focused on the blade, Maisy was unfazed for a few seconds. Then she glanced up at Toichero and smiled. "I think my mother would have liked that custom. I've got more brothers and sisters than a Choctaw sow has piglets."

The Japanese couple failed to understand the allegory, but Nellie and the cops did, coloring rosier than before.

Browning cleared his throat. "I believe we've taken up enough of your time, Mr. Koki, Mrs. Koki." He bowed slightly to both of them. "Thank you for your gracious hospitality." He slid his chair away from the table. "We'll be going now."

Once outside, Nellie Sharpe leaned close to Maisy and spoke softly so only the actress could hear her. "Maisy, did you notice that Mrs. Koki looked a little queasy and quite pale at times as you talked to her and her husband?"

"I certainly did, Nellie. I noticed her condition the other day when we were first here."

"Do you think she might be with child?"

"I've seen that look on all my older sisters. She's either expecting or she's got a serious illness she's not telling anybody about. Not even her husband."

* * *

When they came in sight of the dock, the four members of the investigating team were incredibly happy to see Tsu-chin and his water taxi waiting patiently for their return. So was Tsu-chin who waved excitedly at his return fares as they approached him at a leisurely pace.

Maisy responded in kind for the group. "Let's not question him until we reach the Wilmington wharf."

Browning nodded in agreement. "That's the right idea, Maisy. If we start asking him questions now, he just might leave us here to catch the next ferry. Not that I'm against taking the ferry, but because it's sundown already and the moon hasn't risen yet. We might be cops, but I still don't like the notion of being here on Wilmington's waterfront after dark."

Maisy voiced her approval. "Works for me, too, Eddie."

The boatman took a few steps toward the team, his tobacco-stained teeth showing his joy to see them. "You come back just in time, Picture Lady. Tsu-chin begin worry about you no come back. Think you to take ferry back to main dock."

Maisy shook her head. "We wouldn't do that, Tsu-chin. We said we'd come back, so here we are."

Tsu-chin focused on Browning. "Same price go back. Five cents each. You pay?"

"Yes, I pay." Browning dug into a trouser pocket for the money, found it, and presented it to Tsu-chin. "You wouldn't have a receipt handy, would you, Tsu-chin?"

The boatman's brow furrowed. "What is receipt?"

"Oh, never mind." Browning glanced at his partner. "I've got a witness that paid the fare, right, Bill?"

"Witness to what, Ed?"

"You're a funny man, Ingram. A real laugh-a-minute riot. You should be in Vaudeville."

Maisy plugged in her two cents. "Browning and Ingram. Now there's a catchy name for comedy act. All you need now are uniforms and rubber nightsticks, and I think I could get you jobs working at the studio." She looked skyward and waved her right hand across a make-believe marquee. "I can see it all now. Mack Sennett's Keystone Cops. Not exactly headliners, but just comical enough to keep the audience in stitches."

Browning frowned at her. "Get in the boat, Miss Malone, and try not to rock it."

The investigators found seats on the water taxi and remained quiet most of the way across the harbor to Wilmington dock. As soon as the boat was tied up, Tsu-chin gave them another grin and thanked them for their much needed patronage. To his surprise, none of the passengers made an effort to debark the craft.

"What wrong, Picture Lady?"

Maisy looked him straight in the eyes. "We'd like to talk to you about a couple of things, Tsu-chin."

"Okay, we talk. What about?"

"About you seeing a man leave the *Blackfin* on the morning of the big wind. Do you remember that morning?"

"Yes, I remember. I see man leave tuna boat and head down alley between houses."

"Did you recognize him?"

The boatman shook his head. "Not see his face. Not see face of other man go into alley ahead of him either." Seeing the sudden amazement on the faces of all four passengers, he felt like he had just said something he should have kept to himself. "I say wrong thing?"

"No, Tsu-chin, you didn't say anything wrong. It's only we heard from Willie that—"

"Willie? Who Willie?"

"He was our driver the last time I came here, and you took Mabel and me over to the island."

"Oh, yes. Driver of big car. I remember. Nice fellow. You say his name Willie?"

"That's right. Willie told us you had seen a man leave the tuna boat and go down an alley between houses, but he didn't say anything about another man already being in the alley ahead of the man you saw leaving the boat. And now you're telling us about this man in the alley ahead of the man leaving the tuna boat. Is that right?"

"Yes, that right."

"Did you see his face?"

Tsu-chin shook his head. "Too dark see his face. Too far away across harbor."

Browning pointed out a fact. "But there are street lights over on the island. You couldn't tell who either man was?"

"No, not see faces."

Maisy took a turn. "Did you see them come back to the *Blackfin*?"

Again, the boatman shook his head. "No, I go below after seeing one man leave boat. Go to sleep. Not see anybody come back to tuna boat."

"So why were you up so early that morning, Tsu-chin?"

"Tuna boats wake me when they come from San Pedro. I get up to see if anybody need be taken to island. I see two Japanee fishermen get on *Blackfin*, then see *Blackfin* go over to island."

"Did you recognize the fishermen?"

He shook his head. "Not know them. They Japanee. Not my friend."

"One last question, Tsu-chin. Do you have any other knives on your boat other than the one you carry with you?"

"Yes, have knife for cut up fish. Knife for cut up vegetables. Knife for put butter on bread. Knife for cut meat I cook. You want see?"

Maisy shook her head. "No, I don't think that will be necessary right now, Tsu-chin. Besides, we really should be going. We have a train to catch to get back to Los Angeles."

The investigators left the water taxi and walked toward the railroad depot in Wilmington. Of the four, only Browning appeared to be puzzled.

Maisy noted the look on his face. "Something bothering you, Eddie?"

"Why didn't you accept his offer to see his other knives?"

"He made the offer a little too quickly, Eddie, which tells me he might be hiding something."

"Like what?"

"Oh, I don't know. The murder weapon perhaps."

The next morning Maisy awakened a half hour before dawn and immediately telephoned Mabel, hoping to catch her at home before she left for the studio.

"Hello."

"Oh, good. You're still home."

"Maisy?"

"Yes. I tried calling you last night, but you weren't home, or you weren't answering."

"Both. Mack took me out to dinner, and by the time he brought me home, I was too bushed to answer any calls. I don't recall hearing the phone ring, so you must have called before I got home. So what's up, Maise? Did you and Eddie learn anything new on your visit to Rattlesnake Island yesterday?"

"As a matter of fact, we did."

Mabel was excited to hear the news. "Really? Did you figure out who killed Masi Tanaka?"

"No, not yet, but I think I've got it narrowed down a bit."

"Really? Who do you suspect did it?"

"Well, it's a short list."

Disappointment softened Mabel's voice. "A short list? Let me guess. Mr. Koki and who else?"

"I'd rather not tell you just yet, Mabes."

"Why not? Don't you trust me?"

"Of course, I trust you."

"Then why won't you tell me?"

"Because I want to be a hundred percent sure before I tell anybody."

"Not even Eddie?"

"Not even Eddie."

Mabel paused a second. "So, where do we go from here?"

"Well, I assume you're going to the studio shoot some more of that film Mack is making. What's the title again?"

"*The Sleuths at the Floral Parade.*"

"Oh, yes, now I remember. And they'll be shooting at the parade in Pasadena tomorrow. Do you think there might be a part in it for me?"

"Of course, there will. Either Mack puts you in it, or I won't finish it."

"Well, I'll be there just in case he needs an extra. What about decorating the Cadillac? Do I have to be there for that?"

"Well, since designed the decorations, I would think you should be there to supervise the job, don't you?"

"Yes, I suppose so. When will we be doing the decorating?"

"After we finish shooting at the studio, I should think. Aren't you coming in today?"

"No, I have other plans. I'm going to the library to do some reading."

"You're not going to investigate anything today?"

"Depends on what I learn at the library."

Mabel giggled. "Oo! That sounds delicious."

"I'll tell you about it this evening." Maisy paused a second. "Can you do me a favor, Mabes?"

"Sure, if I can."

"I'd like to save myself the price of a train ticket to Pasadena. Could you have Willie pick me up on his way over there?"

"Certainly, Maise."

"Will you be with him?"

"Sure. I want to help with decorating the car."

"Good. See you then."

* * *

Right from her first visit to the Los Angeles Public Library a week after her September arrival in the City of Angels, Maisy thought its location was odd. Always an inquisitive person, she asked as politely as she could why the library occupied most of the third floor and the roof garden of the six-story Hamburger Building, which was also the home of Hamburger's Department Store. The librarian replied that former City Librarian Charles F. Lummis had found the new structure perfectly suitable for the library because of its address in the city—801 South Broadway, which put it in the epicenter of the burgeoning population of the metropolis—and the floor space it offered, an area more than three times that of the library's previous location. Better still, patrons could readily reach the store and the library by the Pacific Electric, the Inter-Urban, and Santa Monica lines. Besides providing more room for the library's collection of books and study materials, the Hamburger Building also proffered more space for readers to sit. For Maisy's purpose, the library contained separate rooms for reading general literature and for studying reference materials. To the latter, Maisy went on this last day of 1912.

Once in front of the reference desk, Maisy greeted the librarian on duty with all the due respect one would give a good friend with a warm and charming smile. "Good morning, Miss Gleason."

Celia Gleason, an assistant city librarian born 43 years earlier in Canada and raised in Vermont, returned the feeling. "And good morning to you, Miss Malone. Not filming today?"

"No, not today. We're decorating the studio's car this evening for *The Tournament of Roses* parade tomorrow in Pasadena, so I have the day off from filming."

The thought of knowing someone who might be in the parade excited Miss Gleason. "Will you be in the parade, my dear?"

"No, I won't, but I will be there to see the parade because Mr. Sennett is filming the studio's car as well as much of the rest of the parade as possible. I will be in some of those scenes, mostly as a spectator, I would assume."

"That should be interesting."

"Most likely."

"So what brings you here this morning, Miss Malone? To the reference room, I mean?"

"Well, I read in *The Los Angeles Times* last week that you will be taking on a new position at the first of the new year, so I thought I would like to come by and wish you well in your new post as County Librarian."

"That's very thoughtful of you, Miss Malone. Thank you."

"You're welcome, Miss Gleason. And since I'm here I thought I would like to do some reading about Japan and the Japanese people. I recently met several Japanese immigrants here in Los Angeles, and I found them to be interesting. So, I wish to learn more about their culture in order to broaden my knowledge of people who immigrate here to America. Do you have any books on Japanese history and Japanese culture?"

"As a matter of fact, we have. You're actually in luck, Miss Malone. We have just recently received word that a new second edition of the 1904 original edition of *Europe and the Far East* by Robert K. Douglas will soon be available for the library to publish. We have the earlier version here in the reference room. Better than that, we also have the fifteen volume set of *The Book Shelf Scrap Book of Japan* by E.G. Stillman, Kazuburo Tamamura, and Baron Franz von Stillfried."

Maisy grinned and let her head bobble with delight. "You never cease to amaze me, Miss Gleason. Your knowledge of the books in this library is really beyond belief."

The librarian allowed herself a brief twinkle in her eyes and the smallest of smiles. "It's my duty, one might say, to possess such knowledge, Miss Malone. I might add that I take great pride in my work."

"I can see that you are quite unassuming about your achievement."

"Thank you, Miss Malone. I try not to be immodest. Such expression would be most unbecoming of a librarian."

Maisy continued her patronization. "Yes, of course, Miss Gleason. I would expect nothing less of you."

"So, would you like to find a table and chair and seat yourself? And I will have a runner locate the books I have mentioned and bring them promptly to your table."

"Certainly. Thank you, Miss Gleason."

Within a few minutes, Maisy had found a table and chair far from the other patrons of the reference room. She seated herself and waited patiently for the first book to be delivered by a teenage girl runner. To her delight, the volume was the work of Robert K. Douglas, *Europe and the Far East*. She opened it to the table of contents and searched the chapter titles until she came to those that covered the most recent history of Japan, beginning with the opening of the island nation to trade with the European nations and the United States of America by the implied military threat by the American Navy under the command of Commodore Matthew C. Perry in 1853.

As she read each chapter, Maisy summed up the information in her own words and committed it to memory. Within two hours, she finished the pages she wanted to read in the Douglas book, then took a short break before she opened the first of fifteen volumes to *The Book Shelf Scrap Book of Japan*.

Much to Maisy's delight, this incredible work consisted of photographs of everything Japanese from portraits of common people to those of royalty and nobility, peasants to samurai, landscapes to cities building their way from the pre-European influence era into the 20th Century. She flipped through the pages of the first volume, merely giving each one a quick scan before moving on.

Maisy flipped pages, read the captions, and absorbed as much as could, foregoing lunch and only leaving her chair once in the afternoon to answer a call from Nature. To help her memory, she wrote down several notes on the sheets of paper she had requested from the runner. Finally, at a quarter to five, Miss Gleason came by her table.

"Pardon my interruption, Miss Malone, but the library is closing early today, at five o'clock, for New Year's Eve."

"Oh, yes, of course."

"Were you able to learn much from these books?"

A smile spread Maisy's lips as she began folding and gathering the sheets of paper where she had written her notes. "Oh, yes, I did. I found them to be quite helpful."

"I'm glad to hear it. One can't have too much knowledge, you know."

"So very true, Miss Gleason. You never know when some tiny tidbit of knowledge will come in handy during a conversation."

"Isn't that a fact?" The librarian paused a few seconds as Maisy put her notes in her handbag. "Did you learn anything specific about Japan's culture or history?"

"Well, I found the *samurai* to be very interesting."

"The *samurai*? I don't believe I know that word. What does it mean?"

Maisy reached deep into her memory for a brief summarization of the facts she had only learned that very day. "Okay. The *samurai* were the hereditary military nobility and officer caste of medieval and early modern Japan from the 12th Century until their abolition in the 1870s. They were well-paid retainers of the *daimyo*, which were the great feudal landholders of Japan. They had high prestige and special privileges, such as wearing two swords, which I found to be particularly intriguing. They cultivated what they called the *bushido* codes of martial virtues, such as their indifference to pain and unflinching loyalty to their clans and the emperor. They engaged in many local battles. During the rather peaceful *Edo* era from 1603 to 1868, they became the stewards and chamberlains *daimyo* estates, where they gained managerial experience and education in the finer arts, such as poetry and painting. By the 1870s, they made up five percent of Japan's population. Then came the *Meiji* Revolution, which put an end to their feudal roles and turned many of them into military and naval leaders as well as businessmen. Some of them resisted the modernization of Japan, which led to the *Satsuma*

Rebellion and their final defeat in 1877. Their memory and their weaponry remain prominent with their descendants to this day, a fact that interests me a great deal."

"Really? How so?"

"Well, in my family back in Oklahoma, we still talk about how our Deaton ancestors came to America and brought along their distaste for outsiders who wanted to stifle our freedom. The Deatons came to America in the early 1700s. Back in Britain, they lived along the border between England and Scotland. They feuded with people on both sides of the border. To put a stop to that, their English and Scottish landlords shipped them to the colonies, where they continued feuding throughout the Revolutionary War. Those that supported the losing side in the war picked up and moved to Canada, while the winners and their descendants are still here in the United States."

"I must say, Miss Malone, your knowledge of your family history is quite impressive. How is it that you know it so well?"

Maisy grinned. "When the old folks talked, I listened. They made me proud to be a Deaton. Our Deatons settled first in Virginia, then moved to North Carolina and on west to Alabama, Mississippi, and Arkansas before finally settling in the Choctaw Nation part of what is now Oklahoma. In spite of living in all those southern states, none of my Deatons ever owned a slave. Not even those few who served in the Confederate army during the War Between the States. My grandfather was conscripted into the Arkansas militia just months before the end of the war, but he didn't go willingly. He was part of an artillery unit that never went into battle. He was proud of not ever shooting at another human being."

The librarian's eyes became a little misty. "I must tell you, Miss Malone, that I will be a little sad to leave the City Library, if for only one reason. I will miss out little chats when you come in to read. You are a most charming and interesting young lady."

"Thank you for saying that Miss Gleason. I will miss chatting with you as well. Where will your new post be located?"

"We will be setting up the County Library on the tenth floor of the Hall of Records. I will only have one assistant to start with, but we will be terribly busy setting up the library because we will be starting with nothing more than a desk and a couple of chairs and a single bookcase with no books until I order them. You must come see me on an occasion, Miss Malone, if only to see how we progress in building a new system for the whole county."

"I will certainly do that, Miss Gleason. I promise."

* * *

When she exited the Hamburger Department Store building, Maisy was more than surprised to find Mabel sitting on the passenger side running board of the studio's Cadillac. "What are you doing here?"

Mabel stood up. "I called your apartment, but when I didn't get any answer there, I figured you were still at the library. So here we are."

Perplexity screwed up Maisy's face. "We?" Then she saw Mack's driver for the parade, Beverly Griffith, standing behind the vehicle smoking a cigarette. "Oh, hello, Mr. Griffith. I didn't see you there."

Griffith flicked the unfinished butt in the gutter. "That's okay, Miss Malone. I'm still working on making my mark in this town, so nobody notices me yet."

"I'm sure that will change in due time."

"Do you really think so?"

"Let's just say I've got a hunch you'll be somebody important before you call it quits."

"I hope you're right, Miss Malone."

Mabel joined the conversation again. "I've only known Maisy for about four months now, and in that time, I've learned when she has a hunch about something, it usually comes true."

Griffith beamed with joy. "Well, okay then. Get aboard, ladies, and I'll take any place you want to go."

"Maisy, let's both get in the back seat so we can talk during the ride to Pasadena."

Their driver opened the passenger side rear door to allow the two young women to enter the car.

Maisy went first. "Good idea, Mabes. I've got lots to share with you about Japanese culture and history." She slid herself over to the driver's side of the Cadillac.

Mabel followed Maisy into the car. "Is any of it pertinent to your investigation into Masi Tanaka's murder?"

"Maybe. Maybe not."

Griffith closed the door behind Mabel, then hurried around the rear of the vehicle, opened the driver's door, and slid himself in behind the steering wheel.

The starlet clapped her hands like an excited child. "Oh, goody. You've got me on pins and needles. So, let's hear it. Tell me, tell me."

The driver started the engine, checked around for other traffic, then eased the Cadillac away from curb in the direction of Pasadena.

* * *

By the time they reached the parade staging area in Pasadena, Maisy had revealed almost everything she had learned about Japanese culture and history that day at the City Library. The single most important item she made known to Mabel was a photograph of a group of *samurai* warriors that had a most interesting caption.

"It was called *The Warrior Friends*."

"*The Warrior Friends*?"

Maisy nodded a bit vehemently. "Yes, *The Warrior Friends*. *Sensō no tomodachi*. That's how you say it in Japanese, I think. We'll find out for certain when we speak to one of our Japanese friends again."

"Okay. But is this photograph important?"

"I'm not sure yet. All I know for certain is five of the Japanese men we know have the same family names as five of the *senshi* in the picture."

Mabel was perplexed. "Five of what?"

"*Senshi*. That's Japanese for warriors."

"Okay. So does that mean for us?"

"I'm not certain of that either."

Frustration put a little growl in Mabel's voice. "So what are you certain about?"

"I'm certain I don't know yet who murdered Masi Tanaka." Maisy held up her hand in front of Mabel's face"
"Enough questions for now. We've got a car to turn into a ship tonight, right?"

Mabel slumped in her seat. "Yeah, okay."

Director Pathé Lehrman instructed cameraman **Irving** Willard and his backup crew to be in Pasadena before daybreak and ready to roll film as soon as the cast members arrived at parade staging area. The actors and actresses met at the Santa Fe Station at 7:00 a.m. in order to board the first special train, leaving at 7:30 for Pasadena. Mack Sennett counted heads, thought about handing each person a quarter to pay for his or her round-trip ticket, but canceled that idea and gave Milo Cole a sawbuck.

"Go buy tickets for everybody and hand them out." The studio head added a thought. "And bring me *my* change."

The whole crew boarded the train and occupied a group of seats in the middle of the coach on both sides. Mabel and Maisy, being the only women in the crowd, sat together.

Mabel nudged Maisy with her shoulder. "I'm rather excited about being in the parade."

Maisy countered. "I'm excited about seeing the parade. I hear it's really something to see. Can you imagine every entry is made up of flowers?"

"I know. Where do they get all those flowers?"

"One of the ladies I talked to last night said they come from all over southern California and some from as far away as Arizona and Portland, Oregon."

"I only hope I can keep my composure when we're filming. I'll be so excited about the parade."

So chatted the two actresses during the ride to Pasadena.

Flowers, floats, and floral designs. Everything about the parade, and not a word about the murder of Masi Tanaka.

Once they arrived in the *Crown of the Valley*, the translation of the city's name from the Chippewa words *pasa dena*, the movie people went straight to the staging area to join Beverly Griffith who had spent the night sleeping in the back seat of the studio's decorated Cadillac. They found him awake, already dressed in his chauffeur's uniform, and ready to drive the car in the parade.

"This *Tournament of Roses* parade is quite the deal. It's been six months in the making. I understand it will be half again as long as any previous parade here in Pasadena. I hear it's supposed to be five miles in length. Can you imagine that? Five miles long. I can't wait to drive in it. We'll be one of seventy-five to a hundred floats in the parade. And the flowers! I was told it's taken a total of two hundred fifty tons ... tons, mind you ... can you imagine that? Two hundred fifty tons of all sorts of flowers to make up the floats. It costs nearly a half million dollars to pay for all the floats, bands, horses, automobiles, and flowers. We start right here and go out on Orange Grove Avenue at 10:45 a.m. We go north on Orange Grove to West Colorado Street, turn right to go east to Fair Oaks Avenue, south on Fair Oaks to Dayton Street, east on Dayton to Raymond Avenue, north on Raymond to Colorado again, west on Colorado to Fair Oaks again, north on Fair Oaks to Holly Street, then east on Holly to Raymond Avenue again, south from there to Colorado Street yet again, east on Colorado to Catalina Avenue, south on Catalina to California Street, and east on California to Tournament Park. The tail end of the parade should be at the park by 1:30 p.m., maybe sooner if all goes well along the route. The first event at the park will the first heat of the first chariot race. All in all, it should be a wonderful afternoon."

Sennett didn't appear to be as excited as Griffith. Calmly, he stuck to the business at hand. "Did Pathé's camera crews check in with you this morning?"

"They came by here just before sunrise, Mr. Sennett."

"Did they mention where they were going to set up?"

"Mr. Willard said something about having the second crew set up on Colorado Street, while he would take his camera to California Street so he could get into Tournament Park before the first chariot race gets set to start."

"Did Irving mention anything about any other movie companies filming the parade and the events at the park?"

"Yes, sir, he did. He said he saw camera crews from at least fifteen movie companies here filming scenes for either comedies or dramas just like you're doing here."

"Did he name any of them?"

"Yes, sir, he did. If I recollect right, he said Thanhouser, Kaybee, Pathé, and Universal had crews here."

Sennett's head bobbed. "What about news weeklies? Did he say anything about them being here?"

"Yes, sir, he did. He mentioned Pathé, Gaumont, and Mutual having crews here."

"That sounds about right. I hope they shoot some footage of our boys in action, especially when we're shooting *Sleuths*." He waggled a finger at Griffith. "That's free publicity, Bev. Free is always good. Keep that in mind while you're working for me."

"Yes, sir."

Sennett turned to his actors and actresses. "It seems we have more than two hours of time on our hands, so let's go over the script before Pathé comes back from setting up his cameras. This shouldn't be too hard since we already filmed some scenes back at the studio. Let's start with Mabel and Maisy having their little chat."

* * *

As soon as she was done rehearsing her one scene with Mabel, Maisy left the staging area to find a decent spot to watch the parade. No such place existed because the sidewalks were already well filled with eager spectators by the time she arrived on Colorado Street. Disappointed by the lack of a good vantage point, she settled with joining Irving Willard and his camera crew on Raymond Avenue. Fortunately for Maisy, the cameraman had a director's chair for her to sit on.

"Thank you, Irving. I have to tell you; my legs were about to give out on me."

"Yes, I could see that you were tired, Maisy. Walking here from the train station while carrying this camera equipment put some wobble in our legs, I'll tell you. At least we've had some time to squat on the curb. You just stay there and enjoy the parade."

Maisy noted how crowded the streets were with spectators on both sides of the thoroughfares. First, those like camera crew sitting in compact rows on the curbing, then those folks standing for the full width of the sidewalks, and in back of these people standing on the seats or the running boards of their automobiles, visitors mostly from other southern California cities.

The first division of the parade was headed by Division Marshal Eric Kobbe and his aides, followed by the Pasadena Municipal Band and children from Pasadena city schools.

The place of honor next was given to the Royal Rosarians, who came all the way from Portland, Oregon to bring New Year's greetings from their city's Rose Festival. The chief Royal Rosarian rode in a car covered with smilax vines studded with deep red Portland roses. After their leader came the Portland men, four breast and a hundred strong. They wore suits of white flannel and carried their typical red roses. At their front, marching alone, was their flower bearer, holding aloft an immense bouquet of the mammoth blossoms. In a second car rode the Royal Rosarians mascot and a dainty little girl in a nest of Portland roses, with the legend, "Just a Bud," swinging above her on a pennant.

Seated in a car that blended beautiful shadings of lavender and pink was Pasadena Board of Trade. Fragrant jelly stalk, centurias, and carnations formed the main portion of a huge floral basket. At the corners were four smaller baskets filled with violets. A golden arch rose from the rear of the automobile.

A great peacock formed one of the attractions of the Merchants' Association of Pasadena. Composed of violets and yellow begonias, it rested on a mound of 500 pink carnations. The vehicle was lavishly adorned with ferns, pink and white roses, and asparagus plumosus.

The Whittier State School entry followed with its band a group some thirty-four boys wearing dark uniforms brightened with sprigs of green and floral boutonnieres.

Next came "The Melting Pot of Nations." The patriotic theme was carried out by five floats typifying ships and embodying the historical past and a prophecy of the future. It represented the combined efforts of all the schools of Pasadena. Girls representing the different nations were grouped about the final ship. A canopy of golden begonias occupied the center of the ship. High school girls in tiers and in colonial costumes sat beneath the broad folds of the canopy. The Goddess of Liberty sat on the topmost tier, holding the reins of state, represented by lines of white and gold tulle.

Pasadena High School was well represented by a floral swan that towered fifteen feet in the air. The float was built of smilax under a fore portion of white carnations that were gradually blended into a mass of light yellow jonquils, which were in turn blended into deep yellow begonias. The interior of the float was made of deep yellow marigolds. Many outriders on horseback in white and yellow colonial costumes, long-tailed coats, knee breeches, white hose, and buckled pumps accompanied the float.

So went the parade for an hour and a half. Floats, bands, riders on horseback, decorated cars, marchers, and children strolling behind the various divisions. Seeing all these youngsters moving so casually among the parade's main participants seemed odd to Maisy at first. Then she saw one little girl dart forward all of a sudden and pick up a rose blossom that had fallen from a blanket of roses draped over a horse's neck. The child gave it a quick scan, then placed it in a beach pail she carried in her left hand. This particular action stirred Maisy's mind to wonder why the child had done this. As she considered the thought, her view fell on yet another youngster carrying a beach pail who took a few quick steps to where a carnation blossom lay on the street. She also put the flower in her pail. This action brought Maisy's attention to other children carrying pails, some of them swinging them slowly, others spinning around and allowing the pail to fly at the end of an outstretched arm. One little boy swinging his bucket nearly struck another tike in his head.

Maisy gasped aloud. "Good lord!" She popped erect from her seat in the director's chair. "That's it! That's the weapon! That's what—" She intentionally ceased speaking as she realized Irving Willard had stopped cranking the camera and had shifted his focus on her.

"Something wrong, Maisy?"

"No, Irv, nothing's wrong. Seeing that little boy swinging his pail like that and nearly hitting another kid just brought back a childhood memory that's not so ... pleasant."

"Oh?"

Maisy tilted her head to the right and then to the left. "Yes. My baby sister Cora Lee climbed up on a kitchen chair one day when she wasn't much more than a toddler. I was supposed to be watching her to keep her out of mischief. Well, before I knew it, she lost her balance and fell head first at a cast-iron pot on the floor. She hit the rim and split her head open with a gash about three inches long. She bled like a stuck pig, and I got the whipping of my life for letting her climb up on the chair in the first place."

"That sounds horrible."

Quite intentionally, Maisy slipped into her southern drawl. "It was. I couldn't sit on that chair for a whole week, my hind parts hurt me so much."

Willard gave her a stare. "I meant your baby sister. Was she all right?"

"Oh, yes, she survived. Daddy got her to the doctor in town in time for him to put a dozen stitches in her scalp and saved her life. For the longest time, Daddy kept her close to him just to make sure she was right in the head. The rest of us thought she was okay, but he still kept her close by him pretty much right up until he died two years ago next week. I missed his funeral because I was in England working on the music hall circuit. You know. Like Vaudeville? My mother wrote to me over there. It took months for the letter to catch up to me. By the time, the one she sent telling me about Daddy's passing, the one telling me about Cora Lee marrying Basdon Smith arrived as well. Cora Lee was only fourteen when they tied the knot. Basdon is six years older than she is. Mama wrote that Cora Lee missed Daddy so much that she needed a much older man and couldn't wait to finish growing up to find one. So, Basdon was the one. He was one of the reasons I left home when I did. He had his sights on marrying me, and I was having none of that until I was all grown up and had seen a lot more of the world than just Bryan County, Oklahoma."

"What's wrong with your voice, Maisy?"

She grinned at the cameraman. "Nothing. It's just how I talk when I'm talking about home. I've been away from there for five years now. I'll be twenty on my next birthday. I'll be twenty, and my baby sister is already a mother." Maisy frowned and shook her head. "I know what's going through head, Irv Willard. You're thinking Cora Lee was the bride at a shotgun wedding. Well, I hate to disappoint you, but she and Basdon were married in March of '11 and their baby was born in July of '12. Better than fifteen months after they tied the knot."

Willard blushed with embarrassment. "Well, I've rested my arm long enough, so I'd better get back to filming the parade."

"And I've stretched my legs long enough." Without another word, she sat back in the director's chair, relieved that Willard hadn't asked her what she had meant when she blurted out, "That's the weapon."

* * *

Although the last but not the least entry in the *Tournament of Roses* parade for 1913 was the display made by Pasadena's Fire Department. The fire engines and the chief's wagon were elaborately and beautifully decorated with smilax, poinsettias, pink roses, and ferns. As with all of their predecessors, these heroes were followed by several children with pails picking up any and all of the fallen blossoms from the final few floats. After the now exhausted youngsters came a disorganized parade of spectators nearly a half block behind.

Seeing this gap in the throng, Maisy stood and joined her fellow onlookers along Raymond Avenue who stepped off the curb and into the march to Tournament Park, leaving Irv Willard and his Keystone Studio camera crew to complete the last of their filming from this location before they joined the other crew and the Keystone players at Tournament Park where they would film the events being held there that afternoon.

When the steady stream of spectators approached the intersection with Colorado Street, the vanguard turned left to go west. A hundred feet along the main thoroughfare of the parade's route Maisy heard her name being called from what seemed to be a great distance away, only because of the cacophony rising steadily among the joyous celebrants of the day. When she looked in the direction of the voice reaching out to her, she soon saw Ed and Nealy Browning standing on the north side curb ahead of her, both waving their arms to draw her attention to them as the detective shouted her name once more. Delighted to see these two friends so unexpectedly, Maisy waved back at them until she was sure they had seen her gesture. Positive that they had made a connection with Maisy, the Browning's stepped into the street and began working their way toward their motion picture friend. To make the distance between herself and the couple, Maisy began inching her way toward them. When they met up at a third of the width of the street, Maisy took each of them by an arm.

"I wondered if you two might be here this morning. I'm so glad to see you here. Some parade, don't you think?"

Nealy leaned against Maisy. "Oh, yes, it was wonderful. All those flowers on all those floats and automobiles. Your studio's car was very tastefully decked out as a ship."

"You saw it as a ship?"

"Yes, of course. I mean, the way it was decorated with lavender trimmed in pink, and the driver in his nautical suit."

"Actually, that was the new driver at the studio in his chauffeur's uniform. But if you say it was a nautical suit, then it was a nautical suit."

Browning patted Maisy's hand that was clutching his left arm at the elbow. "We thought you might be in the Keystone car with Mabel and Mr. Sennett and Mr. Mace."

"Sorry. I'm not a main attraction yet."

Nealy tugged Maisy's arm. "Well, they did see us and waved right at us. That was a thrill enough for me. But Mr. Fuddy Duddy here was disappointed you weren't with them. He's been worried about you all day. And yesterday."

Maisy looked directly at Browning with her face pinched up with curiosity. "Worried about me? Whatever for, Ed?"

"I had some news for you, and I wanted to gloat about it. I called you at your apartment several times and got no answer. I called the Keystone studio, and Milo said you had the day off."

"I did have the day off. I spent it at the city library reading."

"I thought it was something like that, so I called your apartment in the evening as well. Still no answer. So, I thought your telephone might not be working, so I sent an officer by your place to see that was the case. He said there was no answer when he knocked on your door."

"Mabel picked me up at the library at five o'clock, and we went to Pasadena to decorate the Cadillac."

"Did you stay there all night?"

"No, we both went home to get some sleep, we were so tired."

"Okay, where were you this morning?"

"We had to meet Mack and the rest of cast at the Santa Fe Station at seven o'clock to catch the seven-thirty train to Pasadena. I've been here ever since we arrived here around eight o'clock. So what's this news you want to gloat about? You didn't catch Masi Tanaka's killer, did you?"

Browning grinned like a Cheshire cat. "Not just the killer. We also found the murder weapon."

"You found the killer and the murder weapon?"

"That's right. The killer is in jail this very minute. The coroner tested the knife for Tanaka's blood and found it was a match."

Maisy squinted at the detective. "You said knife. Are you sure it wasn't something longer, like a short sword perhaps?"

"It's a knife all right. The blade on it is only nine inches long."

"In Japan, Ed, that would be a short sword that a samurai warrior would carry."

"Okay, it might be a short sword. So what?"

"So where did you find it?"

Browning puffed up like a fat cat after eating. "On the Chinese boatman's water taxi. I had the boys at the San Pedro precinct get a search warrant, and they found it under his bed yesterday morning."

"Do you mean to tell me you have Tsu-chin locked up in jail?"

Again, the big grin on Browning's face. "That's right. So I guess I won our little bet, Maisy."

"Don't go counting your winnings just yet, copper. You may have the murder weapon, but I'm positive you've got the wrong man locked up in your jail.

"

"**S**o how do you know Tsu-chin is the wrong man?"

"Because Milo and I searched his boat when we went back to San Pedro Friday evening. We searched it from top to bottom, and we didn't find anything even slightly resembling Japanese short sword. All we found were the knives he told us about when we questioned him on Monday."

"That doesn't mean anything. He could have hidden the knife in another place we don't know about, and then brought it back to his boat after we questioned him on Monday."

"I don't think Tsu-chin is that clever or that dumb. I tell you, Ed. You've got the wrong man in jail."

"Well, if you're so sure about that, then who's the killer?"

"I don't know that for certain just yet, but I've got it narrowed down a bit. But before we take this any farther down the road, I'd like to take a look at that murder weapon."

"What for?"

"I want to see who it belongs to. And you might send some of your officers to Mr. Garrido's home in San Pedro and tell him his ships are to stay in port until further notice. They can also tell him you would like him and his daughter and the entire crew of the *Blackfin* to meet us at the Koki boardinghouse at ten o'clock tomorrow morning."

"What if they ask why they should be there?"

Maisy shrugged. "Tell them we want to question them some

more. While your men are doing that, I want your one woman officer … Alice Stebbins Wells … I believe that's her name."

"It is."

"Have her come along with us."

"For what reason?"

"Gee whiz, Eddie, you ask more questions than I do. Just bring her along, will you? We just might need her. And when all this parade business is finished, I'd like you to come with me to speak with Mr. and Mrs. Tanaka, Yoshi Yamaguchi, Enji Nakamura, Mr. Masemoto the barber and his wife, and the marriage broker Iwaturo Oura. We won't be long."

"I suppose you want to tell them to be at the Koki boardinghouse tomorrow morning as well."

Maisy smiled and winked precociously at Browning. "Now you're catching on, Eddie."

* * *

As Maisy had requested of them, all of the people closely involved with Masi Tanaka when he was alive were waiting for her at the Koki home and boardinghouse when she and Mabel Normand arrived there with Ed Browning, Bill Ingram, Nellie Sharpe, Alice Wells, and four male officers of the San Pedro Precinct, two of them taking guard positions at each of the two exits from the meeting room where the boarders ate their meals and otherwise relaxed. Nellie, Mabel, Maisy, and Alice—in that order—sat on kitchen chairs behind the detectives.

Browning took the lead because he was the senior authority in the investigation of Masi Tanaka's murder. "Thank you to all of you for being here. I'm sure you're all anxious to know why we brought all of you here. Well, it's simple. We have found the weapon that was used to murder Masi Tanaka."

This revelation brought on several different reactions. Gasps from some. Mumbles from others. Whispers. Outright words of disbelief and of complaint for having taken so long to find it.

Browning turned to his partner. "Bill, would you mind showing it to everyone?"

"Sure thing, Ed." Ingram took a step forward to stand next to his fellow detective. He reached inside his coat and pulled out the item that had been used to kill Tanaka. To be certain all could see it, he held it chest high in front of him. "This is it. A Japanese short sword known as a ... what? Anybody here know what it's called in Japanese?"

All the Japanese men except one tried to feign ignorance. The one who differed from the others held up his hand.

Ingram nodded at the man. "Yes, Mr. Tanaka. Do you know what this is?"

"Yes, I know. It is a *yari tantō*. I have one almost exactly like it."

Browning asked the next question. "How did you acquire your *yari tantō*, Mr. Tanaka?"

"My father gave it to me the day I left Japan to come to America."

Maisy stood and squeezed herself between Browning and Ingram. "How did your father come to own your *yari tantō*, Tokutaro-san?"

"His father gave it to him."

Maisy continued to pursue this line of questioning. "And how did your grandfather come to own it?"

"It was made for him."

She pointed to the weapon Ingram was holding. "But you said it was almost exactly like this one. How can that be?"

Tanaka sat up straighter. "My grandfather was a samurai warrior and a great leader. His *yari tantō* was one of seven made for him and six friends. The only difference between them is the family name each one bears."

"Was your grandfather Tanaka Tosa who fought and died in the Boshin War?"

The candy store owner tilted backward he was so taken aback by her question. "How did you know that Miss Malone?"

"I read about him in a book in the City Library the other day. I know much about him and his friends and the man who betrayed them. We can talk about that later. For right now, I believe Detective Browning has something else he wants to ask you."

The sergeant cleared his throat. "Thank you, Miss Malone." He turned to Tanaka. "Then, sir, would you say your *yari tantō* is a family heirloom?"

"Yes, Detective Browning, I would say that because that is exactly what it is. It is a reminder that my grandfather and his father before him and his father before him were all samurai warriors in the service their emperor."

"So this *yari tantō* is not yours then?"

"No, it is not."

"How can you be so sure of that, Mr. Tanaka?"

"My *yari tantō* is locked in a very safe place in my home. I saw it this morning before we left to come here."

"Did Masi also have a *yari tantō*?"

"No, he did not. Mine was given to me because I am the oldest son."

Browning nodded. "I see. Then to whom does this one belong?"

A hush stifled the air in the room. Eyes shifted from side-to-side to see who might claim ownership of the short sword. Seconds passed like minutes before Yoshi Yamaguchi stood up slowly and bowed to Browning. "I believe it could be mine, Detective Browning, sir."

"Is there any way you can positively identify it as yours, Yoshi?"

"Yes, sir. If it is mine, then my family name will be on blade just below handle."

"Really? Let's see if you don't mind."

Yamaguchi nodded his approval.

Ingram drew the dagger just enough to expose the *ricasso*. "There's something here, Ed, but it's written in Japanese." He showed it first to Browning, then to the man directly in front of him. "Mr. Koki, can you read that for us?" He pointed to Japanese inscription on the blade.

The landlord twitched, leaned forward, blinked, then focused on the exposed portion of the short sword. "Name is Yamaguchi." He straightened up.

Browning focused on Yoshi. "Are you certain it says Yamaguchi?"

Koki nodded. "Yes."

The detective shifted his focus back to Yoshi. "So, this is your *yari tantō*, isn't it, Yoshi?"

"Yes."

A collective gasp hissed among the gathering.

Panic struck Yoshi. "But I did not kill Masi, Detective Browning. Masi was my closest friend. I did not kill him."

More mumbling and whispers flooded the room.

Maisy spoke up again. "Yoshi-*san*, when we questioned you last week, you said you and Masi boarded the *Blackfin* when it stopped at the Wilmington dock to take the two of you aboard. Is that right?"

"Yes, Miss Malone, that is right."

"And the last place you saw Masi was in the crew's quarters. Is that right?"

"Yes, Miss Malone, that is right. I go to make coffee for everyone. When coffee ready, I take cup up to bridge for Captain Garrido."

Maisy focus on the *Blackfin*'s captain. "Is that right, Captain?"

"Yes, Miss Malone, that's right. Yoshi brought me a cup of coffee just like he does every time we go out to sea. He stays on the bridge as an extra pair of eyes as we leave the harbor. Once we clear the channel and pass Dead Man's Island at the end of the breakwater, Yoshi leaves me alone on the bridge, and another crew member comes up to give me a break from the helm. That's exactly what happened that morning of the twenty-third."

Just then, Officer Orval Barney poked his head into the room by the back porch door. He nodded at Browning, then backed out of the room, closing the door behind him.

The detective leaned sideways toward Maisy and whispered. "Our guest of honor is here. Should I have Barney bring him in now or do you want to wait a little while?"

She spoke as softly as he had. "Let's wait." She centered her focus on Garrido again. "Captain, can you recall which of your crew replaced Yoshi on the bridge that morning."

The captain paused before replying. "Let me think about that for a moment. Let's see." He paused again. "If I remember correctly, it was Enji. Enji Nakamura." He looked over at Nakamura. "It was you, wasn't it, Enji?"

"Yes, Captain, it was."

"You were wet with sweat, and when I asked you about that, you said you'd been down in the engine room before coming up to the bridge. Remember?"

"Yes, Captain, I remember."

Maisy turned to the first mate. "Rodrigo, is that right? What the captain said, I mean."

Manuelo hesitated to answer as he appeared to be scrambling his memory banks. After several seconds, he spoke. "You know, I can't really say if he was there or not. I was very busy with the fuel tank. That I remember. But who was there besides me?" He shrugged. "Could have been Enji, but I can't say for certain."

"Thank you, Captain." Maisy shifted her focus with a smile at Belinda Garrido. "*Señorita Garrido, ¿cómo está hoy?*"

Surprised by the sudden attention to her, Belinda swallowed hard before replying. "*Estoy bien. Gracias por preguntar, señorita Malone.*"

"That's very good to hear, Belinda. I have a few very important questions to ask you. Please do not be afraid to answer them because your answers will be extremely helpful to this investigation."

"Yes, of course, Miss Malone."

"Would you say you and Masi Tanaka were good friends?"

Belinda answered slowly. "Yes, I would say that."

Maisy nodded. "And as good friends, did you and he confide in each other about … delicate matters?"

"What do you mean by delicate, Miss Malone?"

"Let's say … did he tell you anything that might be considered to be a secret?"

Belinda mulled over her answer before making it, looking to her father for his reassurance that she should respond honestly.

Geraldo Garrido nodded at his daughter. "Answer Miss Malone."

"*Sí, mi Padre.*" She returned her attention to Maisy. "Masi told me he was worried about something that was happening at the Koki's boardinghouse. He said he had suspicions that one of the other men who lived there was … *involved* … with a married woman."

Shock rushed over the room.

Maisy remained calm. "Did he say which man was … *involved* … with a married woman?"

"No, he didn't. He was about to tell me when Rodrigo interrupted us and attacked Masi."

"When the fight between Rodrigo and Masi was over and you two continued your stroll, did he say anything else about the man and the woman he thought were … *involved* … with each other?"

Belinda shook her head. "No, he didn't talk about it again, and I did not ask him about it either."

"Thank you, Belinda. You've been immensely helpful."

A great deal of murmuring rippled through most of the listeners. Four men and two women remained silent and motionless.

Browning and Ingram noted everybody's reactions to Maisy's line of questioning with Belinda Garrido. Then they looked at each other with raised eyebrows.

Maisy turned around and winked at a surprised Mabel. Then she bent over to whisper to her friend. "This is going exactly how I hoped it would."

Mabel smiled back at her friend. "Sure looks that way to me, Maise. Keep going."

Maisy straightened, turned back toward the gathering, and nudged Browning with her elbow against his elbow. "Ed, now's the time for our guest of honor to speak his piece." Then she added one more item. "Oh, and don't forget the bucket."

Browning held up his hands to quiet the people before him. "If you will pardon me, I have to go outside to get a couple of things. I'll be just a moment." Without another word, he went to the back door, opened it, and leaned out to speak to Officer Barney. "You can bring him in now, Orv, and don't forget the bucket."

Barney held up his right hand to show Browning he had the pail in it. With his left hand, he held the upper arm of Tsu-chin the boatman. "Let's go, you, and don't try no funny business."

Those gathered in the big room all had their eyes pinpointed on the rear door, wondering what Browning was bringing inside with him. When they saw Tsu-chin being led by Barney, again they hissed out a collective gasp of total surprise. This was immediately followed by another round of murmurs and muttering.

Browning walked back to his spot beside Maisy in front of the assembled suspects and witnesses. Barney guided Tsu-chin ahead of him, hiding the bucket at his right side and then behind him when they reached a place beside Browning.

The detective raised his hands a bit to get everyone's attention. "I believe most of you, if not all of you people, know this man, Tsu-chin, who operates a water taxi around the harbor. Tsu-chin is here because he witnessed something particularly important to our investigation. That and the fact that we found Yoshi Yamaguchi's *yari tantō* hidden beneath the mattress of his bed on his boat when we exercised a search warrant two days ago. We arrested Tsu-chin for the murder of Masi Tanaka—"

Before Browning could complete his sentence, the room erupted with a cacophony of sounds, all expressing surprise and disbelief.

The detective raised his hands again to silence the crowd. "Upon receiving more evidence in the case, we have dropped the charge of murder and have brought him here as a material witness in the case." He patted the boatman on his shoulder. "Tsu-chin, tell everybody what you saw on the morning of December twenty-third."

Tsu-chin's anxiety for the moment was quite obvious to everyone in the room. He hesitated to speak as he trembled and licked his lips to keep them moist.

Browning patted his shoulder again. "Go ahead, Tsu-chin. Tell us what you saw on the morning of December twenty-third. Everyone's eager to hear you."

"I-I wake up early because I know Japanee fishermen come from Los Angeles to board tuna boat *Blackfin*. I think maybe they might need Tsu-chin take them across harbor to board tuna boat. But tuna boat come to Wilmington dock to meet Japanee fishermen. I watch *Blackfin* cross harbor to fuel dock. See more Japanee fishermen board tuna boat there. I think I go back to bed, but then I see one fisherman jump onto dock and run toward houses. I not see his face. Just as he go into alley between houses, one more fisherman jump off *Blackfin* and run same way. I not see his face. Then I think this not right, so I stay awake just in case fishermen not get back to tuna boat before it leave for ocean. Then fishermen need Tsu-chin to take them to catch tuna boat before it go out of harbor. Little while go by and then one fisherman come back and board *Blackfin* just before it go away from fueling dock. I wait to see if other fisherman come back. He not come back. I wait long time. Still, he not come back. I see *Blackfin* make turn to leave harbor. I think fisherman missed boat. I tired, so I go back to bed. That all Tsu-chin know."

Maisy edged forward. "Thank you, Tsu-chin. That was very well said and especially important to our investigation."

Browning looked at Officer Barney. "You and Tsu-chin can go back outside now."

The boatman hesitated to move. "Tsu-chin want stay. Okay?"

The detective looked at Maisy. "All right with you, Miss Malone?"

"Sure, let him stay. He's been immensely helpful to us, so why not?"

Browning sighed, then looked at Barney. "You can stay, too, if you want. Stand over there by Officer Wells. You, too, Tsu-chin."

Before speaking, Maisy waited for her witness and the policeman to get to their places next to Wells. "So, two fishermen left the *Blackfin* and ran toward the houses, disappeared into an alley between them, and only one of them returned to the *Blackfin* before it got underway that morning. So, who were these two fishermen? We're very certain the one who didn't come back to the *Blackfin* was our murder victim, Masi Tanaka. So, who was the other man?" She paused intentionally for dramatic effect. "Before we answer that question, let's pose another question or two. Why did they leave the boat? And where were they going? Since all the fishermen on the *Blackfin* live in the same place, it's obvious they were headed to the Koki boardinghouse. But why? Could they have forgotten something they needed for their fishing trip? That seems like the most logical reason for them to jump off the boat and run back to the boardinghouse." She focused on the seven fishermen all seated together. "Have any of you men ever jumped off the boat and run back to the boardinghouse because you forgot something?"

Katusmi Kubota and Toyoshiga Takagi each raised a hand but very cautiously.

"Okay. Did you do this without telling someone before you left the boat? Or without asking permission from the captain first?"

Both men shook their heads.

"So, each of you told someone or asked the captain for permission to leave the boat before you left it, right?'

Both nodded again, relieved that they had given honest answers.

"So, who left the boat besides Masi Tanaka? We know it wasn't Yoshi Yamaguchi. He was making coffee, then he took a cup up to the bridge to Captain Garrido. That leaves ... Mr. Kubota, Mr. Takagi, Mr. Izuzoa, Mr. Sujuki, Mr. Harada, and ... Mr. Nakamura. Can each of you tell me where you were on the boat from the time you boarded that morning until the *Blackfin* left the fueling dock?"

Kubota, Takagi, Harada, and Sujuki each said they went to their bunks to get more sleep. Izuzoa said he was helping the first mate with the fueling.

Manuelo spoke up. "That's right, Miss Malone. Hamsabo ... Mr. Izuzoa was with me in the engine room."

"Thank you, Rodrigo." Maisy smiled slightly and focused on a very nervous Enji Nakamura. "So, Enji, that leaves you as the only man who could have left the boat either before or after Masi Tanaka. Would you mind telling us why you left the *Blackfin* that morning?"

Nakamura twitched and shifted on his chair. "I saw Masi jump on dock and run toward houses, so I run after him."

"Why did you run after him?"

The fisherman appeared lost for an answer, then struggled to give one. "I just … curious about why he leave boat." Enji shifted his view on one exit, then the other.

Maisy leaned forward a few inches. "I don't think you were that curious, Enji. I think you left the *Blackfin* before Masi did, then he left to follow you. Isn't that right?"

Before Nakamura could answer, Browning had a question. "Mr. Koki, when we visited you the other day, you said you saw Masi walked past your bedroom window on the morning of December twenty-third. Are you still certain it was Masi you saw?"

Koki paled. "Yes, I am certain it was Masi."

"What did you do after you saw him?"

"I go to bed."

Maisy took a different tack in their questioning. "Mr. Takagi, how long have you lived here in the Koki boardinghouse?"

"I come here two years back."

"In all that time, have you noticed how many rowboats have been tied up to the pylons on the beach out back?"

"Yes, six."

"Would you agree with that number, Mr. Harada?"

The fisherman nodded rapidly. "Yes, six."

"Do any of the rest of you fisherman disagree with that number?"

To a man, they shook their heads in the negative.

Maisy turned to the uniformed policeman in their line. "Officer Barney, did you count the rowboats tied up to the pilings on the beach?"

"Yes, Miss Malone, I did."

"How many are out there now?"

"Five, Miss."

"Thank you, Officer. Now would you please hold up that item in your left hand for everyone to see?"

Barney raised the bucket shoulder high in front of him.

"Where did you find that bucket, Officer Barney?"

"It was hanging on a nail on the back wall of this building, Miss."

"Have you touched any part of it other than the handle?"

"No, Miss, I haven't."

Maisy turned and faced Hatsenke Koki. "Does this bucket belong to you, Mrs. Koki?"

The woman shook with fear. "*Hai.* I mean, yes."

"Officer Barney, would you please hold the bucket higher so you can see the bottom of it without touching any part of the bucket other than the handle?"

The policeman complied with Maisy's request. "Detective Ingram, would you please look at the rim of the bottom of the pail and describe what you see there? You, too, Office Barney."

Both men studied the bottom rim of the pail for several seconds.

"Detective Ingram, what do you see?"

"There's some built up black stuff on most of the rim, and then there's about three inches of very dark red stuff that I'd say could be blood."

"Officer Barney, do you agree with Detective Ingram?"

"Yes, Miss, I do."

Before Maisy or Browning could ask another question, Toichero jumped to his feet and pointed to the pail. "That fish blood. Hatsenke work at cannery sometime. She take pail to cannery with her. Sometime fish blood get on pail at cannery."

Browning had a response for the landlord. "When was the last time your wife worked at the cannery, Mr. Koki?"

"When Mr. Garrido's boats come back from sea."

The detective shook his head. "We stopped at the cannery on our way here, Mr. Koki. We asked the bookkeeper when Mrs. Koki last worked at the cannery, and do you know what he told us?"

Koki sat down slowly, knowing he had been caught in a lie. He peered feebly at Browning. "Maybe I make mistake."

"Yes, I believe you did, Mr. Koki. Mrs. Koki hadn't worked at the cannery since a week before Christmas, had she?"

The landlord shrugged. "Could be."

Maisy took the lead again. "Let's get back to the rowboats, Mr. Koki. You owned six rowboats, according to your residents. But now there's only five tied up outside. What happened to the sixth one?"

Koki shrugged again. "I don't know. Someone steal it, maybe."

"It's been missing for at least three days, Mr. Koki. In all that time, you didn't notice it was gone?"

Koki remained silent and motionless.

Browning turned to Maisy. "I think we've taken this far enough, so why don't you sum it all up for everybody?"

"You're right, Eddie. We've made your case."

Maisy cleared her throat. "By now, I think most of you have come to one conclusion or another about who murdered Masi Tanaka. But I'm certain you would like to know how and why he was killed. And how his body wound up miles from here on the beach at Castle Rock. Well, here goes."

"**As Miss Garrido said, Masi Tanaka told her how** he suspected one of the other *Blackfin* fishermen was involved with a married woman. Unfortunately, he didn't tell her their names. The question now is, who are these people?"

The gathering muttered among themselves in response to Maisy's question.

"We know for certain that the two men who left the *Blackfin* on the morning of December twenty-third were Enji Nakamura and Masi Tanaka. The question is, who left first? The next question is, why did they leave the boat?"

Another round of mumbling by her listeners.

Maisy paused to let the audience quiet down. "It's my contention that Enji Nakamura left the *Blackfin* first and Masi Tanaka followed him. If Enji left first, why did he leave the boat? It's my contention he was going to the boardinghouse to see someone. So, who was that someone? Mr. Koki or Mrs. Koki because they were the only two people there. I believe he was going there to see both of them."

All but the Kokis whispered among themselves.

"Masi Tanaka followed Enji because he suspected Enji Nakamura was planning to see Mrs. Koki because he was the fisherman who was involved with a married woman and she was that woman."

The responses by the group in front of the police and Maisy grew louder now, while the Kokis squirmed in their seats.

"Enji and Mrs. Koki met outside, behind the boardinghouse, where she gave Enji the *yari tantō* that belonged to Yoshi Yamaguchi. They were surprised when they saw Masi come around the corner. Enji and Masi began to argue, and then they began to fight. Mrs. Koki then went up on the porch and retrieved her pail. She came back down from the porch and hit Masi in the head with the pail. I am certain that when the coroner examines the blood on the pail, he will confirm that the blood is a match for Masi Tanaka's blood and that the rim on the bottom of the pail is a match for the gash on Masi's head."

A collective gasp hissed from the audience.

"But the gash on Masi's head didn't kill him. It only stunned him. Seeing Masi was only hurt by the bucket, Enji then took the *yari tantō* and stabbed him in the chest with it, killing him almost instantly."

The gathering remained still as they waited for the next words to come from Maisy.

"Realizing what they had done, Enji and Mrs. Koki panicked for a moment before they heard Mr. Koki calling out to Mrs. Koki from inside the boardinghouse. Mrs. Koki then took the knife from Enji and told him to run back to the tuna boat. She then went back into the boardinghouse where she met her husband who was headed outside. She told him a story that Masi had tried to force himself on her. Or some other such fairytale." She looked at Toichero. "What was the story she told you, Mr. Koki?"

The landlord was speechless. So was his wife.

"Whatever it was, Mr. Koki believed her, and then he went outside to find Masi dead on the beach. His first instinct was to believe his wife. In his mind, Masi had done whatever it was she told him. But then he realized that something had to be done about Masi's body. He couldn't just let him be found there on his beach. That would certainly cast suspicion on him. So, he had to get rid of Masi's body. What to do was the question. The howling wind that morning gave him an idea. He would put Masi's body in one of his rowboats with the thought that the wind would push it out into the outer harbor and then out to sea. But then he had another thought. What if his rowboat was found at sea with Masi's body in it? That wouldn't be any better than having Masi's body found on his beach. So, he got into the rowboat with the body and rowed it toward the mouth of the harbor with the idea of throwing Masi's body into the water near Dead Man's Island. That was a better plan except for one thing. The closer he rowed toward Dead Man's Island, the choppier the water became. It became so choppy that as soon as he threw Masi's body into the water the boat became lighter and was driven against the rocks of Dead Man's Island. We know this because Officer Barney here had Tsu-shin take him out to Dead Man's Island this morning where they found the wreckage of Mr. Koki's rowboat. Mr. Koki couldn't save his boat, but he did save himself by crawling onto the island. Then he waited until the sky grew light enough for him to see the breakwater before walked atop it back to the railroad bridge where he used to cross back to Rattlesnake Island and the safety of his home.

"Mr. Koki thought he and his wife would be above suspicion until Detective Browning and I visited the boardinghouse the other day and asked the other fishermen about their knives. Then we asked Mr. Koki about the knives in their home. Because both Mr. Nakamura and Mr. Yamaguchi were still in Los Angeles, Mr. Koki knew we couldn't look into their belongings in the bunk room upstairs. He knew, if we did that, then we would find Mr. Yamaguchi's blood-stained *yari tantō* that Mrs. Koki had returned to the place from which she had taken it to give to Mr. Nakamura. Mr. Koki then took the murder weapon and hid it on Tsu-chin's water taxi because if it was found there Tsu-chin would get the blame for murdering Masi Tanaka.

"This is really going to hurt you, Mr. Koki, but your wife and Enji Nakamura planned to murder you that morning and dispose of your body in the same manner in which you had originally thought you would dispose of Masi Tanaka's body. They would kill you and put your body in one of your rowboats and push you out into the harbor where the wind would drive the rowboat out to sea. Enji couldn't row you out there because if he did, then he wouldn't have enough time to get back to the *Blackfin*.

"Now most of you are thinking that Enji Nakamura and Mrs. Koki were planning to murder Mr. Koki because of their love affair." Maisy shook her head. "No, their reason for wanting him dead goes much deeper than that.

"Remember what Mr. Tokutaro Tanaka said about his father being a samurai warrior who was killed in the Boshin War? Tanaka Tosa and five of his friends were betrayed by one of the seven friends. The family names of the five friends who were also killed at the same time in the Boshin War were Yamaguchi, Nakamura, Masemoto, Oura, and ... Hamada. Mrs. Koki's family name is Hamada. She is the granddaughter of the Hamada who was killed in the war. Enji is the grandson of the Nakamura who was killed." Maisy focused on Mr. Oura. "And Mr. Oura the marriage broker is the son of the Oura who was killed. Until I read the names of the samurai friends, I had never thought of Mr. Oura as being involved in the murder of Masi Tanaka. Of course, I'm certain he hadn't planned for Masi to be murdered. That was never part of his plot, a plot he started when Mr. Koki came to him and asked him to find him a picture bride back in Japan. Mr. Oura is not a killer, but he is very clever. He arranged for the photographs he showed Mr. Koki to be of ... how should I put this? ... young women who were not very attractive. All but one. Hatsenke Hamada. He convinced Mr. Koki that she was the one for him. Why did he do that? Because Mr. Koki's father was the man who betrayed his six friends during the Boshin War. Since Mr. Koki's father was killed in the Satsuma Rebellion eight years later, the six betrayed friends could only be avenged by their descendants. And the only way they could avenge their ancestors was to kill the only son of the man who betrayed his friends. Toichero Koki."

Maisy then faced the boardinghouse landlord. "The real tragedy for you, Mr. Koki, is by trying to protect your wife you made yourself an accessory to their murder of Masi Tanaka."

Browning stepped forward again. "Enji Nakamura and Hatsenke Koki, you are under arrest for the murder of Masi Tanaka. Iwaturo Oura and Toichero Koki, you are under arrest for being accessories to the murder of Masi Tanaka." The detective turned around. "Officer Wells, would you please take Mrs. Koki into custody?" He turned back to his partner. "Detective Ingram, would you and Officer Barney please take Enji Nakamura and Iwaturo Oura into custody?" He faced the last of the accused. "Toichero Koki, would you please come with me?"

As the police escorted their prisoners from the premises, Mabel took Maisy by an arm. "How do you know all this stuff about the Boshin War and the something or other Rebellion in Japan in 1877?"

Maisy smiled back at her friend. "I keep telling you, Mabes. Los Angeles has a wonderful public library, and I'm one of their best patrons. What do you think I do when I'm sitting around waiting for my few seconds in front of the camera? I read."

ABOUT THE AUTHOR

Larry Names has had 43 titles published to date, 25 of them novels, and the remainder non-fiction all dealing with sports teams or sports figures. He resides in central Wisconsin with his wife Peg on a family farm that has been in his wife's family since 1854. They have a son, Torry, and a daughter, Tegan; and three grandchildren; Nora, Maverick, and Kieryn. Larry has four children from his first marriage: daughter Sigrid, son Paul, daughter Kristin, and daughter Sonje.

The author was born in Mishawaka, Indiana and has lived in nine different states during his life and went to eleven schools growing up. He is an avid researcher and traveler.

Please visit the author's website: www.larrynames.com and Facebook page: Larry Names Fan Page.

LARRY NAMES

Book List

NON-FICTION

LAMBEAU YEARS, THE, PART ONE, THE HISTORY OF THE GREEN BAY PACKERS, VOL. 1
LAMBEAU YEARS, THE, PART TWO, THE HISTORY OF THE GREEN BAY PACKERS, VOL. 2
LAMBEAU YEARS THE, PART THREE, THE HISTORY OF THE GREEN BAY PACKERS, VOL. 3
SHAMEFUL YEARS. THE, THE HISTORY OF THE GREEN BAY PACKERS, VOL. 4
LOMBARDI'S DESTINY, PART ONE, THE HISTORY OF THE GREEN BAY PACKERS, VOL. 5
BURY MY HEART AT WRIGLEY FIELD: THE HISTORY OF THE CHICAGO CUBS
 -WHEN THE CUBS WERE THE WHITE STOCKINGS, PART ONE
GREEN BAY PACKERS FACTS & TRIVIA, 1ST EDITION
GREEN BAY PACKERS FACTS & TRIVIA, 2ND EDITION
GREEN BAY PACKERS FACTS & TRIVIA, 3RD EDITION
GREEN BAY PACKERS FACTS & TRIVIA, 4TH EDITION
CHICAGO WHITE SOX FACTS & TRIVIA
OUT AT HOME BY MILT PAPPAS, WAYNE MAUSSER AND LARRY NAMES
HOME PLATE BY STEVE TROUT, DAVE CAMPBELL, AND LARRY NAMES
DEAR PETE: THE LIFE OF PETE ROSE

FICTION

SHAMAN'S SECRET, THE
LEGEND OF EAGLE CLAW, THE
BOSE
BOOMTOWN
COWBOY CONSPIRACY
PROSPECTING FOR MURDER
TWICE DEAD
THE OSWALD REFLECTION
IRONCLADS: MAN-OF-WAR
IRONCLADS: TIDES-OF-WAR
TEGAN O'MALLEY – THE TRAVELER IN TIME
TEGAN O'MALLEY – STOWAWAY ON TITANIC
A TWO REEL MURDER – STARRING MACK SENNETT & MABEL NORMAND – A MAISY MALONE MYSTERY
MURDER ON RATTLESNAKE ISLAND – STARRING MACK SENNETT & MABEL NORMAND – A MAISY MALONE MYSTERY

With others
HUNTER'S ORANGE
PK FACTOR, THE
As Bryce Harte/Larry Names
CREED #1: CREED/A TEXAS CREED
CREED #2: WANTED/TEXAS PAYBACK
CREED #3: POWDERKEG/TEXAS POWDERKEG
CREED #4: CREED'S WAR/KENTUCKY PRIDE
CREED #5: MISSOURI GUNS
CREED #6: TEXAN'S HONOR
CREED #7: BETRAYED/TEXAS FREEDOM
CREED #8: COLORADO PREY
CREED #9: CHEYENNE JUSTICE

CREED #10: ARKANSAS RAIDERS
CREED #11: BOSTON MOUNTAIN RENEGADES

AUDIOBOOKS
CREED #1: SLATER CREED, THE
CREED #2: TEXAS PAYBACK
CREED #3: POWDERKEG
CREED #4: KENTUCKY PRIDE
CREED #5: MISSOURI GUNS
CREED #6: TEXAN'S HONOR
CREED #7: TEXAS FREEDOM
CREED #8: COLORADO PREY
CREED #9: CHEYENNE JUSTICE
CREED #10: ARKANSAS RAIDERS
CREED #11: BOSTON MOUNTAIN RENEGADES
IRONCLADS: THE TIDES OF WAR
A TWO REEL MURDER – STARRING MACK SENNETT & MABEL NORMAND – A MAISY
MALONE MYSTERY
OSWALD REFLECTION, THE
PROSPECTING FOR MURDER
SHAMAN'S SECRET, THE
BOSE
BOOMTOWN

KINDLE EDITIONS
THE OSWALD REFLECTION
BURY MY HEART AT WRIGLEY FIELD: THE HISTORY OF THE CHICAGO CUBS
 -WHEN THE CUBS WERE THE WHITE STOCKINGS, PART ONE
PROSPECTING FOR MURDER
A TWO REEL MURDER–STARRING MACK SENNETT & MABEL NORMAND – A MAISY MALONE
MYSTERY
TEGAN O'MALLEY – THE TRAVELER IN TIME
TEGAN O'MALLEY – STOWAWAY ON TITANIC
IRONCLADS: TIDES OF WAR
CREED #1: A TEXAS CREED
CREED #2: TEXAS PAYBACK
CREED #3: TEXAS POWDERKEG
CREED #4: KENTUCKY PRIDE
CREED #5: MISSOURI GUNS
CREED #6: TEXAN'S HONOR
CREED #7: TEXAS FREEDOM
CREED #8: COLORADO PREY
CREED #9: CHEYENNE JUSTICE
CREED #10: ARKANSAS RAIDERS
CREED #11: BOSTON MOUNTAIN RENAGES
LAMBEAU YEARS, THE, PART ONE, THE HISTORY OF THE GREEN BAY PACKERS, VOL. 1
LAMBEAU YEARS, THE, PART TWO, THE HISTORY OF THE GREEN BAY PACKERS, VOL. 2
LAMBEAU YEARS THE, PART THREE, THE HISTORY OF THE GREEN BAY PACKERS, VOL. 3
SHAMEFUL YEARS. THE, THE HISTORY OF THE GREEN BAY PACKERS, VOL. 4
LOMBARDI'S DESTINY, PART ONE, THE HISTORY OF THE GREEN BAY PACKERS, VOL. 5
COMING SOON!
LOMBARDI'S DESTINY, PART TWO, THE HISTORY OF THE GREEN BAY PACKERS, VOL. 6